HOT PUCK

ROUGH RIDERS HOCKEY SERIES

SKYE JORDAN

1

Beckett Croft angled to stop just inches from the referee, spraying ice over the prick's skates. This guy had been favoring the Anaheim Ducks since the first puck drop.

Leaning in, Beckett pinned the ref with all the frustration that had built up over the first two periods of the game.

"You've *got* to be *fucking* kidding me." Beckett kept his voice down, but it took more control than he thought he had left. "Donovan wasn't even close. Decker faked that trip. You ought to at least call him on embellishment."

As the Washington Rough Riders' captain, Beckett was the only player who could talk to—or in this case, challenge—the ref's calls. Normally, he handled his job with stoic intensity. Setting an example for his teammates was an important part of the position, one he took seriously. But so was calling bullshit.

"Don't tell me how to do my job." The ref grabbed the puck from another member of his four-man team. Before he skated away, he warned, "If you want to stay on the ice, Croft, lose the attitude."

"Fucking A." He blinked sweat from his eyes as he skated into the face-off formation. "This is bullshit."

Tate Donovan, one of their highest scorers, glided past on his way toward the penalty box with "Even it up, Beck."

"You know it."

Beckett had two major jobs on the ice—protection and punishment. He was one of the team's two designated enforcers. And Donovan was right, this was a good time to even up the score—if not on the board, where they were already tied with the Ducks two-two—certainly on the ice, where the ref had fallen short.

There was more than one way to seek justice.

With twelve minutes left of the second period, Fall Out Boy blasted over the arena's speakers, background to the announcer's voice hyping the Rough Riders' lineup. And while the fifteen thousand fans filling their home stadium in downtown Washington, DC cheered with steadfast belief in their team, Beckett's chest tightened with each second that ticked past.

His team was approaching the middle of their season and the acclaimed Winter Classic. They *needed* this win to advance into the finals. Beckett himself was approaching the end of his contract with his team, and he needed this win just as badly to secure his personal and professional goals.

The puck dropped. Savage chipped it to Hendrix. Hendrix smacked it to Saber. Saber swept toward the Ducks' goal and passed to Beckett.

Decker appeared on Beckett's flank, blocking the goal. And goddammit, he was fucking sick of this guy. He faked left, drove right, and flew behind the net, passing to Savage.

Savage took the shot. The smack of the puck echoed off the ice. A sound that pumped adrenaline through Beckett's blood.

The Ducks' goalie, a fresh young hotshot from Canada, blocked the puck, and Saber grabbed the rebound while Beckett bullied the Ducks' defenseman out of his teammate's path. He pushed toward the opposite end of the rink in time to witness Hendrix out-skate one Duck, out-stick another, and swing toward the goal.

Energy buzzed like live wires between the players. Everyone's focus was honed and intense. Cheering in the stands had faded into white noise. All Beckett heard was the rasp of his breath and the beat of his heart or the occasional call from a teammate.

In split-second intervals, Beckett saw Hendrix set up, take stock of those around him, pull his stick back—

Decker's angle of approach shifted, and the Duck drove toward Hendrix. Beckett pushed every ounce of power he owned into his thighs, driving his skates forward. But he didn't reach the men before Decker slammed Hendrix against the boards so hard, the Rough Rider came off his feet, banged his head on the glass, and broke his hockey stick.

Yet the refs remained silent. No roughing call.

Before Hendrix had even gotten back on his skates, Decker was driving the puck toward the Rough Riders' goal.

This was fucked. It was also over. Beckett was done watching the other team pummel his teammates without consequences.

Fury put speed into Beckett's skates. Donovan blasted out of the penalty box and immediately crowded Decker toward the wall. Beckett angled toward the bastard, lowered his shoulder, and threw all two hundred pounds of himself—along with a decent amount of momentum—into the Duck.

The clatter of equipment filled Beckett's ears a split second before Decker hit the boards. Then the thunder of the Plexiglas rumbled through his ears and rattled his brain, followed by ravenous spectator approval.

Adrenaline gushed through Beckett's system, and he used it to catch up with his teammates. He traded the puck a few times with Saber and Donovan as they jockeyed for an opening between the Ducks' pipes. Decker intercepted a pass between

Hendrix and Donovan and ran the puck toward the opposite end of the rink. The fans howled in disappointment.

"No fucking way," Beckett said under his breath.

He sprinted across the ice as Decker set up for a play. Beckett saw three moves ahead, the way a chess master spied a checkmate in the near future with perfect accuracy. He pushed every ounce of strength available into his legs. In his peripheral vision, Beckett saw Donovan come up on his left. Savage on his right. Perfect positioning to grab the puck and go.

He braced himself and hit Decker hard, driving them both into the boards. Their bodies slammed with thundering impact, drowning out their curses and the cheering crowd. The puck was long gone, swept down the ice by Beckett's teammates.

Decker's frustration finally exploded. Instead of heading back into play, the Duck twisted and hammered a right hook at Beckett's face. He dodged the punch, and the momentum swung Decker ninety degrees. His skate blade caught on Beckett's, and before he could untangle himself, Beckett went down hard, hitting the ice on his ass. The impact nailed his tailbone, driving a steel shaft of pain straight up his spine. Every molecule of air in his lungs froze. Beckett hadn't even reclaimed his breath before Decker shoved him backward. Beckett's helmet cracked against the ice.

Hard.

So hard, a burst of black filled his vision, immediately followed by blinding white light and stabbing pain.

Beckett tried to push Decker off, but his arms wouldn't move. He ordered his body to twist and roll. Still, he didn't move.

His brain hurt. Bad.

His head felt wobbly. And light. Like it was floating off his neck.

Overhead, the goal siren echoed through the arena. The

dome erupted in earsplitting applause. And even though the sounds came to him from a distance, like he had cotton stuffed in his ears, Beckett felt a sliver of gratification.

We've got the lead was his last thought before his mind went dark.

2

E den Kennedy frowned at one of the dozens of EKG strips her boss had collected for her to study.

She sat cross-legged on the gurney pushed up against a cement wall in the lower level of the Verizon arena and laid the tape above her textbook, where she flipped through the pages dedicated to EKGs and the pathology found within the various strokes.

Her partner on the ambulance tonight, Gabe, a die-hard hockey fan, had his face all but pressed up against the glass that surrounded the rink. That left her free to focus on all these squiggly lines.

She rested her elbow on her knee and her forehead in her hand. "This is way too much like reading ink blots."

Eden barely heard her own words over the noise rocking the stadium. She'd gotten pretty good at tuning out almost everything and everyone when she needed to focus on the job or her studies, but this noise was wearing on her concentration and her nerves. And as each hour of study time for tomorrow's midterm dwindled away, her stress mounted. She was now at the tearing-her-eyelashes-out tension level.

"I think we've got something." Gabe's yell barely registered beneath the dense foam plugs she'd stuffed in her ears upon arriving at the stadium.

Eden lifted her gaze from the EKG strips to shoot a glare at Gabe, who stood ten feet away, but he was still focused on the rink. The only reason she'd agreed to work this extra shift was because he'd promised her nothing *ever* happened. He'd promised her she'd get all sorts of extra study time. But since he wasn't looking at her, Eden followed suit and ignored him. It was going to take a hell of a lot more than that vague warning to get Eden to take him seriously.

The announcer's voice rose over the noise and seemed to vibrate inside her body.

Eden cringed, squeezing her eyes shut and holding her head with both hands. "God, I *hate* hockey."

Her words were once again sucked into the chaotic void beneath the metal dome.

"Eden," Gabe said again, louder this time as he turned toward her. "I think we're going in."

"I doubt it," she muttered.

The teams had physical therapists and team physicians. Gabe hadn't hauled a guy in yet this season, and it was already November. Besides, these were professional hockey players. A notch above MMA fighters in her book *only* because at least they played a game in between fights that required some skill. Considering their brutal tendencies, Eden couldn't fathom a reason to bring them in, barring a heart attack, stroke, broken bone sticking through the skin...

"*Eden.*"

"Jesus." Eden slapped her textbook closed, pushed off the gurney, and wandered toward the mouth of the tunnel running beneath the stadium to meet Gabe. As she neared the rink, the cold wrapped around her, and she pulled her uniform jacket tighter.

The stadium had filled since she'd last looked, and a sea of royal blue created a thick tiered ring around the ice. "Damn. There are way too many people in our society who will pay to watch a fight."

"They're paying to watch hockey," Gabe told her. "The fights come with the territory."

Whatever. "This shift was supposed to be a cakewalk."

"This never happens…" He trailed off as a man in slacks and a Rough Riders warm-up jacket stepped onto the ice in dress shoes. With a referee on either side of him, he held their arms for support as he jogged across the ice to the group huddled near the arena's far wall. "That must be the team doc."

Before Eden could ask what happened—hoping this was all a dog-and-pony show for the fans—the announcer spoke.

"Beckett Croft took a hard fall in a scuffle with the Ducks' Andrew Decker."

Jeering rumbled through the crowd.

"Look." Gabe pointed to the Jumbotron where a replay flashed over the screen.

The announcer continued to commentate. Eden didn't understand the hockey language, but she did understand fight language—unfortunately so.

On the screen, the guy in blue rammed the guy in white against the glass with so much malice and intention and force, Eden's stomach coiled into a knot. White retaliated, shoving back Blue, who then tripped over White's skate. Blue hit the ice tailbone first.

Eden tensed and winced. Her hand instinctively moved from her hip to the base of her spine. Then White followed Blue to the ice and shoved him back. Blue's head hit so hard, his helmet bounced. Referees stepped in, blocking sight of the players on the video.

Eden crossed her arms, trying to squeeze ugly feelings from her body. "Did I already mention that I hate hockey?"

Gabe didn't answer. He was riveted to the replay.

"Guess there's job security in perpetual human stupidity," she muttered.

"Bet he shakes it off," Gabe said, never looking away from the ice. "He's one of the toughest in the league."

Born and raised in Philadelphia, Gabe knew all about these East Coast winter sports and was a rabid Rough Riders fan. When their employer, Capital Ambulance, won the contract to transport Rough Riders players to the hospital in the event of an emergency, Gabe had jumped at the chance to staff as many of those shifts as he could grab. And then started begging, borrowing, and stealing the rest.

After working for the company for nearly two years, Eden had seniority, but she'd taken a huge step back and let the others claim these light-duty runs. She didn't need any unnecessary exposure to violence or reminders of how it could slip into a life and ruin everything.

She heaved a sigh and looked at the scoreboard but couldn't tell what any of the numbers meant. "How long until this is over? I've still got a lot of studying to do."

"Excuse me." Gabe and Eden turned. A man in his midforties came toward them from the tunnel. He wore nice slacks with a dress shirt, a tie, and a royal-blue warm-up jacket emblazoned with the Rough Riders' logo. "I'm Paul, one of the Rough Riders' assistant coaches. Doc Danbar wants Beckett to go in."

Perfect. Eden heaved a breath but shoved her midterm to the back of her mind.

"Fine." She returned to the gurney, grabbed the rails, and pushed it forward, then took one handle of the backboard and picked up the C-collar. "Let's do this."

The thought of having fifteen thousand pairs of eyes on her while she packaged this so-called elite athlete onto the backboard and then the gurney gave her butterflies. But, hell, she had to do what she had to do, right? And the sooner they dropped this loser at the emergency room, the sooner she could go home and find some peace to study.

She glanced at Paul. "Do you have those grates for our shoes so we can walk on the—"

The crowd broke into cheers so loud, the noise drowned her words. She glanced toward the glass and found this Beckett guy gliding to the sidelines with the help of the team doctor and a referee.

"What the hell?" Eden threw the hand holding the C-collar out to the side. Her accusatory gaze shot to Paul. "He shouldn't be on his feet. He could have a spine injury."

A smile broke out over Paul's face. "No one keeps Beckett Croft down if he doesn't want to stay down."

Eden had dealt with her share of uncooperative and even combative patients over the years, but she really wasn't in the mood to deal with one tonight.

If the idiot wanted to risk becoming a paraplegic, who was she to try to save him from himself?

She tossed the board and the C-collar back onto the gurney. "Where do we pick him up?"

"Locker room." Paul gestured for them to follow and started into the tunnel.

Gabe took control of the gurney, and Eden fell in beside him.

"Start your mental recorder," she told Gabe under her breath. "We don't need some big shot coming back later, blaming us because this Beckett guy's in a wheelchair. I want every detail of this call in the report."

Gabe gave a single nod. "Got it." They slowed as Paul paused at a door, entered a code, and stepped through. "Hey," Gabe asked Eden, "think I could ride in the back with him?"

Eden shot him a you-can't-be-serious look.

Gabe shrugged and smiled. "I'm dying for his autograph."

"And I'm dying for my paramedic's license." Which

included a certain number of patient cases or hours as an EMT. Eden had opted for cases over hours since she worked at one of the busiest ambulance companies but couldn't give a lot of hours.

"I'll give you the call on paper," Gabe offered, hopeful.

"Which would require you to *lie*."

"I would never lie." He pushed the gurney through the doorframe and shot a smile at Eden over his shoulder. "I'd just very carefully word my report."

She was grinning at his excitement as she stepped into another hallway.

"I'm *fucking fine*, goddammit."

The man's bellow erupted from the next room and echoed off the concrete walls, startling Eden to a stop. Unease prickled over her skin. The fear response was automatic and still came now and then when she least expected it. Less and less as time passed and Eden's life moved on, but the paramedic program was wearing her out. Fatigue kept her from compartmentalizing as well as she used to. Stress broke down her professional barriers more easily.

Eden rolled her gaze to the ceiling, searching for strength and patience.

"This is *fucking bullshit*. They need me on the ice. Do I look like I need to go to the fucking hospit— Ah, *goddammit*."

Eden heard the pain in the man's voice and smirked at Gabe. "Still want to ride in the back with him?"

She didn't wait for his answer before stepping into the next room—obviously the main locker room. The space was large and well-appointed, with lacquered blue benches lining the walls. Each cubby space had been assigned with a brass nameplate. The team's logo—a stylized image of a horse's head wearing an intense expression—was everywhere: painted on walls, cut into carpet, carved into wood. A lot of money had been dumped into this space.

She took a quick glance around at the half-dozen men standing in a semicircle around Croft. He'd dropped to a seat on a bench in the middle of the room and was holding his head in both hands. His hair was dark, drenched, and standing up in every direction. He'd stripped off his jersey, and shoulder pads lay on the bench beside him. His muscles stretched a red long-sleeved shirt around thick biceps and across cut deltoids.

Eden wasn't a small woman. At five foot seven, she worked out and carried her own tight frame of muscle. But in this room, surrounded by these men, she was acutely aware of the power surrounding her—and not just the physical power. Croft himself wielded a significant influence over these men. Men who she guessed wielded their own authority in other circles.

This room reeked of power and money and testosterone.

Eden knew all about that bullshit—and it meant less than nothing to her.

She rounded the bench and stepped between two of the men to stand in front of Croft.

"Mr. Croft," she said in a professional but compassionate tone. "I'm with Capital Ambulance. After that hit, we need to stabilize your spine as quickly as possible. You shouldn't be moving until you've been assessed by a physician. My partner and I are going to take you to Georgetown University Hospital."

"*Fuck.*" His bitter anger cut into Eden's stomach. She stood her ground, hoping she hadn't flinched externally. "Give me a fucking minute. I'm gonna be fine. Jesus Christ, you're all making something out of nothing."

Everyone had the right to refuse medical care, and as far as her responsibilities went, she could walk away at any time after a mentally sound patient said no. But there was a bigger, more ethical part of her job. The part that drove people to seek this work in the first place: the desire to take care of others who couldn't take care of themselves in times of trauma or stress or illness. And she believed it was part of her *ethical* job to recognize those who truly needed a doctor's wisdom and guide them into skilled hands.

Considering this man hadn't even stayed still after taking such a bad hit to the head, she'd definitely put him in the poor judgment category.

"You have to go, Beckett." The team doctor delivered the assertion with what Eden thought was an overabundance of consideration. They were dealing with a grown man, not an angry two-year-old. "It's concussion protocol."

"*Fuck protocol*," Croft yelled, pushing to his feet. His sheer size—around six foot three and at least two hundred pounds—made Eden take a step back. Made her gut flutter with alarm. "I wasn't out more..." His words drifted away. His gaze went distant. "I wasn't... More than..."

"Gabe." Eden alerted him to Croft's imminent drop. Gabe moved behind Croft, while Eden stepped closer and held out a hand. "Mr. Croft, you need to—"

He swayed, his eyes rolled back in his head, and his body went lax. All in the span of two seconds.

Eden got ahold of his forearms just as he pitched sideways and backward. She wasn't able to do much more than guide him toward Gabe's arms. The other men in the room jumped in, adding support to get Croft onto the floor and saving him from another crack to his skull—though Eden thought that might have helped knock some of Croft's stupid loose. On the upside, this took the decision of whether or not to go to the emergency room out of Croft's hands.

Eden took a quick pulse at Croft's wrist while the team doctor hovered and the other men in the room twittered with concern. When she found Croft's heartbeat steady and strong, she nodded at Gabe, who worked the C-collar into place around Croft's neck.

"Doc," someone called behind them. "Looks like Kristoff's going to need stitches."

The doctor turned that direction with a disbelieving "*Again?*"

"We've got this," Eden told him. It wasn't like he was helping anyway. "Go ahead."

The doctor moved on to his next patient, and Eden started on the straps attached to the backboard.

She kept a watch on Croft's face, anticipating trouble if he regained consciousness before they had him secured. He reminded her more of a boxer than a hockey player, with the ugly green-and-yellow resolving bruise shadowing one eye and an inch worth of fresh stitches across the same brow. A few days' worth of beard darkened the lower half of his face, but the balance and strong, squared angles of his features made him undeniably attractive.

Eden tightened the strap over his hips as Croft's lashes fluttered. She met Gabe's eyes and lifted her chin toward the opposite side of the gurney. "Rail."

Her partner lifted the metal arm while Eden untwisted the final strap for Croft's chest.

He opened his eyes and looked around, dark eyes flooded with confusion. Urgency created tension along Eden's shoulders. She wanted to get him tied down before—

"What the—" Croft jerked his legs against the straps, and fury cut across his face. A look that brought back nightmares and chilled the pit of Eden's stomach.

"Everything's fine, Mr. Croft," she said, sounding surprisingly calm. "We'll have you out of this in—"

"*Now.*" He pulled himself upright and twisted to grab for the strap at his thighs. "You'll get me out of this *right fucking now.*"

In her mind's eye, she saw the spinal column as she'd studied it so intricately. Saw a potentially chipped vertebra cutting into his spinal cord. Saw delicate nerve endings wedged and compressed as he twisted and fought. She was momentarily caught between the urge to swear at him and the desire to throw her hands up and let him ruin the rest of his life.

"Mr. Croft," Gabe said in what Eden called his dad voice, "you need to lie down."

But Croft obviously had no respect for any kind of authority. He pulled on the strap in Eden's hand.

"Mr. Croft—" Gabe repeated.

The buckle pinched Eden's fingers, pain sliced through her hand, and her fraying patience snapped.

Eden planted her knee on the gurney at Croft's hip, steadied herself with one hand on the edge, and pulled herself up to his level. Slapping her free hand to the center of his chest, Eden pushed him straight back and against the pad. An *oomph* drifted out of him, and he stared up at her with a mix of shock and confusion.

"Whoa, sugar." He held up his hands, his dark eyes making a quick sweep of her body. "I usually save the rough stuff for the second date, but since you're so good at it, I'll compromise this time." He met her gaze again, and his mouth lifted in a half smile. "Bring it, baby."

A smattering of relieved laughter rounded the room. Eden experienced relief and embarrassment, frustration, and, yeah, a twinge of excitement. Because, okay, he was pretty hot when he smiled. Even for a hockey player.

Gabe stepped to the opposite side of the gurney, and in Eden's peripheral vision, she noted his nervous gaze darting between them. "Mr. Croft, she's probably not the one you want to tangle with. I'm far more congenial."

Both Eden and Croft tilted their gazes toward Gabe.

Eden lifted a brow at him. "Really?"

Her partner smirked back. "Just trying to defuse the tension."

It worked. When she and Croft locked gazes again, he was grinning. And damn, the boy had a smile that could melt steel.

"Are you done fighting and arguing and generally being an ass?" she asked, far less forceful than she'd been a moment ago, but stern enough to let Croft know she wasn't backing down. "Are you going to let us do our jobs?"

"I don't usually let anyone get between me and the ice"—his voice was warm and his gaze playful as he wrapped a hand around her wrist—"but I might make an exception for you."

She didn't get a chance to tell him how full of shit he was before he tried to pull her hand away and sit up. But Eden already had her weight balanced over him and used the miniscule advantage to keep him down.

"Look, we both know you could toss me across the room if you wanted. And I really have more important things to do than fight with you, Mr. Croft. I want you to hold still long enough to hear me out so you can make an informed decision."

His mouth quirked again. "I've really got more important things to do than listen to your advice—"

"If you haven't already completely fucked up your spine," she said, forging ahead anyway, "continuing to move in the presence of an injury could do even more damage. So if you really love hockey and the rough stuff on the second date, you'll hold still until we can get you to the hospital and make sure you didn't do irreparable damage to your head, neck, or back. An injury like that could not only keep you from the things you love most, but it could keep you in a wheelchair for the rest of your life."

When she finished, the deep stillness in the room registered. For the first time since she'd entered the locker room, her lungs filled completely, and a sense of control returned. Her head cleared, and Eden scanned Croft's face as if seeing it for the first time. Dark brown hair, rich brown eyes, bruises, stitches, sweat. And, man, he was handsome in a rough, almost brutal sort of way.

She eased back, but his big hand remained wrapped loosely around her wrist.

"So, what's it going to be?" she asked. "Back on the ice for five minutes tonight? Or back on the ice for five years starting tomorrow?"

He relaxed into the gurney but didn't release her or break her gaze. The faint crinkles at the corners of his eyes told Eden he found her amusing.

But then he confused her by saying, "I want to talk to Donovan before I leave."

"On it," someone behind her said, followed by the shuffle of movement as one of the men left the locker room.

Eden lowered her feet to the ground but had to continue leaning over the gurney with her arm in his grip. His gaze seemed to relax too, now scanning her face with a kind of intimacy that made her self-conscious.

"You're a smart man," she told him.

"And you're a pretty little firecracker."

Pretty? Hardly. She went makeup-free on the job, her hair pulled back into a boring bun. All very efficient and utilitarian, but definitely not pretty. But the compliment still created a hot little buzz low in her body.

She glanced down at his big scarred hand still circling her wrist, surprised at how gentle he could be after seeing what he'd done on the ice. But she'd known that kind of man before. The kind who could stroke a cheek as expertly as he could hammer it. "Think I could have my hand back now?"

Instead of releasing it, he stroked his thumb across the sensitive skin of her wrist, and heat coursed up her arm. "About that date—"

"There was no mention of a date." She picked up the one remaining strap with her free hand. "Will you let me snap this? Just until we get you into the ambulance?"

"If you'll talk date with me."

Strangely enough, she got more come-ons as an EMT than she ever had as a cocktail waitress. "I was asking as a courtesy. You heard the doctor. You have to go in."

"You're pretty tough for a girl..."—he glanced down, where her name badge rested at her breast—"Kennedy. That a first or last name?"

The way the man could create heat with nothing but the slide of his eyes was unnerving. More so when she'd spent years building barriers he seemed to blow through with no effort.

She fastened the final strap over his chest and smiled. "Planning on filing a complaint?"

"The only complaint I've got is that you're not taking me seriously."

She lifted the gurney's metal arm. "After that hit? Everything you say is suspect."

He grinned—a big, high-on-life grin that blasted heat straight through Eden. His straight, white teeth contrasted with his dark stubble, and his gregariousness beamed like a beacon, sizzling in the air. "You wouldn't say that if you knew how many times I've hit my head over the years."

"Or maybe I'd say that explains a lot."

"Good one." His gaze lowered to her chest again. "Any relation to *the* Kennedys?"

"*Pffft.* Right. I'm really an heir to the Kennedy fortune. I do this on the side to create purpose in my life."

Croft laughed. Eden met Gabe's you-always-manage-to-win-them-over smirk with a shake of her head. He took the foot of the gurney as they maneuvered out of the locker room and into the cement tunnels toward the ambulance waiting in the bowels of the stadium.

Another player ran up alongside them, still in full uniform and gear, including helmet and skates. "You scared the hell out of us." This had to be Donovan. He looked a few years younger than Croft and walked along with them through the corridor. "You okay?"

"Fine. Fucking concussion protocol. Listen…" Croft barely took a breath, and his gaze held Donovan's with surprising intensity considering how lightly he'd been flirting with her only minutes ago. "Don't let this sidetrack the guys. Get them to channel the emotion into the game and hold the momentum."

"Got it."

"With me out, the Ducks will bring in Souza," Croft said.

"Leftie."

"Cut everything off," Croft instructed. "Don't give them one fucking inch…"

He continued to coach Donovan until they reached the ambulance and loaded him inside. Even then he called, "Lead with your sticks, rebound, and keep them out of our zone."

Gabe moved around to the driver's door, and Eden took hold of the back door. Before she closed it, she glanced between the men. "Anything else?"

"Focus on the game, Tate. You got this. You guys got this."

The other man nodded, glanced at Eden, and grinned, then told Croft, "Stop giving Kennedy such a hard time. Behave for a change."

She offered Donovan a nod before she shut the door, then smiled down at Croft. "I like him."

3

Beckett's head throbbed like a mother. The next time he saw Decker on the ice, that man was going to curse the day he was born.

His pain didn't help tamp down his annoyance with this little hottie twittering over Donovan. She was supposed to be swooning over Beckett, dammit. Only, Kennedy obviously hadn't gotten that memo.

"I'm going to put an ice pack on your head." Kennedy's voice had softened since Beckett had stopped bullying her.

She laid a cold compress over the crown of his head toward the back where he hurt most, and the cold spread over his angry skull like soothing fingers. Beckett sighed with relief.

"How long until we get to the hospital?" he asked.

"Gabe?" she called toward the front.

"Maybe fifteen minutes," the driver replied. "Depends on traffic."

"I don't mind a longer, quieter ride, if you know what I mean," Beckett called back. "I think the siren might split my head open."

"Roger that."

He glanced at Kennedy again. "My phone's in the locker room. Do you have one that I can use to pull up the game?"

She slipped the blood pressure cuff around his arm with a silly little fat-chance grin.

"Hey, Gabe," he tried. "Can you get the game on the radio?"

A laugh bubbled out of Kennedy. A sweet, light bubble of laughter that felt like a stream of carbonation through his gut. One that helped him focus on something other than the pain in his head.

"Sorry, boss," Gabe said. "The only radio we've got connects directly to the hospital."

"That sucks." As did the occasional stab deep in his brain when he raised his voice. But it wasn't anything he hadn't dealt with before. Or wouldn't deal with again.

"Tell me," Gabe agreed.

After monitoring his pulse and blood pressure, Kennedy stood and bent over him. "I'm going to check for anything abnormal along your spine."

She gripped the opposite rail with one gloved hand and slipped the other between his body and the backboard. Her gaze went distant, and her fingers gingerly followed the length of his spine from the edge of the collar to his hips. Then she stretched across him and repeated the action on the opposite side.

Teasing her helped keep his mind off his head. Off the fact that he was missing the game. Off the realization that everything was out of his control. "I think you missed a spot."

Her gaze lifted and focused on his eyes. She was only three or four inches away and the instant intimacy shot a current through his chest that zapped his gut. He grinned, and an answering smile whispered over her mouth before she rolled her eyes.

She'd taken off her jacket, but her uniform shirt did an excellent job of cloaking any femininity hiding underneath.

This close, Beckett caught the very subtle scent of something fruity and light. His synapses had obviously gotten scrambled in that mix-up on the ice, because he was catching some wickedly *hot* vibes from this woman. And there was definitely nothing outwardly sexual about her.

Except maybe her sassy, take-charge attitude. That was pretty damn sexy. Plus, that face... There was no missing all that delicate bone structure and quiet symmetry. Her hair was the color of straw and wound in a tight bun on the back of her head. Her cheekbones were high but soft. Her lips a pale blush and full. She definitely wasn't the smokin' hot, overtly feminine woman Beckett usually gravitated toward. He'd definitely changed over the last year—in dozens of different ways—but he was still a four-inch-fuck-me-heels kind of guy. A tight dress, makeup, and perfume kind of guy.

And Kennedy certainly wasn't that. In fact, Beckett couldn't even imagine her dolled up. Yet, he couldn't stop looking at her. He'd just gone too long between hookups. This year had been brutal on his extracurricular activity.

"I don't feel anything obvious," she said, dropping back to a seat and scribbling notes on a clipboard.

"Then you weren't touching the right place."

She smirked but didn't look up.

"Do you think we could lose the strap on my arms?"

Her gaze rose to his, narrowed.

"There's no point in me causing trouble," he assured her. "The game's almost over by now, right?"

She reached out and freed the buckle holding the strap across his upper body. Beckett sighed and repositioned his arms. "Thank you."

She reached out and slipped two fingers into his hand. "Squeeze."

He'd barely gotten started when she said, "That's good," and moved on to the other. Then jotted more notes.

"Is Kennedy a first or last name? You never answered."

"Last." She stood again, set her clipboard down, and rounded the foot of the gurney, where she started unlacing his skates.

"If you're gonna undress me, you can start up here."

She grinned at him, her head tilted, her gaze flirty and hot around the edges. "I like to take my time."

"And I like the sound of that."

When she tugged off a skate, Beckett's mind refocused. "Hey, can you make sure my skates stay with me?"

A more authentic smile curled her lips, making Beckett's focus cling to them. To their pretty shape. Their plumpness. The dip in her upper lip. "You sound like my last patient, only he was six, and he wanted his blanket."

"So you'd be nicer to me if I was six?"

"I *am* being nice, and somehow I think a big part of you still *is* six."

He laughed and watched her hands move on his laces. The sight created a strange tug in his belly. He couldn't remember anyone ever lacing or unlacing his skates for him. "They're my favorite pair."

She pulled off one skate and set it on the gurney beside his leg, then met his gaze—the first time she'd looked at him without a flare of anger darkening her expression. Her eyes were a warm bluish green. "How many pairs do you have?"

"Um..." He had to think about that. "I'm not sure. More than the other guys. Five? Six? I like to keep them. I'm sentimental like that."

"Eight," Gabe said. "I read it in *Sports Illustrated*, so it has to be true, right?"

Kennedy met Beckett's gaze, and they started laughing at the same time. Her face glowed and her eyes sparkled. Oh yeah, she was a beauty all right. And they shared a moment of intimacy that dug in and held on to something inside Beckett. One he really wanted to explore.

Preferably in bed.

Kennedy placed her hand on the ball of his foot. "Push."

After he obeyed, she repeated the movement with the other foot, then pulled his skates into her lap while she made notes. When she finished, she tucked the laces inside the skates and asked, "What makes these your favorite?"

He would have glanced toward the cab but couldn't move his head, so he slid his eyes that direction. "Do you know, Gabe?"

"Nope. You've got me there."

He met Kennedy's eyes again and could see by her softened posture and easy grin he was slowly gaining her approval. "I was wearing them when I scored my two hundredth goal in the NHL. I also have the ones I was wearing when I scored my hundredth and my first."

"Huh. Sentimental." She looked at the skates again, gave a nod. "Who'd have guessed?" And moved on with questions. "Do you have any allergies to medications?"

She huh'd away his two hundredth goal in the NHL? What did it take to impress this girl?

"One for one," he said. "I'll answer one of your questions, then you answer one of mine."

"You're forgetting the whole this-is-my-ambulance, you're-on-my-turf-now thing." She moved her hands in a circle, indicating the inside of the rig. Then asked again, "Do you have any allergies to medications?"

"No," he answered. "Do you have a boyfriend?"

Her hands dropped against the clipboard, and she heaved a sigh.

"No," Gabe answered for her. "She doesn't."

Beckett started laughing.

"Hey." Kennedy tried to shoot a glare toward the front of the vehicle, but she was grinning. "No ganging up allowed." She returned her gaze to the clipboard. "Have you had any surgeries?"

"Torn right ACL, bad left rotator cuff. What are you wearing under your uniform?"

Kennedy rolled her eyes. Gabe was the one who burst out laughing this time.

"Dude," Beckett called toward the front, "if you know the answer to that, we're going back to the boyfriend question."

"You two are hil-*ar*-ious," she said. "Do you have any other medical problems?"

A slow, dark laugh stuttered past his lips. "I've heard some people consider an erection lasting more than four hours a 'problem.'"

Gabe's laughter rolled into another, deeper round.

"Okay." She put her pen down, but she was grinning, and laughter shook her shoulders. Beckett liked the fact that she could lighten up after such an intense show of passion earlier. He got that. It was the same as his on-ice, off-ice personality shift. "We're done. And, oh look, there's the hospital. Lucky me."

"You owe me an answer," he said. "Do you always work the games?"

"Nope. I'm covering for someone tonight."

"Bummer." A true lick of disappointment irritated him. "Not a hockey fan?"

"I like hockey about as much as you like being pulled out of the game to go to the hospital."

Gabe added, "Truth."

That was a *real* bummer. "Did you watch tonight?" Beckett asked, hoping she'd seen some of his impressive plays.

"Nope, I was reading."

Reading? Instead of watching hockey? He couldn't even fathom the possibility.specially not when she had one of the best views in the stadium. "You know a lot of people would kill to watch the game from where you guys stand."

"So Gabe tells me."

Beckett should cut his losses right here. She wasn't his type, she wasn't fawning over him, and she didn't like hockey. Three strikes.

But after Gabe got out of the truck, he couldn't keep himself from asking, "Do you feel the same about hockey *players* as you do about the game?"

Didn't this make the most pathetic picture ever? Trying to chat up a chick who was barely tolerating him, while riding in an ambulance trapped in a neck brace, tied to a backboard?

But Beckett had always been a sucker for a challenge.

"I couldn't say," she said. "I don't know any hockey players."

"You do now."

"Hardly. We met thirty minutes ago."

"Not only did we meet, but we've had our first fight *and* made up—all in half an hour. The next step is always makeup sex. Imagine where we could take this given a couple of uninterrupted hours."

She was smiling, her pretty eyes holding his with the first flicker of real interest when Gabe opened the back doors. The movement broke the momentary trance, and Beckett tried to think of a way to get it back while she and Gabe lowered him to the ground.

"Why don't you give me your number," Beckett said, "and we can finish talking about this another time?"

"Thanks, but I'm going to pass." Kennedy looked at Gabe over Beckett's head. "I'll let you take him in while I straighten up the back." She lowered her gaze to Beckett's and reached out to squeeze his lower leg with a quick, sincere "Good luck to you, Beckett Croft" before disappearing into the ambulance.

Beckett exhaled heavily as Gabe pulled him across the

parking lot. "I can't remember the last time a woman *wouldn't* give me her number."

"Eden's definitely not most women," Gabe said. "She's better. Way better."

He lifted his gaze to the man at the head of the gurney. "You got a thing for her, man?"

"Nah, we're just friends. But she's really an awesome chick. She'd be worth the trouble if you wanted to make the effort."

Beckett looked up at the night sky and thought of Lily. He instantly realized the logistics of hooking up with the feisty EMT would be as impossible as finding job security in the NHL. So he kept his mouth shut, relaxed into the gurney, and absorbed the disappointment the same way he sucked up a bad game.

Once Gabe transferred Beckett to the nurse on duty, he shook Beckett's hand.

"Hey, thanks," Beckett said. "When they unhook me, I'll sign this jersey and send it to your work."

"Wow." Gabe's face lit up. "That would be beyond awesome."

"Least I can do. Thank Kennedy for me, would you?"

"You bet. Her first name is Eden, by the way. Stay safe."

Gabe retreated from the room. Beckett was still thinking about Eden—and what a perfectly fitting name that was for the first woman who'd tempted him in quite a while—when the doctor came in for a quick assessment and ordered a CAT scan. While Beckett waited to be transported to Radiology, the nurse gave him a phone to call home.

His sister answered on the second ring with a cautious "Hello?"

"Hey, it's me."

"What number are you calling from?"

"The ER. They took me from the rink before I could grab my phone."

Sarah's exhale sounded relieved. "Are you trying to knock *all* your brains out of your head? You know you can't have all that many left after twenty-five years in hockey."

"Yeah, pretty sure I'm running on empty." He closed his eyes as the *thump-thump-thump* radiated through his skull. "I'm at Georgetown. Going to be home late."

"Do you need me to pick you up? I can have Mom come watch Lily—"

"No, no. I'll have one of the guys get me. I'm sorry. I know you have to work in the morning. I'll do what I can to hurry this along." He craved the sound of his daughter's sweet voice. "Lily's probably passed out, isn't she?"

His sister laughed. "Barely stayed awake through dinner."

Beckett grinned. "So she liked dance class?"

"Well, she pirouetted to bed and fell asleep in her leotard, so, yeah, I'd say she's hooked."

The image of his five-year-old twirling herself into bed, her blonde head of corkscrew curls flying, made him laugh. The pressure hurt his head, but his heart still swelled, and he sighed. That kid was the best thing that had ever happened to him. Yeah, his social life had hit a wall when Lily's mother had abandoned their daughter almost a year ago now and Beckett had taken over full-time care. But for every hour he missed out on with a woman like Eden, he only had to think of every moment with Lily to quell his disappointment.

"Have I told you lately how much I appreciate you?" he asked his sister.

"You tell me all the time. Don't give the doctors trouble. Let them check you out, then get your butt home."

"Yes, ma'am."

"Beckett?"

"Yeah?"

"Make sure you wake Lily up to say good night when you get home. I promised her."

He smiled. "I always wake her. She just doesn't always remember."

"And, um," Sarah hedged, "Kim called tonight."

The mention of Kim Dixon made Beckett's smile fade. That explained Sarah's suspicious tone when she'd answered.

A fist of anger and fear closed in his heart. Lily's mother had only called three times over the last ten months, and each time it had been for money, not Lily. She hadn't made any effort to visit their daughter in all that time. Kim hadn't even alluded to missing her.

On the flip side, it had taken two months for Lily to stop asking for her mother. Three months to shake the neglect-induced illnesses she'd arrived with. And four months to stop waking almost every night with nightmares.

"What did she want?" he asked, his voice gravelly with anger and dread.

"I don't know. I didn't answer," Sarah said, disgust in her voice. "I saw her number and let it go to the answering machine. If I talked to her, I would only have caused problems."

Lily had quickly become a bright spot within his tight-knit family. She'd bonded with her cousins as if she'd been born a Croft, not introduced to Beckett only three years ago when she'd already been two years old.

Luckily, Kim's relationship with the Raiders' star running back was going well, which meant Beckett's custody case had proceeded smoothly. If things between Kim and Henderson went south, Beckett knew she'd be back, demanding Lily—and not because she suddenly wanted to be a mother. She wanted Lily because having Lily meant she also had access to Beckett's money. No Lily, no money. And Kim was all about the cash.

"I'll take care of it," Beckett said.

"You don't think she... I mean, she couldn't really..."

The heartbreak in Sarah's voice stabbed at Beckett. Not for the first time, he recognized the price of bringing Lily into the family so completely. If Kim got custody back, his wouldn't be the only heart broken. And seeing his family hurt would be a double blow.

"She probably wants money," he assured Sarah. "And I'm doing everything possible to make sure she stays out of Lily's life permanently."

"Of course you are." Sarah exhaled. "I'm sorry. I'll see you when you get home."

Beckett disconnected with his sister and thought a moment, then dialed his attorney.

Fred Henry picked up on the third ring. "Hey, Beck. Did you mean to dial my number, or is your vision crossed? You hit the ice pretty hard."

"Not that hard. I just found out that Kim called my house tonight while I was at the game."

"Uh-oh." Fred's voice dipped into a troubled tone. "How much did she want this time?"

"I don't know. Sarah's watching Lily tonight, and she didn't answer the phone."

"Smart. And where are you?"

"Georgetown University Hospital, but I'm fine. Listen, I don't like her calling so close to the custody hearing. Can you put Toby back on her?" Fred's investigator was amazing at digging up information. "I want to know how solid her relationship with Henderson is right now."

"You got it."

"Have you contacted her aunt yet?" Beckett asked. His mind filled with an image of the old woman who'd appeared on his doorstep dragging Lily by the arm. His daughter had been filthy and bawling and utterly distraught. The memory still stabbed his heart with a fiery dagger.

"The nursing home she went to closed, and the patients were scattered. They won't give out information to anyone who isn't next of kin, so Toby's tracking her family to find out where she went."

A jumpy feeling Beckett usually only got before big games made his nerves stand on end. "I'd feel better if we upped the resources on this. Lily's settled in school, she's come out of her shell, she's got friends, she's tight with her cousins, she's got my family doting on her." *She owns my heart.* "Do what you need to do to locate her aunt and get her statement recorded. I'm *not* letting my daughter go back to living like an unwanted pet."

4

E den pushed through the front door of Capital Ambulance at six p.m. and slid out of her parka. After a full day of school, she was tired, but still excited about her shift.

The building sat on a corner in downtown DC a few blocks west of the White House in an area of large office buildings and newer brick townhomes. Once a single-family home, the building had been renovated by the company into an industrial ambulance station with living quarters for the crew.

She relaxed into the warmth of the space as she walked through the foyer and stepped into the front office, a room that doubled as a secondary living space for the staff. Tori, one of her favorite coworkers, sat on the arm of a recliner, chatting with Tommy, one of the EMTs Eden and Tori were relieving for the night.

Eden stopped and smiled wide, offering an excited "Guess what today is."

Tori pushed to her feet and threw her hands in the air. "Your last day. Yay!"

She ran to Eden, and they hugged, then laughed over their excitement for such a minor milestone. All the EMTs at Capital were great, but she and Tori had become best friends, and Eden loved their shifts together.

"What?" Clint, Tommy's partner the night before, stepped in from the kitchen, his voice giving away shock and concern. "Eden, you're not leaving us."

Tori pulled away but kept an arm tight around Eden's shoulders. "No way. Well, at least not yet. Today's the last day she needs to qualify for the paramedic didactic program." She turned her bright smile on Eden. "We're going to get you those last five patients tonight even if we have to go trolling the homeless alleys for them."

"Man," Tommy said, pushing from the sofa, "that sounds like a blast. Sorry I can't stay. I've got a hamster to wash."

Clint wandered that direction, pushed his arms into his jacket and picked up the duffel sitting by the door. "Is that what the flowers are for? We thought maybe it was your birthday or something."

Flowers. Eden took a fist straight to the solar plexus.

A chill raced through her belly. Her breath whooshed out, and her smile dropped. She glanced at Tori and forced enough air into her lungs to ask, "What flowers?"

Her friend's smile had disappeared too. Tori shook her head. "I just got here."

Eden's hands fisted so hard, her nails bit into her palms. She hadn't been notified of any parole hearing, and John wouldn't be released for at least ten more years without one.

She glanced between Tommy and Clint. "Who... Who sent them?"

"Don't know," Clint said. "Kylie was here when they came."

Kylie, another EMT, wouldn't be coming on again until tomorrow night.

Tori picked up the slack for Eden with an upbeat "Then we'll have to investigate."

"They're in the rec room," Tommy said, picking up a backpack on the floor beside the chair. He started for the door with "Try not to stir up too much trouble tonight, ladies."

Clint followed Tommy out the door while the two men agreed to meet up for a game of hoops the next morning.

As soon as the door closed behind them, a deafening silence hung in the air.

"Were you notified?" Tori asked, her voice vibrating with the same tension humming inside Eden. "Is he out?"

"No." Eden's throat tightened. Her heart beat too quickly. "I don't know."

If he knew where she was, she'd have to get a restraining order. She'd have to watch her back even more than she did already. If he showed signs of following through on the threat he'd made while they'd dragged him from the courtroom, she'd have to relocate. She'd have to put her life on hold—again—and just when she was so close to moving up and moving on.

Tori reached out and gave Eden's arm a reassuring squeeze. "One step at a time. You've handled this before. You can handle it again."

But she shouldn't have to, and the thought that she might stoked both fury and terror. She exhaled and gave Tori a nod, then headed toward a larger room in the back of the house.

The staff had designated this as the rec room because it was where all their entertainment was housed—television, stereo, movie collection, Xbox, Nintendo, video games, ping-pong table, dartboard. Every EMT brought some form of distraction to pass the time in this home away from home.

Eden stepped down into the room, and her gaze immediately latched on to the only bright spot—a bouquet sitting on the poker table. Her feet halted, and her chest squeezed.

"Holy shit," she breathed. The arrangement was both elaborate and extravagant—a huge spray of lilies and lilacs, foxglove and delphinium, and more roses than she'd ever seen together at one time.

"Good Lord." Tori's voice broke into the fear clouding Eden's mind. "That's...ridiculous."

Eden couldn't make her feet move forward. Her heart pounded in her ears. Fear tumbled through her like a waterfall.

Tori slid a hand over Eden's shoulder, and she flinched. Shame and anger heated Eden's face, and she dropped her gaze to the floor. "Sorry."

"Do you want me to open the card?"

Eden took a breath, then blew it out in a slow stream. Tears of fear burned her eyes. She threaded her fingers together and twisted her hands. Then she cleared her throat and said, "Please."

Tori moved toward the flowers and searched among the blooms for a card. It would be just like John not to leave one. After all the bouquets he'd sent the morning after to smooth things over—as if flower petals could heal cuts and bruises and scars on her psyche—he knew she would assume they were from him.

Eden crossed one arm over her middle and lifted her other hand to the back of her neck. She threaded her fingers into her hair and ran her fingertips over the scar there.

Tori plucked a small white envelope from the middle of the bouquet. "Jeez, almost couldn't find it in this forest."

She tossed a nervous look at Eden, then tore the envelope and pulled out the small card. Eden closed her hands into fists, her gaze intense on Tori's expression.

Her dark brows pulled down, and she shot a look at Eden. "You're definitely not telling me something. Who's...*Beckett*?"

The name hit Eden sideways. *Beckett?* Beckett Croft had sent her flowers?

That was even harder to believe than John finding a way to send them from prison. Croft had seemed too focused on the challenge of getting Eden to swoon over him to think outside himself. Even if he'd considered a thank-you gesture as patients occasionally did, a full week had passed since then, and he was already playing again. Eden had seen his return to the ice on the news.

She released a long breath of relief, but she was still shaky. "What does it say?"

Tori lowered her gaze to the card and read. "'We had a rocky intro. I'd like a chance to show you my better side. I sometimes chill at Top Shelf after home games. Or call me for a more private meeting.'" She flipped the card over. "'Our schedules probably aren't overly compatible, but I'd love to sneak in a stolen moment with you.'" Tori read off a phone number. "And in parentheses underneath it says, 'My personal cell. Please don't share.'"

The knot in her gut unwound a little more, and Eden breathed easier. Her lips tipped up a little when she remembered Beckett's lighter side once he'd been pulled away from the ice. Then heat stirred when she remembered his hard body, handsome face, and overwhelming confidence. Sure, she'd fantasized about him over the last week. Who wouldn't?

"Sneak in a stolen moment?" Tori lifted her hands out to the sides with a what-the-hell look on her face. "What rocky intro? Beckett who? Why didn't you tell me about this? He sounds ridiculously *dreamy*."

He *did* sound pretty damned dreamy. And so did sneaking in a stolen moment with him. Until her mind filled with images of his brutality on the ice.

Eden really didn't feel like rehashing her meeting with Beckett, but by the look on Tori's face... She relented with a sigh. "He's one of the Rough Riders. The one Gabe and I had to take in to the hospital."

Tori opened her mouth to say something, but her gaze hazed over, and after a long, agonizing moment, she finally managed, "Oh..."

Eden had shared pieces of her traumatic past with Tori. She huffed a humorless laugh. "Exactly."

Tori regrouped, pressed one hand to her hip, and tapped her chin with the corner of the card. "Well..." Tilting her head, she lowered her gaze to the floor, her brow pressed into a concerned frown. "Hmm..."

Their pagers sounded simultaneously. Eden was grateful for the distraction. "There's one of my last five." She pulled the pager from her belt and read the call. "Woman down, Dupont Circle."

Tori passed Eden on her way toward the door and their ambulance beyond, holding the card out to her. "We're not done talking about this."

Eden stuffed the card into her pants pocket and followed, pulling up the address of their call on her phone along with potential routes to the location.

She climbed into the passenger's side and fastened her seat belt as Tori pulled out of the garage. "Take 23rd to NW O to 20th. The whole freaking map is red tonight."

"What else is new?" Tori flipped on the sirens while Eden took control of the radio, informing dispatch they were en route.

"You know he's not John," Tori said, continuing their conversation about Beckett as she sped down Q Street toward the heart of DC. "Just because he's a hockey player doesn't mean—"

"He's an enforcer." The last word felt so uncomfortable coming out of Eden's mouth. "Gabe explained it to me. He's the guy on the team who—"

"Fights," Tori finished. "I've heard."

"Figures, right?" The first guy who'd created any kind of interest in her in two years had violence in his blood. "Am I a freaking magnet for these guys or something?"

"It's not like you've dated dozens of guys and they've all been bullies." Tori slowed, checked an intersection, and pushed through. "Do you like him?"

"I don't even know him."

"You know what I mean. Was there a spark?"

"He was an ass the first fifteen minutes, pissed they'd pulled him out of the game. When he calmed down, he was more tolerable, but he was arrogant, cocky. You know the type."

"Sure—successful, driven, good-looking, built. The kind of accomplished guy who's got something to be cocky about."

"Doesn't mean he has to be."

They approached an intersection where cars were stacked at a red light. Tori pulled into the oncoming lane to pass. Once she was on the correct side of the road again, she said, "He had to be tolerable or you would have called him a creep or a jerk or a loser by now. Let me ask it this way, if he *wasn't* a hockey player, would you be interested in seeing him?"

That turned Eden's mind a different direction. As the siren blared in the background, Beckett's smile flashed in her head. Then the way his brown eyes lightened when he laughed. A pang of desire hit Eden. A pang that grew to a craving when she thought of the fantasies she'd created over the last week involving him. "Maybe. I don't know."

"Eden," Tori said, her tone a compassionate reprimand. "It's been two years. You left California so you could have a life, but all you do is work and study. That's not a life."

"I know," she grumbled. She wasn't living, she was existing. Had been from the moment she'd escaped to the East Coast. She kept telling herself she'd venture out when she could cut back on work or when school eased up, but that never happened. And she was tired of the isolation, the stress, the loneliness. There was no fun, no relaxation, no love in her life. Her friends were all from work or school, and they were all superficial. All except Tori. "But, honestly, the thought of that whole boyfriend thing..." She shuddered with an involuntary sound of aversion. "Makes me feel all...boxed in. Makes me want to squirm to get out."

"Screw the boyfriend idea. How about a hookup buddy? He seems like the prime candidate for a booty call. He's hot, he travels, he's got a demanding career. Not to mention he's intensely fit, so you know he can go the distance in bed, if you know what I mean."

Oh man, did Eden know what Tori meant. The thought had heat building between her legs. It had been so long since she'd had good sex. Fun, carefree, fulfilling, *healthy* sex. And, damn, she missed that part of her life.

"Hmmm." Her gaze blurred over the street through the windshield as Tori navigated into a residential area. "A hookup situation does sound like a better option." At least it did until her memory flashed with the look on his handsome face when he'd rammed the other player into the boards. "Maybe just not with this guy. If you'd seen him on the ice, I think you'd agree." She scanned the numbers on the street. "It's the third town house on the left. The one with the shiny black door."

Tori pulled to a stop at the curb and put the rig into Park. "Don't make any decisions right now. Just thank him for the flowers and leave it open-ended. See where it goes."

They both bailed out of the truck to open the back. Tori dragged out the stretcher, and Eden tossed the jump bag on top, then grabbed the oxygen tank and followed Tori toward the house.

"Eden," Tori nagged. "Promise me you'll at least consider it."

"Yes, fine." She took hold of the foot of the gurney and started up the brick steps. A small part of her was relieved Tori made the demand. Because it gave Eden permission to consider something her common sense wouldn't. "I'll think about it."

An older African-American man stood on the porch, holding the storm door open.

"My wife," he said, his voice tight with worry. "She's having trouble breathing."

And just like that, all thoughts of hooking up with Beckett Croft faded into the background.

5

B eckett's whole body felt like one big cooked noodle by the time he filed into the locker room along with his teammates. Their spirited comments over the game mixed with heavy breathing and the *clack, clack, clack* of equipment.

At his space on the bench, he dropped his butt to the wood, uncapped a bottle of cold water, and downed it without pausing. Once everyone was settled, Coach Tremblay gave a short talk, congratulating the team and pointing out their strengths during the game.

The floor then transitioned to Rafe Savage, the player named MVP during the previous win. Rafe pulled the ceremonial Revolution-era tricorne hat, a symbol chosen to represent the team's name, from his locker. The brown leather was worn, the gold trim frayed from the hat's many travels with the team.

Savage stood and worked the leather back into shape as he spoke. "Passing this on tonight is easy. For single-handedly cultivating college funds to support the children of the Blackhawks' team dentist, I hand this over to Beckett Croft." Group laughter erupted around the room, peppered by hoots and hollers. Savage handed the hat to Beckett with a grin and a "Way to clean house, bud."

Beckett felt every one of those hits tonight. But he stood as if he were twenty-two with no scars, and firmly positioned the prize on his head, then posed for a few photos. And since the love of his life was currently ensconced in a Disney-movie marathon with her cousins at her grandmother's house, he said, "I guess drinks are on me."

After showering and changing back into the clothes he'd worn to the stadium, Beckett wandered toward Top Shelf with the other guys, lingering behind to call his mom. Before he could tap into FaceTime and connect, his attorney's name lit up his screen.

He groaned but then purposely twisted his thoughts in a positive direction before he answered. "Hey, Fred. Tell me you've got good news."

"I've got good news and not so good news."

"Hold on a sec." As they approached the bar, Beckett lowered the phone. "Hey, guys, I'll be right in. Open a tab."

When his teammates disappeared inside, Beckett leaned his back against a light post, grateful the icy wind wasn't blowing tonight. "Okay, what have you got?"

"The good news," Fred said, "is that Toby located Kim's aunt at a nursing home in Sarasota, Florida."

"That's great."

"Hold on," Fred cautioned, pulling Beckett's hopes down a little. "While she does corroborate your story about Kim dumping Lily on her and leaving without ever looking back, her health has deteriorated considerably over the last year. If her state of mind is challenged, I can't guarantee her affidavit will be all that beneficial."

Beckett winced.

"Also," Fred went on, "inside sources say Kim and

Henderson are a little on the rocky side. A lot of ups and downs over the last month or two."

Beckett squeezed his eyes closed. "*Fuck.*"

"Hey," Fred said, serious and steadfast, "I'm going to keep a titanium bubble around you and Lily, Beck. I'm giving you the big picture, but worrying, planning, and counterattack are *my* job. Your job is to focus on the ice. Securing that next contract is as important to keeping you and Lily together as holding Kim at arm's length. You've trusted me for years. You've got to trust me now. You know it would kill me to see that bitch get Lily back."

"I know." Beckett exhaled, his jaw muscles pulsing as his teeth clenched and released. "Listen, I'll feel better if we go all the way with this. Don't stop with her aunt. Get all Lily's medical records, get statements from Kim's neighbors, friends, coworkers, talk to her ex-boyfriends, anyone who took care of Lily during that time. I want documentation on not only how Kim abandoned her that one time, but showing it was a pattern of behavior. Because we both know it was a pattern, the same way her calls to me for money are a pattern. And if her patterns hold true, that means her relationship with Henderson is going to fall through. Hopefully that will happen *after* a judge awards me full custody of Lily, but I want all the ammunition I can possibly get in case that relationship goes south before."

"Beck, you know that's going to take an enormous amount of manpower—"

"I don't care what it costs. If you have to put Toby on it full time, three guys on it, five guys on it, whatever you've got to do, Fred, just do it."

"Okay, okay." He used his soothing tone. "I'll do whatever you want, and I'll get it done as fast as possible, but Kim hasn't made any aggressive moves, so I think it's best to play this cool. As if we're confident. As if we'll keep giving her money as long as she wants it. The less flack she gets as we approach the hear-

ing, the less apt she'll be to launch her own offensive maneu-
vers. You have to remember, she's had a whole year to stash
Henderson's cash. There's no telling what kind of resources
she's got now. And there's a lot of talk about you being the
hottest free ticket coming on the market in July."

Beckett dropped his hand and stared blankly at the pedestrians passing on the sidewalk. God, the pressure felt like a vise.
Holding on to Lily, staying close to his family, securing another
contract. It seemed to build and build, with hockey being his
only consistent outlet.

"I hear you," he said.

Fred promised to keep him posted, and Beckett disconnected, then used FaceTime to call his parents' house,
searching for some good to offset the bad.

His mother answered, her familiar smile filling the screen.
She was in the kitchen of his parents' home in the hills of
Arlington. "That had to be one of your best games to date, son.
At thirty-one, you keep getting better."

"Thanks." His mother had sung Beckett's praises since he
first stepped on the ice, but it still made him smile. "It was a
tough game."

"That's an understatement. Keep playing like that, and you
won't have to worry about where your next contract is coming
from."

He pulled up a smile for his mom. "That's the plan."

"I'm sorry we couldn't be there."

"Me too, but after decades, you've seen enough of my
hockey games. You've got something more important to do
now."

"Yes, I do." She stood and walked through the house.
"Listen to this."

She moved down the stairway to his parents' finished basement, and a flurry of giggles floated over the line. Beckett
laughed, and his stress melted. Nothing could relax him like

Lily's love and laughter. In ten short months, her happiness had become his absolute first priority.

"*That* is *beautiful*," he told his mom.

"She's come so far, Beckett." His mom's voice was soft, her expression drenched with love. "She's a completely different little girl from the one left on your doorstep last year."

He smiled, pleased with Lily's transformation. "She is amazing."

"*You* are an amazing father. We couldn't be more proud."

Father.

That reality still seemed to hit him like a fist to the gut, even three years after he'd learned of Lily's existence. The responsibility that title laid on his shoulders stole his breath and touched everything he did. Would continue to affect every decision he made for the rest of his life. And every time he thought of Lily, he welcomed all of it.

"Well, I had an exceptional role model, didn't I?"

She chuckled. "I'll tell him you said that."

"Do." He glanced at the bar. "Can I talk to Lily for a minute?"

"Yes, but don't forget our deal."

"Oh, Mom, really?" he complained, remembering her unrelenting requests for a sleepover with all the granddaughters, sans Beckett. With this Kim turmoil going on, he had an overwhelming urge to stay close to Lily. "What if I come get her after she falls asleep?"

"Then she'll miss waking up with Rachel and Amy. She misses the whole morning routine of lying around in the sleeping bags, eating breakfast while they watch cartoons, getting dressed together, doing each other's hair—"

"God. Fine." He gave up. No one argued like his mother. And it was in Lily's best interest. "Don't worry about me going through withdrawals all night. Why couldn't you schedule this during one of my away games?"

"It had to fall on a weekend night and fit with Sarah's, Rachel's, and Amy's schedules too." She grinned. "Remember, it's not all about you anymore."

He sighed dramatically. But he'd never believed everything was about him. His parents had drilled that into him early.

A burst of giggles erupted in the background, and a sweet ache surged inside Beckett. "Okay, okay, what about this—I'll come over and sleep on the couch. She won't even know I'm there until she wakes up, and I'll let her stay and play with the girls. I promise I won't cramp her style."

"Oh my God, Beckett." His mother gave him a pitying look. "You realize she has to go away to college someday, right?"

"Shit, don't do that to me." He dropped his head and covered his face with his free hand. "That's cruel."

His mother's laughter made Beckett laugh too.

"How do you get through away games?"

He wore himself out on the ice, trained extra hard, and found an occasional hookup—because that had become the only time he could hook up without traipsing strange women in and out of Lily's life. Which was—without question—unthinkable. And, of course, he missed Lily like crazy. But he told his mom, "I think about getting back home."

His mom passed the phone to Lily.

Her dark eyes and button nose filled the screen. "Hi, Daddy."

Beckett's grin slid into his chest and lit him up from the inside out. "Hey, beautiful. How was school today?"

"Good," she chirped. "We finger-painted. I played with Becca and Colby on the swings."

"What did you paint?"

"You skating." Her perfectly smooth brow pulled into a frown, and her little nose scrunched up. "But Colby used all the bright blue, so I didn't have the right color."

He chuckled at her diligence to get his uniform right. "I'm sure it's great. Can't wait to see it. Is Becca over her flu?"

All Lily's frustration vanished. "Yeah."

Something distracted her, and she looked away.

"Are you having fun with Rachel and Amy?"

"Yeah," she said, her gaze still clinging to something else in the room. "We're gonna watch *Frozen*."

"Okay," he sighed. "Give me a kiss, and I'll let you go."

That got her attention. Her face grew comically close to the phone, and the screen went dark as her lips pressed against it for a split second. Then she was gone, and the image jumped all over the room as she ran to hand the phone to her grandmother with a distracted "Bye, Daddy."

When his mother's face finally came back into view, Beckett was already feeling lonely. "How long do I have before she goes to college?"

"Thirteen years. But you'll start losing her to friends, sports, and boys a lot sooner."

Beckett's heart cracked. He huffed a groan and hung his head. "Thanks, Mom. I'm going to drown my sorrows now. Enjoy my daughter enough for both of us."

She laughed. "Oh, you never have to worry about that, son."

Beckett disconnected with an overwhelming amount of love flowing through him. Love right alongside a restless kind of loneliness. He glanced at the doors to Top Shelf again, and his mind drifted to Eden. That was another disappointment he was going to have to push into the background. He'd sent the flowers several days ago, and he still hadn't heard from her.

Almost two weeks had passed since she'd hauled him to the ER. Even without any hockey knowledge, that was plenty of time for her to figure out who he was, how much money he made, and every other intimate detail of his life. At least everything except Lily. He was keeping Lily extremely under the radar until he had full custody. But either Eden didn't care enough to look him up or what she'd found hadn't interested her enough to call, because he still hadn't heard from her. At this point, he doubted he would.

And that was a damn shame. Especially tonight. Because she would be the perfect woman to administer sexual first aid to get him through the lonely stretch ahead.

Since that wouldn't happen, Beckett would have to entertain one of the offers he routinely received on any given night out on the town. Lucky for him, hockey was a popular sport, and smokin' hot puck bunnies were everywhere.

He'd let the night play out. Who knew? Maybe he'd get an offer he couldn't refuse.

6

E den tapped the screen of her phone to check the time and found it five minutes later than the last time she'd checked.

Beckett's game had ended almost an hour ago. She was pretty sure at this point, the closest she was going to get to Beckett Croft tonight was the recaps on the television over the bar. She'd begun to think maybe that was a good thing, judging by the sportscaster's praise of Beckett's work on the ice tonight. In this case, "work" translated into dozens of brutal hits and three fistfights.

Evidently, not only was it okay to fight in hockey, it was encouraged, reminding Eden that even the idea of a hookup probably wasn't a smart move. In fact, she'd started to wonder if it might even border on pathological.

Though, halfway into her second lemon drop, Eden wasn't sure she cared. Right now all she really wanted was a roll with a hot guy. She wanted the wet heat of a man's mouth on hers. Ached for the heaviness of a man's body pushing her into a mattress. Craved the burn and stretch of a man's hard cock inside her.

What she'd really been dreaming of when she'd come here tonight was the idea of reclaiming a little of that spontaneous, sexually liberated woman she used to be years ago.

God, she hoped she still had some. She hoped it wasn't something that shriveled and died when neglected. Because if that was the case, hers was dust in the attic.

A wave of young, handsome men in suits and ties and smart-looking overcoats or parkas streamed into the bar, and Eden's pulse jumped. A few had women at their sides, but most were alone. And they didn't look like businessmen or guys who'd bailed on a wedding reception to find some fun. They were unshaven, their hair was damp, and they had that just-worked-out glow. But it was the Rough Rider jerseys worn by the women at a few of the men's sides and the way the staff and some of the customers greeted them that told Eden for sure that these men were members of the team.

But that didn't matter to her, because the door closed behind the men, and Beckett wasn't among them.

Disappointment tugged at her gut. From her tiny table in the shadowed corner, she scanned the men, searching for one who might make a halfway decent replacement for Beckett. But despite several fine specimens standing at the bar, none interested her.

Beckett had inspired her to dress up, do her hair, even put on a little makeup and come out alone in the hopes of seeing him postgame. No one at the bar even gave her enough incentive to get her butt out of the chair to start a conversation.

And wasn't that just perfect? A battered woman only interested in hooking up with the baddest of the bad boy hockey players? If that didn't scream *psychiatric problem*, she didn't know what did. Which made her wonder where a girl went to get a mojo tune-up.

Evidently, the universe had its head screwed on way straighter than Eden did. Maybe tonight was meant to be more about lessons than action. After all, the realization that she could get past the nerves for the right man was a good first step —even if Beckett hadn't been the right man.

"Not meant to be," she reassured herself and glanced around for the cocktail waitress to ask for her check. "Excuse —" But the woman passed in a blur, and Eden dropped her hand, exhaling, "me."

She fished through her purse and—painfully—parted with thirty dollars. After laying it on the table, she reached for the drink and took one more sip.

When she tilted the glass back, her gaze fell on another man entering the bar, sliding out of an overcoat. Underneath, he too wore a suit, black and well cut for his large muscular build. His dark hair fell in a wave over his forehead, the sides layering out in an effortless sort of roguish carelessness.

Beckett.

Eden's stomach lifted and flipped. Her throat closed in the middle of her swallow, and she had to consciously focus on getting the drink down without choking.

Lord, he was even better looking than she remembered.

He slid a phone into the pocket of his blazer and greeted other customers as he sauntered toward the bar. With an easy smile, he accepted handshakes and slaps on the back and stopped to talk with everyone who wanted a minute. He signed a few autographs and took a few photos, all with an I've-got-all-the-time-in-the-world attitude.

He exuded confidence and ease, happiness and positivity. His face was scruffy, and the way he wore that suit... Damn, he was ridiculously sexy. He stirred all sorts of heat inside Eden she hadn't felt in forever.

Hello, mojo.

Once he'd satisfied fans, Beckett melted into the busy scene at the bar. With one foot pressed to the brass rod near the floor, his forearms leaning on the glossy surface, Beckett relaxed into a conversation with the man Eden had met as she and Gabe transported Beckett to the ambulance. Donovan, if she remembered right.

Beckett laughed, and his bright smile created crinkles at the corners of his eyes. Eden's stomach squeezed so hard, her throat ached. And, holy shit, the first flash of real fear came out of the shadows and seared her gut.

It was *way* easier to think and talk big when what she wanted was a fantasy. Now that he was here in the rock-hard flesh, she suddenly realized he was too much. Too sexy. Too confident. Too charismatic.

Her mind darted to John, just as sexy, just as confident, just as charismatic. It made a sick sort of sense that she would be attracted to the same kind of man. And look how badly that had turned out. Eden should really start off with someone more like a milquetoast and build her confidence from there.

But her gaze slid down the length of Beckett's big body again. His suit covered a crisp white dress shirt pulling across muscled abs, decorated by a deep red tie, pulled loose at his neck. His slacks hugged muscled thighs. She'd spent her life surrounded by men in suits, but she'd seen only a handful who could really wear one well. And she could honestly say she'd *never* seen anyone look as good in a suit as Beckett Croft.

Why all the players were wearing suits was a mystery. But none of them looked like bankers or accountants or IT guys. There was something very different about these men. Something about their posture, their attitude, their vibe. A confident, careless, undeniably attractive swagger Eden had never experienced before.

Tori was right. Eden did need to start living. If she kept hiding, she was only continuing to let John control her—two years later and three thousand miles away. If she didn't at least try for Beckett tonight, everything she'd done to drag herself up from the darkness was wasted.

Eden took a breath and pressed her hands against the table to stand. Before she got to her feet, two pretty women several years younger than Eden approached Beckett. She released her breath and sat again. Disappointment and regret landed heavily in her gut as she prepared to watch him pick up a woman—or two—and get cozy. The weak, scaredy-cat part of her hoped he took them up on their offer. It would give her a legitimate out.

After a moment of conversation, Beckett turned, called two of his teammates over, and introduced them to the women. Then he extricated himself from the conversation and made his way to another area of the bar, where a few guys watched ESPN. As he wandered, he scanned the bar, glancing over the tables.

When his head turned toward Eden's dark corner, she held her breath. How mortifying would it be to have him find her sitting alone, waiting for him, only to have him brush her off because she'd waited too long?

The answer was: *extremely.*

But the bartender drew his gaze before he found her little table, and Beckett reached across his friends to take a clear drink from the other man.

The wave of relief that swept in made Eden realize she couldn't take this roller coaster. She had to do something.

She tapped into her phone's messages. Her nerves were strung so tight, her hands shook. But she wanted to test the waters before she approached him, because the truth was that no matter how badly she might want him, no matter how strong she could pretend to be, she was feeling pretty damn fragile.

She quickly sent a message to the number he'd left on the florist's card.

Hi, it's Eden. Thank you for the flowers. They are exquisite and the gesture was thoughtful. It's been a hectic few days for me, but I wanted to tell you that I appreciated them.

With his gaze bouncing between his friends, the television, the door, and the tables, Beckett pulled his phone from his pocket with a lazy, distracted air. He was lifting his drink to his mouth when he looked at his screen.

His hand froze. His eyes scanned the message. And a smile broke over his face.

The sight uncorked a giddy kind of joy inside Eden. One she hadn't felt in forever. One she also knew was as dangerous to her well-being as it was essential.

He set his drink down, wandered away from his friends, and, still smiling, returned the text.

Eden bit her lip and tried to breathe through the nervous tingles in her stomach as she waited for his message. When her phone dinged, she looked down.

Hey. Good to hear from you. I'm glad you liked them. Thanks for putting up with my shitty mood the night we met. I'm really sorry I was such an ass. I'm leaving town tomorrow for away games. Can I take you to dinner tonight?

She tilted her head with a confused smile and responded. *Little late for dinner, isn't it? Saw the game tonight. I don't know anything about hockey, but the sportscasters have been praising your hitting ability. Not sure if that relates to the guys you ran into the wall or the ones you got into fistfights with.*

She was curious to see how he responded to the topic.

Beckett wandered toward the jukebox, turned his back, and leaned against it, tapping out his response. *It is late, but I figured your schedule probably wasn't the standard 8-5. As for my work on the ice, I do a lot more checking and pushing than fighting, but with some teams like the one we played tonight, fights are inevitable. How about drinks? Or dessert? Or even coffee? I'll bring it to you if you don't want to go out.*

Checking? What the heck was checking?

Eden bit the inside of her cheek. Did she want to chance spending time with a guy who thought hitting and pushing— or this thing he called checking—didn't fall into the realm of fighting? A guy who talked about it with a careless all-in-a-day's-work attitude, then asked her out for drinks in the next breath?

John pushed into her mind, and a nagging ache pulled deep inside her. Eden slid a hand over the discomfort with a soft *"Goddammit."* She *needed* to let the past go. She thought she *had*. But when she darted a glance toward Beckett and found him almost meditatively staring at his phone, waiting for her response, a little voice in her head kept asking, *Why? Why me?*

She looked for the two young women who'd come in earlier and found them cozied up to Beckett's teammates. They were pretty and fit, and Eden couldn't help but wonder why he'd hooked them up with teammates instead of keeping them for himself. Eden truly didn't know whether to be flattered that a man as confident and good-looking as Beckett had shown an interest in her, or concerned that his interest stemmed from some victim vibe she emitted.

Eden? Did I lose you?

His text pulled her out of her own head. God, she was a bigger mess than she'd realized. Coming out to meet Beckett had prodded insecurities she thought she'd overcome. And, man, this really pissed her off. She was sick of living like a goddamned psycho woman, locked in her tiny apartment when she wasn't at school or work.

Still here. She typed, then murmured, "Breathe, Eden." And added *How about if we share dessert? What do you like?*

When she chanced another glance at him, she saw his smile was back.

It would probably be inappropriate to say you, so anything with chocolate and whipped cream would be my second choice.

Tingles erupted all over her body. Good tingles. Tingles that made all the icky feelings disappear.

"Oh God," she whispered, her heart beating hard and fast against her ribs. She pushed herself with "Type, Eden."

Then I'm ordering the Sticky Chocolate Pudding Cake. Make your way over to me in the corner when you're ready to indulge.

She took a breath, whispered, "I can do this," and hit Send.

His smile slowly faded as he read. And it seemed like forever before his head came up. As the waitress passed, Eden caught her attention and placed the order. Beckett looked straight ahead, his brows drawn in a little furrow before his gaze jumped to all the corners of the bar, landing on hers last. Surprise lit his eyes, and his lips moved with something she couldn't hear but what looked like *"Holy shit."*

She rested her chin in her hand and grinned while her belly did somersaults and triple flips.

He pushed off the jukebox and started toward her, dodging other people in the bar with an expression of excitement and determination. Eden stood to meet him, but when he stopped short a few feet away, and scanned her from the top of her head all the way to her toes, a fresh surge of self-consciousness prickled along her limbs.

This was an outfit she wouldn't have thought twice about wearing a few years ago. An outfit she'd worn to parties and events she'd attended with John in Los Angeles. She loved the sweater dress for its soft texture, beautifully stylized pleats, gently flared short skirt, and the way it showed all her curves without clinging like Lycra. Her black suede boots had three-inch heels, rose above her knees, and were adorned with rhinestones.

She used to feel pretty and sparkly and comfortable in this outfit. But now, she wasn't sure it worked—in this city, in this bar, for this guy, or even for the woman she'd become. And the way Beckett was looking at her—like he'd been hit with a puck between the eyes—she was pretty sure her original feeling of going overboard was accurate.

Before Beckett spoke, a young man approached with two drinks. "Bro, you left your drink at the bar." He pushed one into Beckett's hand. "That tonic water's expensive, and the lime? That shit's like gold." Then he turned his smile on Eden and offered his newly freed hand. "I'm Tate Donovan. We met briefly when you were wheeling Beck to the ambulance and he was acting like an ass—"

"She doesn't need any reminders," Beckett cut in, his gaze sharp on his teammate.

"Beckett's right," she said, teasing him with a grin before refocusing on Tate. "I do remember. Good to see you."

"You too. And, *wow*, you look *amazing*. *Way* too hot for this guy." He gestured toward Beckett. "Would you like to join—"

"Donovan," was all Beckett had to say.

"All right, then. Well, if this guy turns back into an ass, you know where to find the good guys."

As he walked away, Beckett glanced over his shoulder and groaned. Eden pulled her attention off his delicious body and the way he filled out that suit to follow Beckett's gaze. She found all the other guys watching from the bar, their expressions filled with joviality and an edge of mischief.

"I didn't think this out very well when I suggested we meet here," Beckett said, returning an embarrassed look to her. "The guys are great, but sometimes they're like—"

"Bratty little brothers who put bugs in your shoes, then make fun of you when you freak out over them?"

He laughed, and the man's smile made her stomach float. "Sounds like you've experienced this."

"From several bratty coworkers who are about as well-behaved as your teammates when we're out together socially."

Beckett set his drink down on her table. "Then you probably wouldn't be surprised to know how mercilessly they've been razzing me about screwing up with you that night you took me to the ER."

Eden's nerves ratcheted higher. They were going to eat her alive if she didn't act. A little voice inside her head started a chant, and it got louder and louder. *Live, Eden.* So she did what she'd learned to do two years ago when fear threatened to immobilize her—she forced herself to push through.

"Well, let's solve that problem right now." She took two steps toward him. Until his heat circled her. Until his scent—something clean and spicy—filled her head.

Live, Eden.

She slipped one hand under his blazer and around his waist. He was warm and hard, and desire flooded in.

Live, Eden.

She met his surprised eyes, skimmed her other hand against his rough cheek, and combed her fingers into his hair.

Live, Eden.

And pulled his head down for their first kiss. *Her* first kiss in two long years.

_____

7

S he took Beckett so off guard, he didn't even close his eyes as she kissed him. He was shocked into stupefaction and froze, as if he'd forgotten what to do with a woman.

The moment seemed to pass in slow motion. Her long lashes lowered as her gaze focused on his mouth, and when her lips touched his, her breath whispered out and her lids closed.

It was the feel of her sweet body softening, her belly, her hips, her thighs all rubbing against his, that finally made Beckett's eyes fall closed. His heart kicked into a sprint. His hands lifted automatically, but he wasn't sure where to lay them. Did he wrap his arms around her? Should he rest his hands on her arms?

Shit, he *had* forgotten what to do with a woman. If this were a normal hookup, he'd know exactly what to do. But he wasn't particularly interested in just a hookup, yet he couldn't give any more of himself with the demands of his career and Lily and the custody issue...

While he'd been lost in all that indecision, he'd missed the kiss. Eden pulled back. Air drifted over his lips, and disappointment clouded his chest.

But she retreated only far enough to shoot a sassy little smile up at him. "To make this convincing, you should probably participate."

God, he was a dumb shit. He'd jumped way the hell ahead of the situation. But he cut himself some slack. It had been a solid four or five months since he'd had sex. Hell, maybe six. He couldn't even remember the last woman he'd been involved with who *hadn't* been a puck bunny. Even the French bicoastal model-slash-actress he'd been seeing steadily before he'd taken custody of Lily had been a fan first, a lover second.

He huffed a laugh and laid his hands on her shoulders, then let his forehead rest against hers. "You blindsided me there. I turned fifteen again for a few seconds, the prettiest girl in school took me under the bleachers, and I didn't know what the hell to do."

She laughed. A light, quiet, little giggle that utterly charmed him. And the urge to really kiss her overwhelmed him.

He stroked his hands down her arms, then back up, tempted by the sweater's softness, tantalized by her warmth beneath. Then he cupped her face with both hands. "Let's try that again."

Her hand tightened in his shirt. The spark in her eyes turned hot. And Beckett held her gaze until their lips touched again. Then he let his eyes close and explored her lips with his. Soft, supple, warm, responsive. In less than ten seconds, he was licking her lips, silently asking her to open. And when she let him in, Beckett's brain did a little spin.

Their tongues touched, stroked. Warm, wet, soft. And his cock stiffened to attention. She tasted like lemon and sugar and vodka. A delicious kind of hunger bloomed inside him. The kind he hadn't felt in a really, *really* long time. The kind that encompassed more than his cock.

He let one hand slide into the silky soft strands of her hair. Opening wider, tasting deeper, he let the other roam over her shoulder and down her slim back, then wrapped his arm low on her hips. Circling his tongue with hers, he pulled her in, letting her feel what she was doing to him. Her quick, soft intake of air felt like lightning through his body.

She pulled back a little, just enough to break the kiss. But she held on tight and looked at him with a dazed kind of hunger that gripped Beckett by the groin and wouldn't let go. "Aren't you one surprise after another?"

He licked her taste from his lips. "I was thinking the same thing about you."

Her gaze drifted past his shoulder. "Looks like one of your problems is solved."

Still holding her, he glanced that direction. All the guys had turned back toward the bar and refocused on their own conversations. He returned his gaze to her with a grin. "I owe you."

A sexy smile brightened her face. "I plan to collect."

"God, I hope so."

He stroked both hands over her back from shoulders to hips. She was trim and tight, with subtle curves that tempted, and his mind darted toward all kinds of naughty, beautiful, sexy things he hoped they had to look forward to tonight.

"About dessert," he murmured. "Are you still off the menu? 'Cause I've got a craving that won't quit."

Eden's gaze turned thoughtful. Her gaze lowered. While one arm remained curved around his waist, the other slid down the front of his dress shirt, where she slipped her fingers beneath his tie and toyed with the buttons. Her tongue stroked her lower lip, leaving it shiny and making Beckett so damn hungry.

"My body wants to jump. Wants to trash all caution and good sense and run with whatever you've got in mind."

The hesitation in her voice dampened his edge of excitement. "But...?"

She lifted her gaze to his, and something new floated there.

Something...nervous. She smiled, but that too was the slightest bit shaky. "Let's start with chocolate, and see how that goes."

This wasn't the reception he'd expected. Not the reception he was used to. He might be turning the puck bunnies down to go home to Lily now, but that didn't mean nights out at local haunts weren't usually filled with a lot more of what the two women who'd hit on him earlier had offered—a little two-on-one action, no small talk, no foreplay, no follow-up required.

But Eden wasn't a puck bunny, which was why he was standing here with her when he'd turned the other women down. Lily's presence in Beckett's life had changed more than his knowledge base about things like educational toys and girl clothes. Lily had changed almost everything, including how he related to everyone in his life—especially how he treated women. And at some point over the last year, Beckett had—unfortunately for his sex life—outgrown puck bunnies.

He smiled at Eden now and gave her waist a reassuring squeeze. "At least one of us has their head on straight."

A waitress skimmed past them and set down the chocolaty dessert, then glanced at Beckett. "Hey, Beck. You were on fire tonight."

"Thanks. How are you doin', Toni?"

"Can't complain. Can I get you two anything else?"

"I'm good," Beckett said, then looked at Eden. "Eden? Another drink?"

"Oh no. I'm half a drink over my one-drink limit. Water would be great, though." When the waitress disappeared behind the swinging door into the kitchen, Eden looked at Beckett. "You do come here a lot."

"Used to come after every home game. Now I stop by once in a while." He glanced at the table where Eden had been sitting and picked up the martini glass, half-filled. He sniffed the drink. The sugary lemon scent made him grin at her. "I thought you tasted kinda like a Lemonhead."

She gave him a silly frown. "Lemonhead?"

"The candy."

"Oh wow." She laughed. "Haven't thought of those in a long time."

"But way sweeter."

"And spiked."

"Amen. You certainly make my head spin." He set the drink down and picked up the cash.

"No." She covered his hand with hers. "That's for the—"

"Tonight's on me." He curved his free arm around her waist and eased her against him. Man, she felt great, all warm and curvy. She smelled good too, a soft floral fragrance that filled his groin with blood. His gaze slid over her pretty face and rested on her plump lips. "Showing up is your only required contribution."

When he pressed the bills into her hand, appreciation shone in her eyes. "Thank you."

He lowered his head for a feathery kiss. "Thank *you*. Seeing you again is the highlight of my night."

That made her smile deepen. Damn, she had a beautiful smile. This woman was racking up points.

But he forced himself to pull his gaze away and glanced down at his second choice of desserts tonight with a contemplative "I think I might be able to swim in that."

Eden laughed. "They said it served two."

"Two hungry hockey players, maybe." This small table wasn't going to work for the cozy chat Beckett had in mind. An open corner booth caught his eye, and he picked up the dessert plate in one hand and slipped his other arm around Eden's waist. "Let's take this somewhere more comfortable."

At the booth, he set the plate down and ushered Eden onto the padded seat. Toni came by with the drink Beckett had left at the table and Eden's fresh water. He pulled his wallet and offered her his credit card. "Can you put this together with her earlier drinks? And those idiots are all mine tonight."

She shot him a knowing smile, took the card, and smacked his arm. "You deserved MVP tonight."

Beckett was returning his wallet to his pocket when Eden said, "Why are you picking up their drinks?"

"It's tradition. In the locker room, after every win, the MVP from the prior win passes on the ceremonial hat—in our case, that's an ugly leather tricorne, à la Rough Riders from the 1800s —to whoever that person deems the MVP for that night's game. Tonight it was me. Since we were going out after, I'm also buying."

"That's pretty cool. Why were you MVP tonight?"

"Record hits in one game."

Her chin tilted up, and she offered a less than impressed "Ah."

Before he'd given it much thought, he said, "I'm going to warn the guys that if they bother us, they'll regret it at practice."

She nodded and grinned, but it was an obligatory kind of smile, and a shadow flitted through her eyes. It lasted only a millisecond, but he'd seen it.

Beckett turned toward the bar, with odd connections firing in his brain, trying to pin down these strange mixed messages he was getting from her. His body was telling him one thing, his brain another, and his gut still another.

While he'd spent decades developing his hockey skills, his true successes lay largely in his finesse. Reading cues, studying human behavior, and understanding habits were as important to him on the ice as knowing how to control the puck. He'd only realized how valuable those skills could also be off the ice in the last few years.

He'd gotten so good at figuring out what women were looking for within a few minutes of conversation, a lot of the guys asked him to screen women before they invested emotional real estate. Women all looked at members of the team differently. Some saw money, some sought fame by association, some simply wanted a good time, quite a few were downright crazy-ass bitches, and others were big-game hunters, shooting for the rock on their finger. And, yeah, he had to admit, a few of the guys had been lucky enough to find women who were truly in love with them despite the shitty schedules, lousy moods, and perpetual career instability.

But whatever he'd seen in Eden's eyes, he didn't recognize.

He stepped up next to Donovan and interrupted his bullshitting with Hendrix. "Hey."

Donovan glanced at Beckett, then immediately looked behind him. "Did you lose her already? Your moves off the ice suck as bad as mine. You have to think about getting a nanny for Lily. You're never going to find a mom for her like this."

The guys all thought that was funny. They thought the way Beckett slapped Donovan upside the back of his head was even funnier. But Beckett wasn't laughing, and he lowered his voice when he told his friend, "You know not to talk about Lily in public."

"Oh shit," Donovan said, glancing around to see if anyone other than the team was sitting nearby. "Sorry, man. I forgot."

Beckett wasn't going to be able to keep his daughter a secret forever, but until the custody hearing was over, Beckett wanted to keep Lily out of the press.

"And I'm not looking for a mother for Lily." His daughter had plenty of wonderful women in her life, Beckett's mother and sister, chief among them. "But I *am* looking for some quality time with this very hot woman, so don't even think about bugging us. I already gave my card to Toni. Try not to max my limit, would you?"

"Got it," Savage said.

"Don't blow it," Hendrix added. "You need some good pussy to keep you fresh for this out-of-town run."

"But not so much that you forget I'm picking you up for the flight tomorrow," Donovan finished.

Beckett rolled his eyes. "If I leave here before you, would one of you grab my credit card, please?"

They made a bunch of jokes about what they planned to do with his card on their trek home—things that included strip joints, drug dealers, and hookers—for which he called them a bunch of dumb fucks and returned to Eden with a chorus of fresh laughter following him.

She had her elbow on the table and her head resting on her hand. Her other hand twirled a fork in the cake. And when she looked up and saw him coming, she brought the fork to her mouth and licked chocolate off the tines in a slow, fluid sexual move. His groin tingled with an influx of heat, and his head filled with Hendrix's "You need some good pussy."

Crude but accurate. His newly acquired single-father status wasn't the only element in his life that had interfered with sex. The truth was, casual sex held a lot of risk for an athlete at Beckett's level. Lily and the complications surrounding her custody were proof of those risks. But there were others too— allegations of abuse, defamation of character, lawsuits. So, yeah, his sex life sucked. Big-time. But if his cock's radar was on target, he might have found exactly what he needed in this beautiful Garden of Eden.

He slid into the booth next to her as she lazily filled the fork with decadence. "Are you playing with that? Or eating it?"

"Little of both. What are they laughing about?"

He narrowed his eyes as his thoughts drifted back to the troublemakers that made up his second family. "Drug dealers and hookers haven't started taking credit cards, have they?"

"What?" She laughed the word.

Beckett grinned and shook his head, dismissing the sideways thought. "Nothing."

The teasing mood vanished when she lifted the fork to his

lips and watched him take the cake into his mouth. By the time he pulled back and licked his lips, his groin was heavy and hot with an infusion of lust. He let the chocolate decadence melt in his mouth. Rich, sweet, moist. His eyes closed on the raw deliciousness of the dessert.

"Mmm." He swallowed and smiled. "Good call, gorgeous."

Beckett picked up a fork and mirrored her position. He collected cake on the tip of the fork, dipped the dark chocolate in whipped cream, and brought it to her lips. "Open for me, Eden."

A slow, sensual smile turned her lips, and she opened. He slid the cake into her mouth and watched those full lips he wanted in so many ways purse around the fork. Her lids grew heavy with pleasure, and his cock throbbed at the sight.

Oh yeah. This woman had seriously great pussy potential. If the way he craved her right now was any indication of how sex between them would be, he'd take a leap and predict it would be explosive.

"I don't think I got a chance to tell you how absolutely gorgeous you look tonight." He took in the way her dress outlined her toned upper arms and shoulders, curved over her full breasts, and lay flat against her abdomen. "That dress is making me crazy."

"Thank you." She glanced down. "It's one of my favorites, but I wasn't sure..."

"It's perfect. Except that it makes me want to run my hands all over you."

She met his eyes again with a little laugh. "Then you're right. It *is* perfect. Tell me about the suits." Her gaze slid over him. "This is the last thing I expected to see a bunch of hockey players wearing after a game."

"It's partly tradition," he told her. "Something all kids do from the very start—shirts and ties in and out of the rink on game day. Those become suits in high school and the leagues.

It's a show of respect—for the game, for your team, for yourself. A symbol you take your job on the ice seriously."

"Interesting." She lifted her finger to his lip, rubbing away some chocolate. Beckett closed his hand over hers and took her finger between his lips, sucking the chocolate off the tip. Her lids went heavy, her eyes dark, and her tongue touched the corner of her mouth.

"Mmm," she murmured, watching his lips as he kissed a path over her palm.

Then he took her hand between both of his as he worked on a *let's get out of here* suggestion that sounded at least a little smoother. As something relatively respectable came to mind, he reached up to push a honeyed curl off her forehead.

But before he even touched her skin, she flinched.

The movement was so quick, so subtle—the soft jerk of her head, the quick flicker of lashes, the slight intake of breath— Beckett almost sensed the recoil more than experienced it. He froze, fingers millimeters from her face. His eyes cut to hers. Any doubt over her reaction vanished at the sight of her averted gaze, the way her lashes hid her pretty eyes.

A cold sensation seeped through the warmth inside him like tendrils. He passed a featherlight touch along her forehead with one finger as he'd initially planned. And when she exhaled and relaxed, his tension eased a little too.

"Sorry," she murmured, almost a whisper.

Beckett put that *let's get out of here* on hold.

"Hey," he said softly, then waited until she met his gaze again. When she did, the woman he'd met in the Rough Riders' locker room was somewhere way, *way* in the background. "Don't apologize for..."

He sucked back words that came out sounding like a repri-mand and reeled in all his thoughts, searching for a new starting point. In that instant, he saw a distinct correlation between his attempt at diplomacy now and all Lily had taught him about patience and compassion and humility since she'd come into his life.

"Okay," he said, "Let's get real for a minute."

She leaned back with an oh-great-here-we-go expression. "Look, I should probably just—"

"Don't do that." He slid his hand over hers. "We've gotten this far. I'm willing to talk a little to see if we can get past this blip. I think you're worth it."

"You don't know me well enough—"

"I know the woman who had the guts to shove around an angry hockey player for his own good. I know the woman who took control of that situation in a professional and, ultimately, compassionate way, then managed to make a friend of that bitchy hockey player by the time you dropped him off at the hospital."

She laughed at the last part.

"And now," he continued, "I know the woman who, despite something less than pleasant in her past, is here taking a chance on connecting again. So, I may not know the little things about you, like what your favorite color is or what you prefer to do on a Saturday night, but I know you've got character. The kind I admire."

"You know my tough side. That's not really who I am."

"You know my tough side too, and you don't even like it, but you're still here, giving me a chance. Which means, like me, you believe there's more than one side to a person. Unless, of course, you're so hot for my body, you're willing to forget everything you hate for a couple of hours to experience my godlike sexual prowess."

Eden broke into laughter. A relieved smile lifted Beckett's mouth, and his shoulders relaxed.

"I love your laugh." He stroked his hand up her arm, over her shoulder. "Let's make tonight all about you. What we do, what we don't do, how fast or slow we go or don't go is completely up to you. Like I said, you've already met your required contribution to the night by showing up."

Her grin was soft. She lowered her chin into her hand again. "You're a lot sweeter than I expected."

"If you were expecting the asshole in the locker room, why'd you come?"

"I..." She held his gaze for a moment, searching his eyes as if he had the answer. "I guess I was ready to take a chance. And I guess I was hoping there was more to you than what I heard on the news."

"The news." He let his gaze drift to her high cheekbone and brushed his knuckles across her skin, pleased when she didn't flinch or shy away. But his mind was searching the latest newscasts for negativity that might have been thrown his way. "I haven't committed any felonies lately, at least none that I know of. What were they saying about me now?"

She gave a little shake of her head as if blowing it off as no big deal. "The sportscaster was as impressed with your hit count this season as your teammates were with your hits in the game tonight. In fact, he and the news anchor marveled at your lack of injuries over the length of your career."

The dots were definitely connecting. He proceeded with honesty but caution. "I'm careful, and I'm good. I've spent all my life practicing to be careful and good. And I have to stay careful and good because my performance as a defenseman determines my salary, my future contracts, and the longevity of my career. And while I may have been more zealous when I was younger, my dad always kept me in check. I was never one of those guys who slammed players without a purpose."

Thoughts churned behind her eyes. "Your dad?"

"Yeah. He coached for decades. Was my coach for most of my life up until I went pro. Even coached me in the minor leagues. He put me on skates at two years old and stayed with me until I got drafted. I was accountable to him for every hit after every game. If I fucked up, I had to look him in the eye and tell him I fucked up and why. I lost control of my speed, I made a bad judgment call, my timing was off, my blade caught on the ice—whatever it was, I had to own up to it."

He laughed, thinking back. "God, it was awful. At the dinner table, we used to argue over what was or wasn't necessary. The rest of our family would—literally—put in earplugs so we could all get through dinner together. No joke. There was this plastic box of foam earplugs on the kitchen counter. Once, my mom and my sister tried to double them up and put two in each ear."

That made her smile deepen, and the darkness gave way to the woman Beckett was so drawn to.

"Anyway," he said, "if you're wondering if there's more to me than the number of my hits—"

"I think you've answered that question in a lot of different ways." And apparently she liked the answer, because she picked up another piece of the cake between her fingers, leaned close, and brought it to his lips. And as she let him lick chocolate off her fingers and watched every move of his lips, she said, "Where does your family live? Is it just you and your sister? Are you as close to your mom and your sister as you are to your dad?"

He was licking her thumb when her questions plucked a strange chord inside him. No woman ever wanted to know about his family. For that matter, no woman ever wanted to hear about Beckett's early playing days either. They wanted to know about his present and his future. They wanted to know about his teammates and their girlfriends and wives. They wanted to know about his salary, his signing bonuses, the big events he attended, what famous people he'd met, where he'd been, and what he did with his money.

Family-smamily.

Beckett lifted his gaze to hers. Those light blue-green eyes were heavy lidded and hot but soft. As soon as he pulled her thumb from between his lips, she leaned in and pressed hers in their place, then sighed as if she'd been waiting forever to rest her mouth against his.

A wild little sliver of desire snaked down his spine. Beckett closed his eyes, slipped a hand around the back of her neck, and opened to her. She responded like she'd been reading his mind. Her tongue slid right into place against his. The rhythm of their kiss was instantaneous and hungry and took Beckett's already interested cock to half-mast. He leaned into her, losing himself in the sweet, erotic taste of heat and woman. The slick, smooth stroke of her tongue. The supple suction of her lips. And, God, the little purr in the back of her throat made Beckett want so much more.

She pulled out of the kiss and pressed her cheek to his, leaving Beckett dizzy. "You sure can make a girl forget her own name." Her nails scraped gently along the back of his neck, and she rolled her head to press kisses to his jaw. "What were we talking about? Your family...right. Where do they live?"

"Wow," he breathed, "that was so *not* where my mind was." He had to force himself to refocus. "They're all in and around the DC Metro area."

"They're so close." She leaned away just enough to smile up at him, a new light in her eyes. She scraped her wet bottom lip between her teeth, then moved even closer and draped one thigh over his. Do they come to your games? And where was your mind?"

He automatically covered her thigh with his hand. Her soft dress felt sinfully delicious. "When they can. They have busy lives too." He couldn't keep his hand still and found her thigh toned and supple and warm beneath the soft fabric. "Eden, I'm having a really hard time thinking about anything other than you right now."

"I'm having the same problem." She pressed a flat hand to

his tie and slid it slowly down his abdomen. "But at least I'm trying."

He took a gooey chunk off the cake with his free hand and braced his elbow on the table as he lifted the chocolate to her lips. "Trying to what? Think about nothing but me? Because I would support that decision two hundred percent."

She was laughing when her lips parted to take the chocolate, but the humor faded as soon as her mouth closed. Her warmth tingled through his hand, and then the gentle suction of her lips tugged on his fingers.

"Damn, you are so beautiful." He listed forward, leaning his head against hers. Watching her lick and suck his fingers clean made his cock flinch and throb, begging for the same attention. Not only had it been a long damn time since he'd had decent sex, but it had been fucking forever since he'd had a woman give him this sort of focused attention. Only now, when the promise of that kind of pleasure glittered on the horizon, did he realize how badly he needed it.

"*Fuck*, you're good with your mouth." His other hand flexed and released on her thigh. He turned his head and put his lips at her ear whispering, "Will you tell me what you have on under your dress tonight?"

She licked the tip of his thumb. "I could, but that would ruin the surprise."

His heart did a three-sixty. He was probably pushing the envelope, but he really didn't know how else to live. It was what he did. It was who he was. "What if I felt it? That wouldn't be looking."

He bent his head and pressed a path of kisses along her jaw. Her fingers curled into the front of his shirt. He tasted the sensitive hollow behind her ear, and Eden tipped her head toward him and sighed.

"God, you are sweet." He lifted an arm over the back of the booth and brushed the hair off her neck, kissing her there.

Then he slipped his other hand beneath the edge of her skirt, opening his hand over the soft suede of her boot top before spanning the inner thigh of her leg draped over his own.

His palm hit the warm, bare skin of her thigh, and the shock of intimacy traveled through his body like lightning. "*Fuck*." In this cold weather, he wasn't prepared for skin-on-skin contact. He pressed his forehead to her neck and let his fingers sink into the supple muscle. "Baby, I think your sexy just blew my circuit."

Her laugh started as a giggle and grew until it shook her whole body. Her happiness added to Beckett's joy until he couldn't stop smiling. And he knew this short time with Eden would count as one of the best dates of his life, even if they never got any further than this.

Then she went and blew another fuse by whispering, "Go ahead. Touch me."

8

Eden hadn't felt this playful or free with a guy since she'd been in high school. High school, when nothing mattered but self-discovery and figuring out what life was all about. And as Beckett's dark eyes latched on to hers while his hand slid up her inner thigh, Eden realized that was really what this stage of her life was about—discovering who she was now, after everything that had happened, after how far she'd come.

The fiery look in Beckett's eyes told Eden she was still attractive, still sexy, still desirable. And she hadn't felt wanted, or even worthy of being wanted, in so long, she'd forgotten what it felt like. Beckett was damn good at reminding her it felt downright intoxicating.

His touch left a wake of tingles along her thigh, and by the time his fingers neared her panties, she was swollen and damp and throbbing. Her sex clenched, preparing for a heavy hand. But Beckett's fingers barely touched her as they brushed past and traced the lace band low on her belly.

"Put your arm around me." His murmur drew Eden's gaze from his mouth to his eyes. "It'll give us more privacy."

Her awareness instantly widened to the dim space around them, to the other customers in the bar, to the waitresses wandering between tables. It was crowded and dark, and everyone was in their own world. The waitresses were working too hard to take time to notice them. And she and Beckett weren't the only couple cuddling up in dark corners.

Eden leaned closer, reached across his body, fisted her hand in the fabric of his jacket, and brushed a kiss across his lips.

He met the touch just as gently, eyes heavy lidded and staring into hers while his fingers explored the fabric of her panties without taking or grabbing. "Lace and satin?" His words sounded like a heavy purr. "What color?"

The throb between her legs intensified to an uncomfortable ache. "Guess."

The corner of his mouth tipped up in a smile. "I think it would depend on your mood."

"What do you mean?"

"The night I met you, I think you'd have been wearing black —kick-ass-and-take-names, all business. Tonight, you seem like more of a hot-pink type of woman."

She grinned and pulled his lower lip between hers for a moment. "Which do you prefer?"

"Both."

"Are you really that easy to please?"

"Not usually, but you seem to be able to please me in all sorts of unexpected ways." He leaned his forehead against hers, then tilted his head and kissed her temple. "Does your bra match?"

His whisper feathered warmth over her skin and made her eyes flutter closed. She moaned softly, lifting her hips. "What do you think?"

"I think it does. You know what else I think?"

"Hmm?"

"I think you're wet."

A flicker of embarrassment heated her face, and she let out a soft laugh. She was really glad she'd had those drinks now. She wouldn't have been able to battle her anxiety over taking this step on her own, and she'd really needed to take this step. Really needed to feel beautiful and wanted again.

"Are you wet for me, Eden?" he asked, his voice a rough, sexy whisper that made her throat tight.

Her pussy surged at his words. "I'm so wet, I ache."

He kissed her beneath her ear. "Do you want me to slide my hand between your legs and feel how wet you are?"

"Yes." The word whispered from her lips, and panic immediately followed. She opened her eyes to check their surroundings again and found his hot gaze staring back at her.

"It's all right," he murmured. "No one's paying any attention to us."

He held her gaze as his fingertips slipped beneath the edge of her panties, and his hand—his big, warm, and rough hand— ever so gently pressed between her thighs. Deep between her thighs. Until his palm rested over her mound and his long fingers slid over her opening.

Beckett let out a long, quiet moan, and his eyes fluttered closed with an expression of such bliss, he pulled Eden that direction too. Her body tingled with anticipation. Her lips parted, but her throat tightened, and no sound emerged.

The feel of a man's hand on her, *this* man's hand on her, in the middle of a crowded bar, yet in secret, was so many things at once, she couldn't define them all. Naughty. Decadent. Thrilling. And the way he opened his eyes and held her gaze added an intensely intimate element that made her feel both exposed and safe at the same time.

"Fuck..." he whispered. "You're so soft." Then his fingers stroked, and she gasped at the erotic sensation. A low laugh rolled through his throat, the sound more wicked than humorous. "And *so wet*."

Her breath whooshed out on a shaky sound.

"Do you like me touching you?" he asked.

"God, yes."

"I haven't been able to stop thinking about this since we met. And it's even better than I imagined. Have you thought of me, Eden?"

"Yes."

"Tell me."

His fingers slid over her again, and Eden's breath caught.

"Focus, Eden. Tell me what you thought about me."

"I...thought about kissing you." He continued to stroke her, slowly, intimately, moving a little deeper with each pass. Damn, she couldn't breathe. Couldn't think. "About...undressing you. Touching you. Tasting you. Fucking you."

She didn't even know what she was saying. His fingers created tingles and pressure and heat that made Eden rabid.

"What about going down on you?" he asked in a rough whisper. "Did you imagine my mouth on you, my tongue inside you?" His eyes fell closed in a look of pure pleasure. His jaw tightened, and his nostrils flared. The sight shot fire through Eden's veins. "Mmm, because if we were alone, I'd wrap your thighs around my head and eat you until you begged for relief."

"Holy shit..." she breathed. "Beck..."

She was too breathless to finish his name. How in the hell had he taken her to the edge of orgasm in, what? Five minutes? Ten minutes? With nothing but dirty talk and touching? His fingers pushed inside, just a little, but he stretched her, and the burn was deliciously breathtaking.

"God..." Her body coiled tighter and tighter. Pleasure spiraled higher and higher.

"Tell me what you want, Eden. I'll deliver."

She was overwhelmed with desire. The kind that made her forget everything else. The kind that made people stupid. The kind she hadn't felt in so long, she hadn't believed herself capable of feeling it ever again.

"I don't... I can't... Never felt anything so good."

"You haven't felt my mouth on you yet. You haven't felt me filling you yet. You haven't felt me driving into you yet. You haven't felt me making you come over and over and over yet."

Unable to find or form words, Eden whimpered.

"There are so many amazing things I want to make you feel."

"Yes," was all she managed to breathe. "God, yes." She was using all her willpower to keep herself still. She was already light years beyond her comfort zone. She'd never even considered doing anything this wild. "Where?"

"I think we should start right here." He lifted his head, pressed his forehead to hers, and murmured, "You're so close, it wouldn't take but another minute to send you into the clouds. Then you can cross 'finger fucked to perfection in a crowded bar' off your bucket list."

When a half laugh stuttered out of her, Beckett leaned in and kissed her, long and slow. His fingers pushed deep. Pressure spread through Eden's pussy. Pleasure tightened her stomach. Then he adjusted and pushed even deeper, until his hand pressed against her body and his thumb lay over her clit. A sound rolled from Eden's throat into Beckett's mouth. A sound of wild erotic pleasure.

As Beckett continued to kiss her with the mastery of Casanova, his fingers moved against the front wall of her pussy, and his thumb rubbed her clit. One move might have led her slowly to the edge of orgasm and tipped her over, but both, while he fucked her mouth with his, completely swamped her with more sensation, more pleasure, more excitement than she'd ever known. And all Eden could do was hold on to him and hope like hell she didn't completely shame herself in public. But this pleasure was so intense and so essential in the moment, she didn't even care enough to worry about it.

When Eden broke their kiss to catch her breath, Beckett slipped his other hand beneath her hair, pulled her head to his shoulder and her face to his neck. She needed to lift and rock and writhe, but Beckett's forearm determinedly held her still while he delivered the slowest, deepest, most minimal fingering Eden had ever known. One she would never have guessed could have delivered such all-encompassing pleasure.

"Beckett..." She panted, her mind fragmented. "Please..."

"Does it feel good?" he murmured at her ear, his free hand clasped on the back of her neck in a possessive, controlling gesture that, strangely, didn't bother her. "Do you like my fingers inside you?"

She choked out a sound. "Beckett..."

She was so close, floating out of orgasm range where all she could think about was reaching the peak, opening up, and receiving that lightning bolt of ecstasy. It had been so long. And she was so hungry.

"I love hearing my name in that breathy voice," he murmured. "I can't wait to hear you when you're grinding against my mouth. When my cock is filling you. When I'm pounding inside you."

The erotic images he created in her head only drove her higher, faster. "Beck..."

"I want to see you in bed, naked, sweating, panting, begging," he rasped in her ear, "free to writhe and scream."

She whimpered. "Need to come..."

"Patience." He smoothed his hand over her hair, and closed it on the back of her neck again. "There's no rush. I'm not going anywhere. I'm yours as long as you want me tonight. And tonight is all about you, Eden. Let go. Relax. This is only the pleasure I can deliver with the tips of my fingers. There's so much more waiting for you."

The awesomeness of his generosity seemed unreal, even in Eden's altered state. But she'd have to think about that later, because she was floating on a plateau beyond the reach of the release she'd grown rabid for.

"You're so ready," he growled in her ear, then added pressure somewhere inside her that pushed her that last step toward the cliff edge.

"Ah..."

And he pushed her again.

Before she got a sound out, Beckett pulled her face into his neck. The orgasm slammed through her in one hard quake, turning all her muscles rigid and shooting intense electrical pulses of pleasure over every nerve. Her cries came muffled against his skin. Lights burst against her closed lids. And shiver after shiver rocked through her, each leaving her a little more spent than the one before.

In Beckett's safe hold, the release probably appeared controlled and subdued, more like an emotional meltdown than the orgasm of the decade. But inside, every cell of her body swelled with light before popping and spilling ecstasy through her until she finally settled into a feathery lightness that felt a lot like pure joy.

9

Beckett had managed to steal Eden out of the bar without anyone from the team giving him a hard time. If they'd noticed, he'd catch shit tomorrow. But he'd take as much shit as they dished out and he'd smile through it all too.

He stopped on the corner where a group of pedestrians waited at a red light. She was already leaning into him, but he pulled her into the circle of his arms and tugged the collar of her jacket closed against the DC wind. "Are you warm?"

She smiled up at him. The same smile she'd been wearing since she'd floated back to earth after that orgasm at the bar, a sort of dazed grin, like she had a secret. "I don't think I'll ever be cold again." She curled her fingers into the front of his overcoat. "And thinking about getting you naked is keeping me all toasty. Skin on skin," she said, her voice throaty. "God, I can't wait."

Her hair blew across her face, and Beckett lifted his hand to push it away. Only when it was too late to stop did he realize he'd probably moved too fast. But she didn't startle or avoid his touch. And that was great progress in his opinion.

Though making her orgasm in the midst of a crowd of dozens was progress too. On a whole different level. The thought of getting her back to his apartment to see what other intimate levels they could achieve tonight was making his cock throb and his mouth water.

"You floored me in there tonight," he said honestly. "I can't remember the last time a woman blew me away like you did."

"Hmm." She laughed softly. "I think you were the one who blew *me* away." She pushed up on her toes, wrapped her arms around his neck, and pulled his head down to kiss him. And, man, he loved the way she kissed.

With 90 percent of his blood currently in his cock, he didn't know exactly why he loved it so much. But he didn't care either. And he couldn't wait to get her back to his apartment and start getting to know every intimate inch of her.

"Why'd you turn down the other girls?" she asked, flipping Beckett's mind upside down.

"What?"

"The two pretty girls who came up to you earlier. You hooked them up with two of your teammates."

"Oh, right. Yeah. They weren't my type." And he really didn't want to go into why. He didn't see any good coming out of that conversation at this moment. He cupped her jaw and stroked her cheek. "Where are you from, Eden Kennedy?"

"California."

"Whoa. You're pretty far from home."

"That's where I'm from, it's not my home. This is my home for now."

"For now?"

She gave a one-shouldered shrug. "I don't know where life's going to be taking me."

"Do you still have family there?"

"Yes, but my family isn't like yours. We're not close."

"Hmm. I'm sorry."

She shook her head. "I've never known any different."

"Neither have I, but I could imagine." He pulled her close

and kissed her forehead. "I don't know what I'd do without my family."

Her hands slipped under his jacket and roamed his abdomen. "I'm glad you have them."

"God, you're sweet," he said for what had to be the fifth time tonight. "Why hasn't some smart guy snapped you up?"

She grinned. "I move too fast. Every minute of my day is filled." She stretched up and kissed his jaw. "This is one of the rare times I give myself a little break."

"I feel doubly lucky now." His eyes closed as her mouth moved down his neck and tingles followed. "Don't you get days off work?"

"Mmm-hmm. But I'm in school those days." She pulled back and lifted a hand to his chin, running her thumb over his lips. "All my spare time is spent studying."

He frowned, thinking back. "Did I miss something? I don't remember anything about school."

Her gaze lifted to his, then flicked past his shoulder. "It's green." They started across the street. "I'm in paramedic school. Between that and work, I'm usually running on empty."

"Really. What school?" He was still trying to envision what that kind of schedule would look like, when they approached his building. He tugged his wallet from his pocket and held it in front of the electronic pad above the door handle.

"It's through Johns Hopkins."

Beckett was staring at her with more realizations and a loose jaw when the lock clicked over. "Hopkins. Jeez. Didn't I see an article about them in *Newsweek*? One of the top five best hospitals in the nation or something?"

Her grin shone with pride. "Third best It changes a little every year, but Johns has been in the top five for over two decades."

"Go big or go home, girl." Beckett pulled the door open for

her. "Just when I didn't think you could impress me any more, you do."

"Thanks." Eden stepped into the warm, still marble foyer and sighed. "Oh, it feels good in here." She shook her hair back and combed her fingers through the windblown tangles, staring at the three ornate crystal chandeliers that lit the foyer. "I love this place. These chandeliers make me think of ballrooms."

Beckett shrugged his overcoat off his shoulders. "You've been in this building before? Did I miss that conversation too?"

She grinned at him. "After two years running ambulance in DC, I swear I've been in almost every building in the city."

"Ahhh." He smiled. "Right." He folded his coat over his arm, then stepped behind her and slipped hers off. He lowered his chin to her shoulder and murmured, "I forget you've got a master key to the most powerful city in the nation."

She started laughing. "A *slight* overstatement."

He curved an arm around her waist and dragged her back against him. She moved willingly, fluidly, molding her body to his. The way her ass rubbed his erection stole his breath and added another punch of heat to his cock. Beckett pressed his mouth to her neck and groaned. Eden's laughter ebbed into a moan as she rocked against him. Excitement, shock, lust... They spiraled together and pooled between his legs.

"God, Eden..." He released her, took her hand, and started for the elevators. "Let's get upstairs while I can still walk."

He tapped the Up arrow, and one of the elevators immediately dinged. He stepped in, turned, and dragged her into his arms, kissing her hard. As soon as the elevator doors closed, Beckett lifted her, and Eden wrapped her thighs around his waist. He turned, pressed her against a wall, and sank in. Her softness cradled his cock, and the groan she let roll into his mouth reached all the way to Beckett's chest and squeezed. One arm tightened around his neck; the other hand drove into his hair. She tilted her head, opened wider, and tasted him deeper, the same way he wanted to fuck her.

Beckett broke the kiss to pull in air and reposition his hands on her ass, his mouth on her neck. "You are one blazing-hot puck."

She pulled back with a silly sort of frown crinkling her forehead, and Beckett realized he'd used a euphemism saved for the locker room. "Do you mean fuck?"

"Same difference." The elevator doors opened. He was breathless, and after the game he'd played, his body ached. But no one could have paid him enough to put her down, and he walked the short distance to his door.

"How is that the same difference?" she asked.

He sighed, knowing she'd never let it go. "On the ice, when we're closing in on a goal and our team controls the puck, when we're right there, passing it between each other, smokin' the other team, knowing we're going to score and that the goal is going to be extra sweet because the other team is dogging us but we still hammer the net, we call that a hot puck. The guys and I made it up."

When he reached his door, her eyes were glazed, her expression hot, her smile a little wicked. "So it's like a sure thing but way sexier."

He grinned. "I love the way you get me."

"I don't know if I'd go that far."

He turned, put his ass—and his wallet—in proximity to the electronic pad, and his door clicked open.

Eden laughed. "That was slick. You must do this a lot."

"Yep," he admitted, teasing her as he pushed inside his apartment, "Every time I carry in groceries or my duffel bag or—"

"Or me." She kissed him, long and deep and wet. "Take me to your bed, Mr. Croft, because I have a feeling I'm not the only hot puck in this apartment."

He hesitated, stupefied a moment that she didn't want to look around. Didn't want to marvel over his apartment. He hadn't brought a woman here since he'd taken custody of Lily, but before that, his hookups had been ridiculously impressed with this place. Eden, on the other hand, didn't even glance around. She brought her mouth back to his and kissed him like she needed him to make it through the night.

Beckett broke the kiss when he almost walked into a wall. "Damn," he told her. "You're making me dizzy."

"Sure"—she pressed kisses to his forehead, his temple, his jaw—"it's all my fault."

"I'm so glad we agree on that."

"I want to eat you." Her teeth closed on the skin near his ear, shooting tingles down his neck. "I want to kiss and lick and eat every inch of you."

"Jesus. Are you trying to kill me?" He paused to press a hand to the doorframe of his bedroom, already breathing hard. He pulled back and looked her in the eye. "You do realize I've already wrung myself out in one *hell* of a game tonight."

"I was wondering when that cocky side of yours was going to show up."

"Maybe I'm hoping you'll get tough with me again."

"That could be arranged." She brought both hands to his tie and deftly unknotted the silk. Something that often took Beckett several minutes to accomplish. "I could get creative with this if I had to—never underestimate the ingenuity of an emergency medical professional. What do you think about that, Mr. Croft?" She let the tie hang loose and started on the buttons of his shirt. "About having your hands secured to your bedframe with your tie, your body all mine to do with as I please?"

A wild, erotic thrill whipped up inside him. "I think that would be a first for me. I also think that would blow my mind in all kinds of new ways. But I'm afraid I don't get out a lot and doubt I'd last very long. So in the interest of getting the most out of the small amount of time we have, I'd opt for the flipside of that idea."

She yanked his shirt from his pants and unfastened the last button, then pressed both her hands to his belly and guided him back toward his bed. When his legs hit the footboard, Eden slid her hands up his chest, grabbed his tie with one hand, and used the other to give him a gentle push. Beckett let himself fall to a sit.

The take-charge Kennedy was back, but this time she was joined by the softer, more sensual Eden. The combination created a unique kind of sexual frenzy inside Beckett. Then Eden pressed one knee to the mattress and smiled down at him. A smile that said *I can't wait to get my hands on you* and turned Beckett inside out.

She slipped the tie around her own neck, released the ends, and lowered to a crouch between his legs. Beckett's breath caught, but she only unlaced his shoes and pulled them off. When she stood again, she lifted her chin toward the top of the bed. "Scoot back."

Instead, he slipped his hands beneath her dress and wrapped his hands around the backs of her thighs, then slid them upward along her smooth, warm, taut skin to the curve of her ass and squeezed.

A sound of desire rolled through his throat, and Eden's eyes fell closed as a wash of pleasure spilled over her face. He fisted the dress at her hips and dragged it upward, pushing at her arms when she held them down with a murmur of complaint.

He broke the kiss, reminding her, "You said you had a surprise for me."

With a little smile, she let him draw the dress over her head and he dropped it on the bed beside him as he scoured every gorgeous inch of her.

"*Holy fuck,*" slipped from his mouth in a raspy whisper.

She was everything he'd hoped for...and so much more. His gaze scoured her body over and over, unable to get enough. She was like a wicked wet dream. Her bra and panties were deep red, like her dress. Edged in black lace, like her boots. Her body filled out the lingerie to perfection. She had curves in all the right places, flat, taut planes in all the others. She was toned and supple and delicious.

He covered the hard thump of his heart with one hand. "This thing feels like it's going to break my ribs."

A smile quivered on her lips. "Same."

"You are..." He shook his head. "I can't begin to find words to do you justice."

"That was pretty good." She pressed a kiss to the center of his chest. "Now *scoot back*," she said with growing impatience.

He reached for her. "But I want to—"

"Uh-uh," she warned him with a hand held palm out. "It's my turn to play with the hot puck."

A grin overtook his face, and he laughed, then shimmied back on the bed. Eden followed on hands and knees, and the sight of her crawling over him, her hair a little wild, in that sexy lingerie and those fucking kick-ass sexy boots, made Beckett start to think Eden might be his hottest hookup ever.

She sat back on his thighs, did something with his tie that created loops, and deftly slipped one of his hands in, then reached for the other.

"Do you know what you're doing here?" he asked, marveling at how quickly and easily and expertly her hands worked.

"Mmm," she murmured, carefully tightening both ends of the loop around his joined wrists. "I use this in the field for restraints all the time. This method is invaluable." When she finished, there was one long end and one short end. She took hold of the long end and said, "Now pull."

Beckett hauled his hands backward and met resistance, but

the knot didn't slip or tighten. And he sure as shit couldn't move his hands. A flicker of unease, of electric thrill, shot through him. "Holy shit."

Eden leaned in and brushed a kiss over his lips. "Don't worry," she murmured with a devilish little smile. "I won't do anything you wouldn't do."

"That does *not* give me any peace of mind."

She pushed up on her knees and leaned toward the headboard, drawing his arms overhead. And Beckett had a moment of *What in the fuck have I gotten myself into?* But then her body pressed against his as she fastened the tie to a slat in the headboard with another knot. Beckett brought his head upright from watching her progress and found her deliciously plump breasts at eye level. With a tilt of his head, they were at mouth level, and Beckett opened wide, taking as much of one silk-covered breast in his mouth as he could.

She uttered a surprised cry, her body jerked, and her forehead dropped against the crown of his head, resting there as he took her nipple between his teeth and treated her to a sadistic massage.

The sounds she made—surprise, pleasure, pain—had Beckett's cock thumping against his zipper. When she shivered, he released her and quickly turned to the other, repeating the pattern. Loving the way her excitement intensified when he bit down and scraped the hard tip with his teeth, he pulsed, pulsed, pulsed it between his teeth. All followed by gentle sucking.

"Strip, Eden," he ordered, breathless. As if he were in a position to give orders. "Give me skin. Give me raw skin, and I'll make you come with nothing but my mouth on your tits."

She made one final tug on the tie at the headboard and pushed back, panting. Beckett immediately tested the restriction, sure he would break right through, flip her beneath him, and blow this deliriously stupid agreement away.

But he met resistance. Unrelenting resistance.

"*Fuck.*"

"I warned you." Her lids were so heavy, they were almost closed. She licked her lips and grinned.

He heaved a frustrated breath. "Maybe we could save this for another time. I'm a little too impatient right now."

"Who says you're going to wait for anything?" She planted her hands on the bed and looked deep into his eyes. "But I should warn you now that I have a not so teeny-tiny oral fixation. And I haven't been able to stop thinking about sucking your cock for days."

Lust surged through him. He dropped his head back and pulled at the tie.

"Please tell me you like having your cock sucked, Beckett."

He lifted his head and met her eyes while her tongue slid over her bottom lip. Sitting back again, she moved her hands to his belt and easily unbuckled the leather, then unfastened and unzipped his pants. All faster than Beckett could. "You're quick with those hands."

"I undress people for a living."

"Huh," he huffed a laugh. "Never thought of it that way."

Tugging his pants and boxers low enough to allow his cock to spring free, Eden exhaled heavily. Her face went lax, mouth fell open. "Thank you, God. I will never lie again, as long as I live."

That made Beckett laugh. But then Eden wrapped her long fingers gently around his engorged cock and stroked, slowly. Pressure and heat exploded in his groin. Beckett arched and moaned.

"I have...another a little confession."

"Jesus." He pressed his eyes closed. "This is *not* the time to tell me that."

"I have been proverbially starved for years. And your cock looks like a prime cut of meat from a sacred fucking cow. I think my teeny-tiny oral fixation just turned into a full-blown obsession."

Beckett started laughing again. Until wet warmth surrounded the head of his cock. He sucked a sharp breath and jerked against the restraint on his wrists. "Fuck."

When he opened his eyes and looked down, Eden was focused on sucking the head of his cock between her lips over and over. Once he was inside her mouth, she swirled her tongue around the ridge, then pulled back, and cool air drifted over the sensitive skin.

A tremor snaked through him. The muscles of his arms flexed, the fabric of his tie pulled. And Eden lifted a naughty smile to him before spending long, slow seconds torturing him with her tongue around the sensitive tip and rim.

Beckett dropped his head back on a loud groan and a few more curses.

When her mouth released him, Beckett opened his eyes and found her leaning over him to reach for the pillow beside his head. He lifted and grabbed the edge of her bra with his teeth.

Eden laughed a little squeal. "Let go."

He grinned. "Uh-uh." Then added a muffled "Take it off."

After a few minutes of tussling to get the fabric from between his teeth, Eden gave in and unfastened the bra. When she leaned back, it slid from her arms and exposed her breasts. Bouncy, full, gorgeous breasts.

Beckett pushed the fabric from his mouth and rasped, "Bring those beauties here. I'm hungry too."

"Sorry. My needs come first." She stuffed a pillow beneath his hips. "Especially since you're a little tied up at the moment."

Beckett growled. Frustration burned through his body.

Eden hooked her fingers in the waistband of his pants and boxers and slid them down his thighs, his calves, then took hold of his socks and pulled them all off in one swoosh. And then stared at his body, a hot smile lifting half her mouth. "Well done, Mr. Croft. Really, *really* well done."

Her approval only made his need more urgent. "Come say that to my face."

Eden laughed at his challenge to draw her closer, but she did come back to him. And she did lower her head and start feasting. Only she didn't start with his cock like he expected. Instead, she pushed his thighs wide, lifted his testicles, and massaged them while she licked at the sensitive perineum behind. Beckett's breath caught. Sensation rocketed through his cock and up his body, out his arms. His hands fisted and jerked against the tie.

But Eden continued to tease him with light pressure from her lips and the warm stroke of her tongue, nearly tearing Beckett from his skin. And when she gently took the skin of his sac between her teeth and scraped, he swore and bowed backward. Both hands gripped the headboard while Eden pulled his perineum between her lips and sucked and sucked and sucked. Beckett's eyes rolled back in his head. His breathing stuttered. Pleasure shuddered through his body.

"Mother*fucker*—"

She slid her tongue across his sac, then slipped one testicle into her mouth, the move gentle and fluid and utterly natural. But the sensations it washed through Beckett blurred his vision and trembled through his body. His mind wasn't working. The words he uttered were fractured and disjointed, making no sense. Just as smoothly as she'd taken the first, she released it, licked the other, then closed her lips around it and rolled it around with her tongue like candy.

Beckett let out a long, deep, tortured moan. Fuck, that was so good, he couldn't even put words to it. He couldn't remember a woman ever doing this for him. And he would have remembered something this mind-blowing.

The sight of her small hand holding his cock, her blonde

head working between his thighs, delivered another jolt of urgent lust. "Eden, can't take anymore."

She hummed in disappointment, and the sound vibrated through his sac and into the base of his cock. Beckett's hips surged, and he choked out a moan. Eden pushed up on one hand. She brought the other to her mouth and met his eyes while she stroked her tongue down her palm, then wrapped her fingers gently around his length and stroked.

Fire blasted through his shaft and spread through his pelvis.

When he caught his breath, he asked, "Are you wet?"

She nodded, a small smile turning her lips. A dazed look in her eyes.

"Take off your panties." When she didn't seem interested in his suggestion, he said, "Let me see your pretty pussy while you suck me off."

She stepped off the bed and hooked her thumbs in her panties, slowly sliding them down her hips, her thighs, and letting them drop. Her pussy was shaved except for one light strip of hair down the center.

Beckett's breath released on a wave. "How the fuck did I get so lucky?" When she returned to the bed, straddling his thighs, he said, "Bring it here, Eden." He flexed and clenched his fingers, aching to touch her. "Let me taste that pussy."

"Mmm, not now. I have work to do here." And she held his gaze, opened her mouth over the head of his cock, then slowly took three-quarters of his length.

Delirium hit. Pure, unadulterated, raw delirium. Beckett's mind turned to a white haze sparkling with sensation. Then she closed her mouth over him and added suction. Excitement lurched toward Beckett's throat. "Fuck, that's good."

She continued to impale her mouth with his cock, all while her beautiful eyes held his. Eyes swamped with lust and hunger. And she was in no rush. Her mouth moved slow and strong, her tongue languid and luxurious.

Eden pulled him from her mouth and stroked his wet length with her hand, shooting more sparks into the fire. His balls felt as heavy as rocks. A coil of heat lay at the base of his spine, ready to explode.

"I could do this all night," she murmured, her gaze lovingly moving over his length. "I think you've given me a cock fetish."

Beckett was pretty damn sure he'd never had a woman give him head this good, and wished he had more control. Wished he could let her do this for him for hours. Hours while he finger-fucked her, while he ate her out in a sixty-nine. While he just lay back and let her pleasure the fuck out of him.

"I love your fetish. But I can't do this all night, baby. At least not tonight."

Her brow furrowed, and her lower lip pushed out.

Beckett huffed a laugh. "Come up here and let me see how wet you are."

When she looked like she might consider it, Beckett pushed. "Let me slide my tongue between your legs." He licked his lips. "Just move a little north."

She scraped her lower lip through her teeth, and a new kind of heat crept into her eyes. She walked her knees to his shoulders.

"That's it," he encouraged. "Mmm, fuck, I can smell you. That's *so* hot. Come here, Eden. I'm just as hungry as you are." His arms flexed, his body writhed, but nothing brought him closer to her. "Little more, baby. Let me get my mouth on you."

She wiggled closer. Beckett lifted as far as he could and stretched his tongue to barely tease her pussy. But it was enough to entice her closer. Enough to close his mouth over her. Enough to get her moving against him. Enough to make her hands clench. Enough to make her mouth drop open and her eyes blaze.

"Spread your thighs, baby," he told her. "Move higher."

With her hands fisted beneath her chin, a look of awe and excitement and a little bit of unease shifting over her face, she moved a few inches higher and pushed her knees wider, placing her pussy directly over his face.

He pursed his lips and blew on her folds, glistening in the dim light. When Eden moaned, Beckett whispered, "Closer. Bring that sweet pussy to me."

She reached out and used the headboard to steady herself, then pushed her thighs wider.

"That's it." Now all he had to do was tilt and roll his head to have her entire pussy at the mercy of his lips and his tongue.

He started with soft, openmouthed kisses all over. When she added her other hand to the headboard, he searched out key spots to use a flicking tongue—her swollen clit, her perineum, her opening. When he had her squirming, he took sections of the delicate flesh and added the scrape of his teeth, then the swipe of his tongue. All while her head hung between her arms and her heavy-lidded eyes watched. All while Beckett watched her watch him eat her, his hands tied and useless. This had to be the most exciting, maybe even the most erotic, thing he'd ever done.

And Eden reveled in it. Her hips rocked to the sensual rhythm of his mouth; sounds of pleasure filled the air. And the look on her face—that was an aphrodisiac all its own.

"You are so damn..." She shivered, and her eyes closed as a wave of pleasure passed through her. "Good at that."

"I love being good for you. I love the way you watch me. It's such a turn-on. I haven't been with anyone this sexy in a long fucking time, baby. Settle in and ride my mouth to the finish. I want to watch you break."

Eden lowered her hands from the headboard to cover Beckett's hands on the slats and threaded their fingers together. Her thighs flexed as she moved her pussy over Beckett's open mouth. With his eyes on Eden's, he sucked and licked deep inside her. Eden held her lower lip between her teeth, moaned and rocked against his mouth, while Beckett deliberately drove her higher.

"Beckett..." she murmured, her voice rising.

He covered her and hummed, loud and long, letting the vibrations shiver through her.

And that sent her over the edge. She cried out. Her pussy clenched and surged. And Beckett growled with lust as the climax bowed Eden's back and twisted her muscles.

As Eden eased back, pressed her face to his neck, and caught her breath, Beckett thought this might very well become the best fucking night of his life.

10

E den's head was still spiraling when Beckett's voice tugged her back to reality.

"Baby, I hate to interrupt your recovery, but do you think you could loosen the tie?"

She had no idea what he was talking about. Eden lifted her head, still disoriented. She had never come so hard. Nor had she ever been so greedy with her own pleasure. But Beckett seemed to make both incredibly easy.

When she focused on his handsome face, his lust-darkened eyes held a wickedly pleased edge. But then she realized his hands were still tied to the headboard.

"Oh, shit. I'm so sorry." She propped herself up on her knees and lunged forward, but her hands weren't working the way they usually did, and it felt like it took forever to get the knot loose. And while she fought with his tie, Beckett's mouth roamed her breasts, licking and nipping and sucking.

"You're not helping yourself here," she told him, but he didn't seem to care. When she freed his hands, Eden massaged his biceps and shoulders. "Do your arms hurt? Are you okay?"

He wrapped his arms around her and sat up. Her legs splayed across his lap, and Beckett pressed a hand to the back of her head, guiding her lips to his for a slow, deep kiss. She softened against him and was rewarded with the delicious sensation of skin on skin.

Beckett pulled back an inch. "I might need some TLC to help me forget about the ache in my shoulders."

"You think?"

His brow pulled in serious contemplation. "I think."

She combed both hands through his hair and rocked her hips, rubbing her pussy over his erection. Beckett's moan rumbled through him like an earthquake.

The man had the body of a god, the face of a dark angel, and the soul of a lover. He wasn't the kind of man Eden should be hooking up with for the first time in years. He was the kind of man a woman got serious about. The kind of man a woman changed her life for.

And Eden would never change her life for a man ever again.

"What did you have in mind?" she asked.

Fire flared in Beckett's dark eyes, tugging at something deep and elemental inside her. His hands stroked down her back, over her ass, and squeezed. "First, and most important," he said, his voice a low growl, "will you wear these boots while I fuck you? They are so smokin' hot."

"I don't think that's too much to ask." Her sex clenched at the thought of him fucking her. "But don't you want me to finish what I started and what you interrupted? Because I'd love to suck you."

"You are mind-blowing. But let's save that for later. I still have so much to explore." Beckett tilted his head and took her mouth with an all-encompassing hunger. And while she was drowning in his kiss, he rolled her to her back. His legs tangled with hers, his mouth explored beyond her lips, and his hands traveled all over her body, sending her mind into a perpetual spin.

The pleasure was so overwhelming, she could only absorb flashes. The feel of his heavy body pressing her into the mattress. The heat of him. The deliciously sexy scent of him. The hunger of his mouth as his lips and tongue traveled over her throat. The sounds vibrating in his chest.

One of his big, warm hands slid down her thigh and pulled it wide, giving him room to wedge his erection against her sex. Sensation rushed her lower body. Eden moaned, bowed, and sank her hands into his hair. Beckett growled in approval, slid his hand back up to her ass, and gripped as he rocked against her.

"You feel so good," she breathed at his temple.

His mouth moved over her collarbone, her shoulder, her chest, then closed over her nipple. Pleasure blasted through her breast and pulled between her legs.

Eden arched, groaned, and pulled at his hair. This wasn't how she remembered sex. What she remembered was more like a Sunday afternoon, mellow and mild and moderately satisfying. This was sex on drugs. Intense, wild, and highly addictive.

Beckett rocked his hips against her. His erection slid along her sex, thick and hard and hot.

"Want you," she said, panting. "So bad. Right now."

He lifted his head and met her gaze. His eyes were hot, his expression fierce. He gripped her waist and leaned sideways, tipping Eden off-balance.

"Beck—"

"Wallet," he rasped, twisting to reach toward his pants on the floor "Need my wallet. In my pocket."

He pulled is wallet free, opened it, and plucked something from the inside fold.

Yes.

Eden's pussy clenched with anticipation. She took the small square from his fingers, but he closed his arms around her and lay back on the bed, dragging her with him. Stealing the condom back, he ripped it open, and rolled it on.

Then he curved his arm around her waist, rolled to his knees, and pulled her into his lap for a slow, wet kiss. The length of his erection slid easily over her slick entrance, and she moaned into his mouth. And while his tongue stroked hers, his hands guided her hips to position himself. He pulled out of the kiss, pressed his forehead to hers, and held her gaze as he pushed inside.

Delicious pressure spread through her pelvis. Her hands slid into his hair and fisted.

Beckett's eyes slid closed, and his fingers dug into the flesh of her hips. "Fuck," he said, voice low and rough and tight. "So good."

The pleasure in his voice rekindled Eden's energy. And the feel of him inside her urged her body to move. She pressed her face to his neck, drew in his masculine scent of musk and spice, and used the strength in her thighs to move over him. Slowly at first, getting used to the stretch, she drew him out, then pushed him deep. Sensations erupted along her walls, spread through her pelvis, making her crave him faster and deeper.

"God, Eden…" His voice shook, and he lifted one hand to clasp the back of her head. "You're so… Baby, I'm…" He pressed his face against her shoulder and lifted into her. "*Fuck.*"

The pleasure in his voice filled Eden with a euphoria she hadn't experienced in forever. "I want to feel you come, Beckett." Her hand slipped to his shoulder, and she dug in to hold on as he moved faster. "Come hard for me."

He growled, pulled his head back, and cupped her cheek, meeting her eyes. "Come with me."

She pressed her forehead to his. "You fucking overachiever."

He huffed a laugh, then covered her mouth and kissed her deep. One arm wrapped low on her hips and pulled her against him, holding her still as he thrust, thrust, thrust, giving her clit as much action as her pussy.

And God, the feel of him filling her, holding her, trying so hard to please her...

Both his hands slid down her back and over her ass. He drew her cheeks apart and pushed harder, deeper, lifting her whole body with his power. His cock pounded something inside her that spurted a thrill through her lower body. A cry erupted from her throat, and her hand tightened on his shoulder.

"I love that sound," Beckett ground out. "Let me hear you, Eden."

When he thrust again, a sliver of pain preceded the blast of pleasure and she cried out louder. Longer.

"Oh yeah," Beckett praised. "God, that's good. I'm gonna come hard for you, Eden."

"Yes," she breathed, lightheaded from the ecstasy flowing through her body. "*Yes.*"

They were both sweating, and Eden's grip on his shoulder kept slipping. He drove harder and deeper and faster until a perpetual cry streamed from Eden's mouth, punctuated by "Beckett" or "Yes."

"Bring it, baby," he demanded in a dark, raspy voice that coiled inside Eden with carnal sensuality. "Come with me."

She whimpered. He thrust. Thrust. Thrust. And Eden broke with a scream and a shudder. Beckett let go at the same time. His strong body tensed and recoiled. Drove, tensed, recoiled. The frenzied, repetitive pattern rubbed all Eden's pleasure spots just the right way, dragging even more climaxes to the surface.

By the time Beckett's orgasm drained him, Eden was sweating and spent, spread limp across Beckett's lap. She was supported by his bulk, enclosed in his arms, and filled with his body. And she felt an inexplicable new weight in her chest. A sense of being owned in a primal, fundamental way she couldn't explain, by this man she'd only meant to use for a quick fling back into life.

She forced herself to lift her head. A quick cleanup, and she wanted to be on her way. Definitely before he brought up the idea of her going home. Talk about an ego crusher.

But when she eased her grip on his shoulders and leaned back a little, her head spun.

Beckett stroked a hand down her hair and gently pressed her head back down. "Stay." The quick rise and fall of his chest mixed with the hard beat of his heart. "This is...perfect. You feel so...perfect. Just another minute."

One of his hands traced circles low on her back. The other twirled a strand of her hair around his finger. His cheek rested on her head. And, other than his heavy breaths, he remained silent. Contentedly, peacefully silent.

Warmth snuck past Eden's defenses, and she relaxed against him again. In those moments, all her senses seemed to flip back on. She closed her eyes to memorize the thump of his heartbeat beneath her ear. Drew deep lungfuls of air to pull in the heady mingled scents of his skin and their sex. Slid her hands over his shoulders, loving the warmth of his skin.

And she was more than a little surprised at how amazing it felt to have a man holding her again. But then, she couldn't remember any man holding her like this...maybe ever, let alone after sex.

Beckett finally took a deep breath and exhaled, but didn't move. "That was fucking amazing, Eden."

The soft words and his awe-filled tone deepened the warmth burning beneath her ribs. She didn't know what to say to that. Amazing didn't begin to describe that experience for her, and she opted to remain silent, pressing her mouth to his for a soft kiss instead. To relieve the ache between her legs, far more noticeable now that the intense pleasure had faded, Eden rose slowly on her knees, easing him from her body.

But he held her close and pulled her back to his lap, searching her face. "Are you okay?"

She laughed a little. "I'm better than okay."

His concern gave way to that killer smile. "Yeah?"

"Oh yeah." She stroked his face and decided to be honest. There really wasn't any risk. He already had an ego the size of Texas. And she wasn't going to do this again. "Sex has *never* been like that for me before."

His smile faded, his eyes softened, and he lifted a hand to stroke her cheek. "I'm glad," he said softly, then nodded. "Really glad." He kissed her, gently, slowly, letting his tongue taste her in languid strokes that made things deep inside her spark and stir. He pulled back and smiled into her eyes. "I'll clean up, then we can nap, and I'll wake you in an hour or two in an unforgettable way."

Eden's lips parted, but before she'd formed any words, Beckett rolled her to her back, kissed her again, then stood from the other side of the bed and wandered into an adjoining room. The door closed, a light flipped on, and the sound of running water drifted in.

Eden groaned, flopped her arms across her eyes, then started laughing. She slid her arms down to cover her mouth and stared at the ceiling. What the hell was this fizzy thing that made her want to giggle? "Jesus."

The humor ebbed, and reality snuck in. What the hell did she do now?

Eden propped herself up on her elbows and the first thing she saw was her suede boots where they still covered the lower half of her legs. And a smile crossed her face. Beckett had made her forget all about leaving the boots on.

She bit her lip and pushed up a little more, glancing around the room for her clothes. Which was the first real look at the space. Upon entering she'd gotten the general impression of a large bedroom with standard furniture—bed, nightstands, dresser. But she'd missed the biggest and most unique feature —one wall of floor-to-ceiling windows. And there wasn't one blind anywhere to be seen—in the middle of a city with half a million residents.

"Shit," she murmured.

"They're mirrored."

His voice made her startle. "Oh my God."

She pressed a hand to her chest and took a few quick breaths to slow the sudden hike in her heart rate.

He reached out and laid a hand on her suede-covered ankle. "I'm sorry."

"No." She shook her head and drew her knees close. "No, I was..." She gestured to the windows. "I completely missed that."

His grin was quick and hot. He crawled onto the bed beside her and kissed her shoulder. "I noticed." He stroked a warm hand down her arm and rested his chin on her shoulder. "I was saying that the windows have a mirrored film. We can see out, but no one can see in, which I love, because this is my favorite thing about the apartment. The way the moonlight and the city lights fill the rooms at night."

He rose onto his knees and leaned over, straightening one of her legs.

"What are you doing?" she asked.

"As wickedly sexy as these are, you'll probably be able to fall asleep better without them on."

He found the zipper on her inner thigh, worked it down her boot, and pulled the boot off. Then did the same with the other, all while Eden was trying to sort out the strange turmoil inside her. Would she be able to sleep beside a man? Did she even want to? Long before she had the answers, Beckett set her boots on the floor and kissed his way back up her body.

Eden had changed her mind about leaving by the time his lips touched the hollow behind her knee. And by the time he'd stretched out facing the windows and snuggled up behind her, his legs all wrapped up in hers, his arm tight at her waist, her head tucked beneath his chin, Eden realized she was in deep, deep trouble.

He settled and sighed, and the sound was so relaxed, so content. But it had the opposite effect on Eden and tension wound tighter inside her. Her emotions winged completely out of control, and tears burned her eyes. Which only made her angry. But she couldn't focus on ripping herself for letting her stupid emotions get involved when he bent his head, pressed his face to her neck, and kissed her there.

"Sex isn't usually like that for me either," he said, his voice whisper soft, then propped his head in his hand. "In fact, I haven't had time for much sex at all this year."

That surprised her. She turned her head to look at him over her shoulder. "Why's that?"

He shrugged and let his gaze drift out the windows. "Busy. This job...during the season, it takes everything."

She had a hard time believing he didn't slip one-night stands or quickies in there somewhere, but she certainly wasn't going to dig under that rock. "Are you really leaving town tomorrow, or was that just a way to get me to respond?"

A grin lifted his lips. "I'm really leaving town. I'm not a liar. I'd rather tell and hear the truth than a lie. We've got a rough five-game run on the West Coast starting tomorrow night in Los Angeles." He dropped a kiss on her lips, lowered his head, and sighed again. "Catch a nap while you can, gorgeous. I plan on taking as much of your ass-kicking brand of sex as you'll give me." His voice turned heavy with fatigue. "Tonight's got to carry me through these tough games next week."

His breathing deepened and evened out within minutes, and Eden was left alone, wrapped up in a stranger's arms, to stare out at the city lights and untangle all the contradictions she'd uncovered in this sexilicious hockey player.

11

Beckett floated to the surface of consciousness again, and a smile immediately lifted his lips. His back and shoulders ached as he rolled toward Eden, but he already knew she could make him forget all about the pain hockey wrought on his body. In fact, Eden Kennedy could make Beckett forget about every last worry weighing on him—his custody battle for Lily, his aging body, how the success of this season would direct the next five to ten or maybe even fifteen years of his life.

When he reached for her, his hand slid across empty sheets.

"Kennedy," he yelled toward the bathroom. "Get your sexy ass back in here. I've got something that needs emergency TLC."

He chuckled to himself, imagining the reaction he'd get for, one, calling her by her last name, two, ordering her to do *anything*, and three, suggesting she was obligated to meet his needs. Those had all become jokes between them over the course of the night. A night that would go down in Beckett's memory.

He relaxed into the bed with a smile. Outside, the morning sun was cresting, and he felt happy and hopeful for the first time in a long time. He couldn't wait to make love to Eden again. Then go to his parents' and cajole Lily away from her cousins and grandparents to grab some one-on-one time with his baby girl before he jumped a plane with his teammates for five intense games in a row.

Life was fucking awesome.

So awesome, he wanted to share it. Thoughts of introducing Eden to Lily brought a mix of unease and excitement. Eden was a natural. She'd be amazing with kids, no doubt. And Lily was a bubble of love. His daughter spun webs of infatuation with everyone she met. Beckett didn't worry about them getting along. He worried about them getting along too well. Because if things didn't gel between him and Eden, he didn't want to think about another woman disappearing from Lily's life.

And wow, he was getting way ahead of himself. But, hell, it had taken him freaking forever to find a woman who even tempted him to think beyond one night. There had been a time when he thought he and Viviana might be able to make a go of it. Back when the thought of kids hadn't ever entered his mind. Back when having the biggest contract and the most gorgeous woman were his top priorities. Back when he'd believed being a badass was more important than strategy.

He'd been another stupid jock, perpetuating the negative view of hockey players everywhere. But everyone had to grow up sometime. And Eden made that idea extremely appealing.

He sighed and rolled toward the bathroom. "Eden, what the hell are you doing in—"

The bathroom was dark. He darted a look at the bedroom door, which stood open. A streak of panic burned through his gut. If she'd wandered the apartment, she'd seen Lily's room. She'd seen Lily's things. Damn, he wasn't ready to go there. His housekeeper did an excellent job of picking up after Lily every day. Beckett always knew he could come home with the confidence that no one who didn't already know Lily lived here, would ever guess. Which was how he wanted to keep things. For now.

"Eden?" He sat up and threw the sheet off. Panic morphed to fear. The fewer people who knew about Lily now, the better. He halted in the doorway and found the living area and the kitchen empty. His gaze fell on the door to Lily's suite. A knot wound tight in his gut, and he whispered, "Fuck."

Beckett turned back into the bedroom and reached for his boxer briefs on the floor. Probably not a conversation he wanted to have naked. But as he pulled them on, he noticed all the clothes on the floor were his. Nothing of Eden's remained. No dress, no lingerie, no boots.

"What the *hell*?" He turned out of his room and cut through the living room toward Lily's suite, calling Eden's name with more than confusion in his voice. He was using the tone he used when he was getting ready to set one of the guys straight. Felt the same tightness in his gut that swamped him when a ref made a bad call against his team. But he didn't understand it.

He didn't understand it until he turned into Lily's room and found the suite as pristine as Mimi always left it. Pristine and empty.

Holding on to disbelief, he lifted his voice and made one last attempt. "*Eden.*"

The apartment remained silent. Eerily silent. And realization settled in. She'd left.

He stood in Lily's room, hands on hips, staring at the carpet with a maddening whirl of panic and anger and an odd sense of hurt kicking up all kinds of dust inside him. He mentally scoured their conversations between sex. She didn't have to work today. Didn't have school today. She'd said she planned on studying all day. Said something about meeting a study partner in the afternoon.

Dammit, she'd agreed to have breakfast with him at his

favorite Irish pub. Had salivated over his description of their Bailey's Irish Cream French toast.

A sickening feeling settled in his gut. He moved back into the living room, looking around as if he'd find some reason for her early disappearance. But nothing about the pristine way Mimi always left the apartment had been disturbed.

Beckett's mood had gone from white to black in the span of two minutes. He scraped a hand through his hair and let out a tight breath on his way to the fridge. Now his mind searched their night for something that had gone wrong. Something that would have made her leave without telling him. Without giving him any idea of where she lived or when he could see her again.

But as he opened the fridge and stared blankly inside, he couldn't pull up any rough spots. Everything between them had been amazing. While they'd both stayed well away from deeply personal subjects, they'd never run out of conversation when their mouths weren't busy in some other highly pleasurable way.

Beckett's eyes fell closed with longing, and an image of her as he'd last seen her filled his mind. He'd rolled to his stomach, and she'd crawled on top of him to massage a few of his sore spots. Then she'd stretched out, pressed her ear to his back, and closed her eyes. Beckett had watched her in the dim reflection of the room's glass wall as she'd fallen asleep there. Then continued to stare until he fell asleep too.

"God*dammit*." He opened his eyes and swiped the orange juice from the shelf. He smacked the cardboard carton on the quartz counter, ripped open the top, and tipped it toward his mouth. He downed several long swallows, but the cool, fresh liquid didn't improve his disposition.

Beckett slammed the carton on the counter again, and this time, the juice sprayed out the top. He swore, grabbed a kitchen towel, and dropped it to wipe up the spill. That was when he saw a note on the bar.

His heart skipped, and he grabbed the paper.

In pretty, neat, swirly handwriting, she'd written, *Thanks for an amazing night*. And signed it *E*.

He stared at it, half expecting some additional message to appear out of thin air. When that didn't happen, he flipped it over. But found the back blank.

"What the fuck?" No explanation. No *call me*. No *let's do this again*. No *can't wait to see you when you get back to town*.

Nothing.

He slapped the note down. "She fuckin' *walked out* on me?"

Just like that? He didn't believe it. Women didn't walk out on him. Even Viviana, who'd bailed at the sight of Lily, had come crawling back within a week with all kinds of excuses, trying to negotiate. When women left his bed, his room, his life, it was because Beckett led them to the door.

He started to crumple the note, but the paper caught his attention, and he stopped. She'd written it on one of Lily's My Little Pony notepads. And the pen lying on the bar was filled with crystals floating in liquid. Neon pink and purple crystals. It had come with the notepad, courtesy of his sister, Sarah.

Beckett imagined Eden getting up for something to drink, venturing through the apartment, and finding Lily's room. And bailing as fast as Viviana had. That both hurt and angered.

He crushed the paper and pitched the ball into the sink. "Fuck it."

Beckett turned into his room, pulled fresh clothes from his drawers, and headed to the shower. He didn't need a woman in his life anyway. Lily filled every square millimeter of his heart.

The long, hot shower relieved sore muscles, reset Beckett's inner landscape to single dad, badass hockey player, and he drove to his parents' house with only a twinge of lingering resentment. Only considered calling Eden and confronting her half a dozen times.

By the time he turned up the long, winding drive of his parents' house on an Arlington hillside overlooking the Potomac, he was only mildly annoyed at how his morning had unfolded. An hour of focused Lily time would straighten him out. An hour of focused Lily time could right any wrong in Beckett's life. And leaving her this afternoon for a week wasn't exactly sitting right with him either.

He parked behind his mother's Lexus SUV and started up the walk. A chorus of giggles erupted somewhere near the kitchen and floated to Beckett. A smile filled his heart. He took a long, deep breath of the fresh Virginia air and soaked in the silence of the countryside. That was all he needed to remind himself his life was fucking awesome.

He chuckled at himself for getting so wound up over a chick he hardly knew. And by the time he'd climbed the stairs and reached for the door handle, he knew everything in his world was about to be put exactly right.

Beckett pushed open the heavy wooden door and stepped into the wide foyer. Straight ahead, the massive living room looked out onto his parents' property and the Potomac beyond. It had snowed last night, and a dusting still clung to the trees and bushes.

Unlike his apartment, his parents' house teemed with life. The three granddaughters giggled downstairs in the finished basement his parents used as a playroom. His mother, father, and sister chatted in the kitchen.

"Something sure smells good," Beckett said, heading toward the kitchen first to say hello. All three members of his family turned to smile at him from the kitchen table. "What did you make me for breakfast?"

His mother was beaming. She always beamed when the grandkids were here. "Lily ate hers *and* yours."

"Man, is she growing," Sarah said. "I swear she's two inches taller than when I saw her last week."

Beckett couldn't stop grinning. "Yeah, she's definitely had a spurt. I'm going to have to buy her new clothes in a few weeks if this keeps up."

His sister and his mother shared a glance. "Shopping with Beckett's credit card." Sarah pumped her fist. "*Yes*."

Beckett was laughing when all three girls raced up the stairs, then squealed through the living room and into the kitchen, where their high-pitched shrieks echoed off the tile and made everyone cringe.

All four of the adults tried variations of "tone it down," but the girls ran around the table and skittered off into the depths of the three-thousand-square-foot house.

Beckett stared after them, hands held out to the sides. "What the hell? Do I have chopped liver written on my forehead today or what?" Then he yelled, "Lily Nicole Croft, get your little tush back here and say hello to your dad."

But the girls continued to laugh and squeal. And for the first time in a year, Lily didn't come running to him. His heart fell to his feet. To cover the second blow of the morning and his true heartache over Lily's show of independence, he dramatically slapped a hand to his chest and hung his head. "Oh my God. I think my heart just shattered."

His mother stood from the table. "Lily, you're breaking your daddy's heart." She paused to squeeze Beckett's arm and grinned at him. "She slept through the night, no bad dreams. She woke and didn't fuss over you not being here this morning. She's making real progress, Beckett."

His mom disappeared into the living room at the same time that their home phone rang. His father called, "I'll get it." And stood to answer, leaving Sarah and Beckett at the kitchen table.

"Thanks for staying over with the girls," Beckett told her.

"Anytime. They all entertain each other so well, I get to read and knit and watch a TV show without interruption. It's like a vacation."

Beckett grinned, but it was pained. "Not easy raising them alone."

Sarah was married to a marine who was on his second tour overseas. Aside from his mother—and possibly Eden, though since she bailed, he'd never get a chance to find out—Sarah was the strongest woman he knew.

She covered his hand with hers and squeezed. "You are an amazing father. The fact that she's not sobbing all over you right now shows just how great a job you're doing. And it does get easier. Raising them alone, I mean. It's already easier than when you got her, right?"

Beckett winced, remembering how broken his little girl had been. "A hundred times easier."

She released his hand and gave him that now-let's-get-down-to-business look.

He groaned. "Oh God. What?"

"Nika called me last night."

Nika Kristoff was the young wife of the team's newest, and youngest, center, Andre. The couple was nineteen and twenty-one respectively, brand-new to the United States, with all their family back in Russia. They already had a two-year-old son and another baby on the way. To keep Andre focused on the ice, Beckett had set up a support network for Nika, which included Sarah.

Beckett straightened. "What? Why? Andre didn't call me. Are they okay?"

"They're fine." Sarah's calm tone reassured him, and he relaxed. "She called because Dmitri put gum in his hair, and she couldn't get it out."

He huffed a laugh, thinking of the couple's two-year-old. "Beautiful."

"Easy fix. Peanut butter, for your future information."

"Good to know. Hope I never have to use it."

"Oh, you will," she said, smirking. "Anyway, when I asked Nika how Dmitri got the gum in his hair, she told me that she'd been cooking for some Russian tradition, I don't know which one, and that while she was busy in the kitchen, Dmitri went unsupervised for about fifteen minutes because Andre took a detour on the way home from the game and ended up at Top Shelf."

Beckett's humor slid away, the same way this conversation was circling the drain. "Uh...huh..."

Sarah sat back. "You've been incredibly discreet with women since Lily came into your life. So hearing that you were all over one last night made my sisterly antennae vibrate."

Ah fuck. "The reason you think I've been discreet with women over the last year," he told her, "is because there haven't been any."

"Seriously? You expect me to believe that? Hello. I get the whole puck bunny thing. I know how hard women chase you guys down."

"I misspoke," he said deliberately, holding his temper. "There haven't been any *here*. I may have hooked up a couple times at away games, but that's it. I can't kiss anyone in public in the greater Metro area now?"

"Sounds like you were doing more than kissing, bro." Sarah lifted her hand to halt the argument she could evidently see coming, because she continued, "I'm saying that you're a dad now. A dad going after full custody of a little girl. You shouldn't be doing shit like that in public. You have every right to mess around however you want to mess around, but get a room."

Beckett exhaled heavily. He was thirty-one years old and his big sister was bitching him out for getting caught kissing a chick in public. Okay, yeah, he'd been doing more than kissing her, which others might have suspected, but no one knew for sure. Either way, she was probably right. He'd lost his head with Eden.

"Now, tell me about her," Sarah said, excitement replacing the censure in her voice. "If you haven't been hooking up much, there must have been something special about this woman. Jesus, Beck, it's about damn time."

"Don't start. I'm well aware of my age. I'm reminded every time I step on the ice or the team picks up fresh meat—like Andre. And I've already got a perfect five-year-old. What more could I want?"

"How about a perfect sibling for that perfect five-year-old?"

His father returned to the kitchen. Beckett gave his sister the shut-up look. Sarah rolled her eyes and dropped her chin into her hand.

"You played great last night," his father said. "How are you feeling about your game against the Sharks next week?"

Beckett didn't want to talk hockey right now. After thirty-six hours without Lily, he just wanted some focused baby-girl time. But another wave of giggles came from some distant place in the house, so instead of interrupting Lily's playtime to fulfill his own selfish needs, Beckett talked with his dad while Sarah cleared plates.

The patter of little feet turned Beckett's head just as Lily launched herself at him. His reflexes kicked in, and he caught her with a "Jesus, Lily..."

But her giggle infiltrated his heart and melted the irritation that came with the shock. So he tickled her, and her laughter spilled out and filled the kitchen.

And Beckett's whole world righted. His entire life turned into sunshine and Hello Kitty and My Little Pony and butterflies and rainbows.

He was so fuckin' lost over this kid.

"You monkey," he said, laughing. "You're getting too big to be doing that."

"Daddy, stop." The words popped out of her on bubbles of laughter. "*Daddy.*"

He propped her on his lap, facing him. He lifted one of her wild curls and pulled it in front of her eyes. "What the heck is going on here? This mop's all over the place. Jeez, the things your grandma and your aunt let you get away with." He let the curl bounce free and stroked his daughter's dewy pink cheek. Love swamped him. Sometimes his love for Lily felt so big, he feared it would overwhelm him. "Did you have a good night?"

"Uh-huh." She nodded emphatically, all her baby teeth glowing. "We watched movies and ate popcorn and colored and played games." Her exuberance faded a little. "Grandma said you're going away today."

His heart pinched. "I am."

She curled her little hand around two of his fingers, as if trying to hold on to him. "For games?"

"Yep."

"Can I come?"

Crap. He kissed her forehead. "Sorry, baby. No family on work trips."

"How long will you be gone?"

God. Would this ever get easier? He brushed more curly fuzz off her forehead. "I've got five games. They're all on the West Coast. I'll tell you the team, and you tell me where they're from."

Her face lit up a little. "'Kay."

"Let's see." He covered her legs with his hands and rolled his eyes to the ceiling. "I'll give you an easy one to start out. Ducks."

"Anaheim," she responded immediately. Not surprising. They played this game a lot.

"And where is Anaheim?"

She threw her arms overhead, her adorable little face scrunched in a furious smile. "*Disneyland.*"

Beckett, Sarah, and their dad laughed.

"And where is Disneyland?" Beckett asked.

"California."

He went through the other four teams, and she got every one right.

"Okay," he said. "Grab me a brush and a hair tie. I'll rebraid this mess."

She pushed off his lap. "Can you do a fishtail today, Daddy?"

He winced a little. "You know they're not my best."

"Yeah. Okay. How about a waterfall? They're soooooo pretty."

"A what? I've never heard of a waterfall." And Beckett knew every braid in existence. Because Lily's curly hair often knotted, braids had eliminated tears early on, and Beckett had stuck with them. He was a master braider and usually ended up braiding not only Lily's hair, but Amy's and Rachel's too.

"We found it on YouTube. It looks super easy."

His brows shot up. "YouTube?" He cut a look at his sister. "*YouTube?*"

She grinned. "Supervised YouTube."

"Oh my God." Beckett leaned forward, pressed his elbows to his knees, and ran a hand down his face. The weight of everything yet to come with his daughter sometimes terrified him.

Luckily, Lily didn't give him time to think about where YouTube could lead. She grabbed his hand and pulled. "Come on, Daddy. We got new nail polish too. All different colors. We'll find one for you that won't match the Ducks or the Coyotes or the..."

While his daughter recited the names of the teams he would play over the next five days, Beckett stood and looked over his shoulder at his sister.

She met his gaze and nodded. "I'll have it ready for you."

Relieved Sarah would have nail polish remover and cotton

balls waiting for him at the door when it was time for him to catch his plane, Beckett relaxed and followed his daughter into the room his mother had decorated for Lily.

Then he settled on the floor with her in his lap and a brush in his hand. And he soaked in the feel of his baby warm and safe in the circle of his arms, her silky hair slipping through his fingers as he attempted this waterfall thing and listened to her chipper voice as Lily chattered on and on about her night with her cousins while sorting through a box of nail polish.

His life was so fucking awesome.

"What about red, Daddy? Are any of the teams you're playing red? 'Cause then we won't use red."

Red, red, red. Eden pushed into his thoughts.

Okay, his life was...mostly...fucking awesome.

12

E den climbed into the passenger's side of the ambulance, snapped her seat belt, and pulled the iPad onto her lap. She opened the report app as Gabe slid behind the wheel.

"Tori owes you big-time." Gabe turned the engine over and started out of the hospital's parking lot. "We haven't stopped all damn night. I'm starving. Want to hit Dairy Queen on the way back to the house?"

"Ice cream? At two a.m.?" Eden tried to tease, but her exhaustion ruined the effect. "Are you pregnant?"

"Come on. We haven't even had time to eat. You've got to be starving."

Eden gave up on the form, flipped the iPad's cover down, and dropped her head back against the seat, eyes closed. Beckett appeared in her mind. Beckett in all his naked splendor. Beckett and those dark eyes that never stopped watching her, never stopped searching for ways to bring her pleasure.

And good Lord, the heights of pleasure that man could drive Eden to...

Heat flooded her pelvis, and her sex throbbed with both craving and discomfort. She was definitely still sore twenty-four hours after the most erotic and moving sexual experience of her life. And not once but all damn night. Eden hadn't been watching the clock, but she'd bet that man had woken her every two hours for an hour of sexual exploration.

But it wasn't the sex that made her heart tight every time she thought of him. That came when she remembered the way he teased her and challenged her. The way he kissed her afterward, long and slow, like savoring dessert after the perfect meal. Or the way he tickled her until she promised to sleep in his arms. Or the way he'd wake, find her out of reach, and shimmy over to curl his thickly muscled arm around her before settling again.

Yeah, those memories made her heart ache.

"I hope Tori's father's okay." She pulled her phone from her pocket and checked for a new message. Eden had covered Tori's shift at the last minute when her coworker's father had gone into the hospital with heart trouble. But there were no new messages. "She hasn't messaged you yet, has she?"

"She'd message you before she'd message me." Gabe scanned the boulevard. "We've got Taco Bell, In-N-Out Burger..."

"Whatever you want, Gabe." She opened her eyes and stared out at the dark streets. "My stomach could use something—"

Their pagers sounded.

"Motherfucking sonofabitch." Gabe pounded his hand on the steering wheel. "Is it a full moon or something? I haven't had a night like this in months."

Eden was too tired to get angry. She dragged her pager into view and read with a heavy sigh. "Woman down."

"How novel," Gabe said, his voice thick with sarcasm. "I wish they could throw a little originality into it. Woman down, scissors up her nose, for instance. Or, man down, ax lodged in trachea."

Even fried, Eden couldn't stop the laughter from rolling out of her. "Stop. I'm too exhausted to laugh."

Her abdominal muscles ached too, but that was all about what Beckett had put her through last night. She'd never looked at sex as a workout until Beckett.

"Just sayin'." Gabe flipped on the sirens, and Eden read off the address and tapped into navigation on her phone.

"Oh, great," Gabe said. "The last time I rolled on that neighborhood, it was for a gang fight with multiple victims. I've never seen so much blood. Would be nice to know if that's what we're rolling into now? Am I right?"

Yes, he was right, but Eden didn't want to egg Gabe on tonight. Searching the map, she named off the best streets to take toward the incident. She was about to put her head back and close her eyes when her phone chimed with a message.

From Beckett.

Are you sleeping?

Her stomach jumped and twisted. It would be eleven p.m. on the West Coast. He'd probably finished playing his first game, and she found herself wanting to know how it went and who won. In the next second, she wondered if he'd hit a bar tonight and pick up another woman and take her back to his hotel room to give her everything he'd given Eden last night.

Of course he would, dumb shit. He'd probably been juggling multiple women at one time since he hit puberty.

She let out a breath and looked out the window, trying, unsuccessfully, to read a million things into the message. When she'd written the good-bye note without any indication she was interested in further communication, her head had been cleared of the sexual haze that had sent her to the bar in the first place. She'd seen their situation for what it was—a chance meeting, a spark, the opportunity to quench that desire. And her first step toward reconnecting romantically with men.

But she didn't want this. Didn't want the headache of

having someone as delicious as Beckett around to constantly tempt her away from her goal. Didn't want the heartache of wanting someone who had as little time to spend cavorting as she did. Didn't want the stress of trying to make something so impossible work just for great sex once in a while. And she really, really didn't want to be worried about someone cheating on her. Or lying to her. Again.

She hadn't decided whether or not she wanted to start a dialogue with him by the time they'd reached the address of the *woman down*, so she stuffed her phone away without responding.

13

B eckett slid toward the bench in the middle of the third period, letting Savage take his place for a few seconds against the San Jose Sharks. He windmilled his burning legs over the half wall and dropped his ass to the bench beside Donovan.

"Hoo-wee," Donovan said without taking his eyes off the ice. "You are earning every penny of that fat paycheck this run. I'm starting to think you being pissed is worth dealing with your moods if this is the result."

On the ice, Andre Kristoff intercepted a pass between the Sharks, spun, passed the puck behind his back, and outmaneuvered three Sharks bearing down on him.

"*Yeah!*" Beckett yelled.

Andre pushed hard into his skates and shot down the ice toward the Sharks' goal.

Beckett stood, braced his hands on the wall. "All the way. *All the way.*"

"Fuck, he's fast," Donovan said beside Beckett.

One of the Sharks' defensemen crowded Andre; the other angled directly for him and closed so fast, the kid never had a chance. The Shark smashed Andre up against the boards like a bug on a windshield, the kid came off his feet, then hit the ice on his hands and knees. He rolled back to his feet and reached for the puck, but the other Shark already had it directed down the ice.

Beckett looked to the refs, waiting for a roughing call, but got nothing.

"Fuckers," Beckett said, body strung tight, stick ready.

"Get in there, Croft," Tremblay barked.

Beckett was over the wall in a split second, driving directly for the defenseman who'd hit Andre. Building up speed, Beckett threw himself into the smaller player, adding a well-placed elbow during the drive.

The guy hit the ice with a grunt, and a "Fucking A."

Standing over the defenseman, Beckett said, "I'm protective of the little guys."

Down the ice, Beckett's teammates scrambled for a goal. He sprinted that direction, cut in front of the pipes, and shoved a Shark's wing out of the way. Savage shot and scored. Misery leaked through the stands. The buzzer sounded, ending the game and adding the fourth win in the Rough Riders' streak.

Beckett celebrated with a group hug on the ice before moving through the standard postgame rituals of the coach's locker room talk, postgame interviews, and, finally, catching a shower.

Because he took the longest showers of everyone on the team, by the time he'd gotten done warming, steaming, and stretching his sore muscles, Beckett was sitting on his bench with a towel around his waist when all the other guys were almost dressed.

He pulled his phone from his duffel while a bunch of the guys talked about grabbing something to eat at the hotel bar. But when Beckett saw that he'd missed one call from Kim and two calls from his sister, alarm instantly tuned out everything else. It was almost two a.m. back east, but he dialed anyway.

"Hey, there," Sarah answered. "I'm glad you called. I have someone here who's having a little trouble sleeping tonight. I think she could use a few minutes of daddy time."

"What's wrong?"

"Um...can't say."

Which meant they had to play twenty questions. "Did Kim call again?"

"Yes."

"Did Lily talk to her?"

"No."

"Did you talk to her?"

"No."

Beckett's mind stretched for ways Kim's call could have upset— "Did she leave a message?"

"Bingo. You're good at this game."

Beckett closed his eyes on a sigh. "Does she want money?"

"Probably, but didn't say so outright," she said cryptically. "I think lunch sounds great. Let's do that when you get home."

Which translated into Kim wanting to see Beckett. "You're fucking kidding me."

"Nope."

He growled, collected himself, then said, "Okay, turn on FaceTime."

He leaned forward, resting elbows on knees, and a second later, Lily's angelic face, lit by the phone's screen, appeared. She was snuggled into bed beside Sarah.

"Hi, Daddy."

The melancholy tone in her voice broke Beckett's heart. "Hey, baby," he said gently, trying to sound upbeat. "Having a hard time sleeping tonight?"

She nodded and pulled a stuffed bear tighter.

"I'm sorry. I'll tell you what, if you get back to sleep soon, I'll

call in the morning and we can spend some time on Club
Penguin together."

Her face lit up like a sparkler in the dark. "Really?"

"Really." He grinned, his heart lightening. "I still have to
beat you at karate."

She smiled and sat a little straighter. The new excitement
washed the shadows away. "And I have enough money to stay in
the Puffle Hotel."

He raised his brows. "Yeah?"

"Yeah. And I'm going to take my Puffles to the pool and the
spa. And the gift shop there has the cutest Puffle hats ever."

"*Ever?*" Beckett asked.

Around him, the guys were laughing at him, and he didn't
give a shit. His daughter was smiling.

"Ever." She nodded emphatically. Then her eyes darted
around the screen. "Where are you? Who's laughing?"

"I'm in the locker room. We just finished the game."

"When can I come to a game?"

Beckett sighed and ran a hand through his wet hair. He
didn't like that idea. The thought of fielding all her questions
about why he was so mean on the ice wasn't appealing. "Uh..."

"Do I hear Miss Lily's voice?" Andre asked.

"Who's that?" Lily asked, perking up and peering at the
screen as if she'd be able to see someone else.

"You can't tell from my voice?" Andre said.

"Um..." Her face scrunched up the way it did when Beckett
asked her to sound out a word. "You sorta sound like Gru in
Despicable Me."

Sarah giggled in the background.

Andre looked at Beckett with his hands held out palms up,
like *who the hell is that?* Beckett shook his head. But a couple of
the other guys busted up laughing.

"She's right," Emet said. "He does." Emet Mattheson had
four kids under the age of eight and glanced at the others on

the team with young kids. "You know that movie with the minions? The little yellow guys?" When others recognized the description, Emet added, "The little girls' father, Gru."

Recognition hit their faces, and they all started laughing.

Andre put his hands on his hips. "*Pffft.*" He gestured for Beckett to hand over the phone. "Let me talk to this little *kisa.*"

"She needs to get to sleep, Andre. I don't think—"

Andre took the phone from Beckett. "Hello, my *solnyshko.*"

Lily's giggles echoed over the phone. "Hi, Andre."

He shook a comically stern finger at the screen. "You do realize now, they will all have a new nickname for me because of you."

"What nickname?" she asked.

"Gru," he said with all his Russian melodrama. "They will always now call me Gru this and Gru that"—more of Lily's laughter rolled out of the phone—"and the name is so perfect to rhyme, I do not know what these men will think of next. I must watch this...despicable movie. Will Dmitri like, you think?"

"Yes, Dmitri will like it."

"All right, then. Maybe we FaceTime you, watch the movie together, the four and a half of us."

More giggles. "Four and a half?"

"Yeah, yeah, you know the baby in Nika's belly. He's still just a half."

"Andre," Beckett finally said, lifting his hand for the phone. "It's the middle of the night there."

"Oh, your papa." Andre rolled his eyes. "Ruin all the fun. Okay, only sweet dreams, *kisa.* Promise me."

"I promise."

Andre handed the phone back to Beckett with a silent *You're welcome.* But before Beckett could grab the phone, Savage swiped it, then backed out of Beckett's reach.

"Hey, cupcake, plain old American Rafe here."

More giggling. "Hi, Rafe."

"So," he lowered his voice to a conspiratorial hum, "don't tell the rest of these yahoos, but I happen to know a thing or two about Club Penguin. See, my niece is big, and I mean *big*, into Puffles."

"*Really?*" Lily's voice held that phantasmic breathy quality of supreme disbelief and hope all rolled into one. "Does she have a *rainbow* Puffle?"

"No, but I do."

Beckett dropped his head into his hands and groaned as his daughter squealed and the locker room burst into laughter.

"*You* went on the *journey*?" Lily asked, breathless.

Beckett stood and took a step toward Savage. Savage, grinning like a little shit, took a step back.

"Uh-huh," he said, moving through an aisle between benches in the center of the locker room to keep Beckett at bay. "And I'd love to tell you all"—Beckett made a grab for the phone, but Savage jumped and spun out of range—"about it next time I see you."

Beckett had Savage cornered now, and he used a low voice when he said, "Payback's a bitch."

But evidently not low enough.

"*Daddy?* Did you say a bad word?"

The guys broke into a classic first-grade "ummmmmm" fest, followed by more laughter.

"Phone, Savage. Don't make me hurt you."

"Daddy..." Her voice held part censure, part concern.

Savage blew her a kiss, "Good night, cupcake."

And he threw the phone to Beckett. He caught it with both hands and a glare for Savage. "*Dude.* Did you just throw my daughter across the locker room?"

Everyone broke into laughter. Everyone except his daughter.

"That's not very nice, Daddy. I thought they were your friends."

The guys filtered out of the dressing room, and Beckett sat back down, focusing on Lily. "They are being very annoying tonight."

"I thought they were nice. I feel better."

"Well, that's all that matters. Do you think you can dream about rainbow Puffles tonight?"

A grin wiped away her frown. She yawned and scooted down in bed. "I'll try."

"I love you, baby," Beckett said, feeling the emotion all the way to the bottom of his feet.

"Love you, Daddy."

They said good night, and Beckett spoke with Sarah a moment before disconnecting. He heaved a sigh and glanced around to see who was left.

Donovan still stood with his back against the doorframe. "What's going on with Kim?"

"Not sure. Probably wants money, but she hasn't asked for it yet. Says she wants to see me."

"I feel for you, man. I know you're in a bad place, but giving her money is like feeding seagulls. Once they smell food, they never stop pecking at you. Next thing you know, you're in a remake of Hitchcock's *The Birds*."

That was exactly how Beckett was starting to feel. "Guess I'll figure it out when I get back."

"Get your lazy ass dressed. You're totally going to get voted slowest dumb shit on the team again this year."

"I'm not gonna hit the bar. Go ahead without me."

Donovan didn't budge. Beckett stood and started to dress.

"She still hasn't texted you back?" he asked.

Beckett knew Donovan had changed topics and was talking about Eden now. He pushed down the lingering hurt and fastened his pants while remembering how quickly Eden had gotten them undone. "Nope."

"Did you try calling?"

He shrugged into his shirt and turned to face Donovan. "I haven't gotten a reply to three different texts, bro. I'm out. I can take a hint."

Donovan scoffed. "You don't even know what a hint looks like. You get every chick you want. You say lie down, they ask where. You've just had to put that on the back burner this year."

Beckett turned his back to Donovan and buttoned his shirt. He knew he was being an ass about this, but couldn't quite get over himself. She sure as shit didn't owe him anything. She never promised more beyond their night—except breakfast. She had promised him breakfast.

"Doesn't matter." Beckett tucked in his shirt, fastened his belt, and threw his tie around his neck. "I can't get involved with anyone right now. Lily's hard enough to handle on my own when I'm *not* seeing anyone. And then there's this unsettled shit with Kim. Throwing a woman into the middle of it..." He shook his head. "Too much uncertainty. That's not fair to Lily."

"Who said anything about getting involved? Who said anything about involving Lily? And why are you jumping so far ahead of yourself?"

"You're one to talk. Serious is all you do."

"We're not talking about me. We're talking about you, and last time I looked, the serious elements of your life didn't extend to women."

Beckett sat to slide his shoes on. The same shoes Eden had untied and taken off him almost a week ago now. God, it felt like a lifetime. Like a fantasy.

"She obviously isn't into getting serious," Donovan went on, relentless. That trait made him amazing on the ice. But right now, Beckett wasn't loving it. "If you hook up with her a few more times, this infatuation will probably evaporate. It always does."

He looked up. "Aren't you going with the guys?"

"I'll catch up. I wanted to talk with you a minute. Lily's awesome and amazing, and I love what she's done for you as a person. But she also put your life into a tailspin. You have so much responsibility on your shoulders this year. I think it's important for you to have an outlet for the stress and frustration. If Eden's not going to make the next move and you're not going to take a bold step, maybe it's time to look for another hookup."

Beckett slipped on his blazer and thought about the women he'd slept with over the years. He could honestly say no one had ever made him want to see them again the way Eden did.

He grinned, closed his locker, and hefted his duffel to his shoulder. "To be perfectly honest, if I'm not going to be seeing Eden, there's no place I'd rather be than lying on my bed in the hotel room, decorating igloos and dressing penguins with Lily." He slapped Donovan's shoulder and turned him toward the door. "But thanks for caring, dude."

14

Eden brushed out her wet hair while avoiding Tori's eyes in the reflection of the mirror in the ambulance company's sleeping quarters. Her friend had come in early for her shift, then cornered Eden in the girls-only space to pin her down about a subject Eden had been dodging all week.

"You didn't return *any* of his texts?" Tori asked, her brow furrowed in frustration. "I swear you take one step forward and two steps back."

Eden tossed the brush into her duffel and ran her fingers through her hair, shaking it out. "How is that two steps back?" she grumbled. "I dipped my toes back into the ocean. That doesn't mean I want to start swimming with sharks."

Tori stabbed a finger at her. "That's *exactly* the problem."

Eden lifted her arms out to the sides. "*What* is exactly the problem?"

"You still see men as sharks."

She rolled her eyes. "It was a—"

"Freudian slip."

"*Metaphor*," Eden corrected, turning away from her friend

and throwing her uniform into the bag. She hated this topic. It brought up a lot of problems she thought she'd dealt with—until now. Until Beckett.

"You stereotype, and you know it. If Beckett were a contractor, would you see him again? Or a mechanic? Or a fireman? Or a doctor?"

Eden made a face. She couldn't see Beckett as any of those things. "I don't know." Frustration frazzled her already frayed nerves. "Maybe."

"You're stereotyping him, and you know it—Beckett's a hockey player; therefore, he's violent."

She turned on Tori, ready to come out of her skin. "I looked into it, okay? I didn't scratch the guy off my list without any thought."

"Ha, your *list*. That's a good one. I've seen you in action. I've seen you go toe to toe with gangbangers, cops; hell, I've seen you tell doctors to get their heads out of their asses. You are not going to get me to believe you're scared of one damned hockey player."

"I *work* with those people. I'm not *involved* with them."

"For an extremely levelheaded, rational woman, you're not making any sense."

Angry now, she turned on Tori. "Hockey is second only to football in its level of violence, and there is a forty percent increase in domestic violence among pro football players. Why, why, *why* would I put myself at a higher risk after what I've been through?"

Tori tossed her hands in the air. "You must be putting all those brains of yours into your paramedic program, because you sure didn't research that information very well."

"What does that mean?"

"It means I did a little research of my own, because I care about you and because I sure don't want to encourage you into a bad situation. And I found that the NHL is embracing a new policy on domestic abuse, which includes required training for all members. They take it very seriously."

"After watching a dozen of Beckett's previous games over the last week, that policy won't make it any easier to sleep at night." Eden massaged her forehead. "I've seen the way he plays. I've seen his hits, his fights. I've seen how aggressive, how physical, how violent he is. I don't care what the statistics say. I've seen the raw anger on his face when the cameras focus in on him. He's intense, and it fuckin' scares me sometimes, okay?"

"You know what, Eden, *you* fuckin' scare *me* sometimes."

"What?" She threw her arms out to the sides. "What the hell are you talking about?"

"When you confront people in the field before law enforcement arrives. You do it all the time. And sometimes it scares me."

Eden was taken aback, and she scanned her memory. "I do that because I've had training, and because it puts distance between us and the creeps. Letting them know we're not going to take their shit keeps both us and our patients safe."

"Which is exactly what Beckett does on the ice. He's had training too. And making sure the other teams know there will be consequences if they come down too hard on his players keeps everyone safer. You don't bring your hostility home. You don't confront random people in the streets. You certainly don't turn your anger on those closest to you. So why do you assume Beckett will?"

She exhaled, crossed her arms, and stared at the floor. Tears stung her eyes. "I *really* like him," she said softly. "And I'm *really* scared of that. I understand what you're saying, but no numbers are ever going to make me feel safe when violence is a way of life for him. And maybe that's a sign that I'm not ready."

Tori shrugged. "Only you can decide."

Eden recognized the look of pity on her face, and she couldn't take it. She opened the bedroom door, and voices from the kitchen signaled shift change. She hiked her duffel over her shoulder, and Tori followed her into the front room, where Eden said good-bye to the two other EMTs in the kitchen.

Tori walked out front with Eden. "You have to be comfortable with your decision, but sometimes you also have to stretch your comfort zones a little."

Eden sighed and shrugged, her mind already drifting to whether she should walk to Metro or catch a bus at the corner. She glanced toward the street to check traffic, and the sight at the curb pounded a stab of shock through her gut.

Beckett leaned on a car at the curb. Waiting.

Her heart kicked into a double beat. Fear tightened her gut and pulled at the muscles along her shoulders. Eden reflexively took a step back. She cut a look in every direction, taking in her surroundings and her quickest exits.

Tori stopped short next to her. "Is that—"

"Yes," she nearly hissed the word.

Tori frowned. "Did you know—"

"No."

"Dayum," Tori said. "He's *way* hotter in person." Tori glanced at Eden, then turned to fully face her with narrowed eyes. "Eden, *stop*." The bite in Tori's voice cut into Eden's rising panic. "Look at me."

Eden tore her gaze from Beckett and focused on Tori.

"He is *not* John. He is a major public figure who would suffer horrible repercussions if he abused a woman. He's here because he's hot for you and because *you didn't answer his texts*."

Eden fought to clear the panic from her head.

"Breathe."

Eden took a deep breath, feeling like she'd regressed years. "I'm okay."

"Good, because if you look a little closer"—Tori's grin

returned along with a spark of excitement in her eyes—"you'll see he's leaning against a *Porsche*."

She didn't see a Porsche anywhere near Beckett, but now that Tori had knocked her head back into place, Eden was kinda focused on the smile lifting his full mouth. He pulled sunglasses off and tucked one arm of the shades into the collar of his Rough Riders jersey.

God, he looked great. So handsome and vibrant. Not a trace of the fury he showed on the ice. She never expected him to make this kind of effort to see her again.

He straightened away from an SUV but didn't approach.

She needed to make a decision. She needed to tell him their one night was over and she didn't want to see him again. Or... Or she had to actually try to give life more effort than a cursory one-night stand.

She swore under her breath.

Tori frowned at her. "How the hell did you ever get into bed with him?"

"Loneliness, desperation, and alcohol?"

Tori rolled her eyes, then turned and approached Beckett, hand held out. "I'm Tori."

Beckett shook Tori's hand. And his smile... His smile made Eden feel like she'd plummeted down the steepest slope of a roller coaster.

She approached, trying like hell not to notice how freaking attractive he was with the morning sun making gold streaks pop in his hair and highlighting a day's worth of stubble on his jaw. He seemed so big, taller and more muscular than she remembered. And he wore jeans and cross-trainers with his jersey. Eden had to admit, the casual look relaxed her a little and allowed her to get her feet moving toward him.

Tori released Beckett's hand. "I'd better see what trouble I can stir up inside. Nice to meet you, Beckett."

"You too," he said.

Then Eden's buffer was gone, and she was standing face-to-face with Beckett Croft again.

His grin widened and softened. "Hi."

She tried to match his smile, but she was too intensely aware of him. "Hi."

"I scared you, huh?" His brow pulled with concern. "Showing up like this."

She lowered her gaze. "It was a little unnerving to find you here."

"I was afraid of that." He stepped toward her, reached out, and slid his index finger down her forearm, then linked it with her pinkie. Tingles spread along her skin, and her lungs tightened up again. "Sorry. I didn't know how else to get ahold of you."

"Yeah." She nodded. "I know."

"Here's the thing, Eden." He stroked the back of her hand with his thumb. "I'm not the kind of guy who sits back and lets things happen to him. I'm the kind of guy who goes out and makes things happen. My mom calls it ADHD, or OCD, or plain old making trouble, but whatever, no one's perfect, right?"

That made Eden laugh and loosened some nerves.

"The truth is, I haven't been able to stop thinking about you for the last six days," he said. "So I couldn't take the thanks-for-the-hookup note or the unanswered texts as proof that you weren't interested. I had to come and see what that looks like up close and personal."

"Yeah." A soft laugh rolled out. "I guess you aren't very familiar with that, are you?"

He winced and chuckled. "Ouch. Has someone been looking into my history?"

"Six days is a long time to think about something."

"Very true. Felt like a damn month to me." He threaded

their fingers together and met her eyes directly, his expression serious. "Tell me you're not interested, and I'll go. I promise not to bother you again."

So charming. So genuine. Oh, what she would give to be able to accept a man at face value again. And she could. She just had to choose to do it.

"I've been—"

"Busy." He nodded, his expression serious. "I know. I kept telling myself you have more important things to do. That both our lives are already way too full. And a hundred other reasons I should have driven home from the airport this morning instead of straight here."

She took a breath. "The truth is...I'm not sure about this. Everything inside me tells me it's a bad idea."

"Fair enough." He seemed to take that in stride. "I'm not sure about this either. What I am sure of is that you promised me breakfast and bailed."

She exhaled a laugh. "True."

"So let me take you now," he suggested, then added, "unless you have school."

"Not till this afternoon."

"Breakfast? Somewhere extremely public? So we can get to know each other better? We can even take your car if you'd be more comfortable driving."

"My car is Metro."

His face went slack a second, but he came back strong. "I can do Metro."

She laughed. "Oh, that deer in the headlights was priceless."

His hand felt so good in hers. Big and warm. Six short days, and she'd already forgotten how good it felt when he touched her. She closed her fingers around his, and her chest knotted at the rightness of it.

She searched beyond those damned blinders and stereotypes and fears, the way Tori had with her research.

And she found solid ground.

Yes, she really wanted to see where this went.

Eden nodded and smiled up at him. "Okay. Breakfast."

15

Beckett's knee jittered as he navigated the streets of downtown DC. His gut was tight, the way it squeezed when he was on the bench, watching other guys play instead of being out there himself.

"Five-game winning streak," Eden said, pulling her gaze from the passenger's window.

Her hair was down and loose. She'd come out of the ambulance company in inky jeans, a San Diego hoodie, and not an ounce of makeup. And she looked freaking gorgeous.

"Mmm-hmm." He wanted to ask if she'd watched or caught that on the news. Wanted to ask if her feelings toward the game had changed. Wanted to ask her if touching him after six days felt as good to her as touching her felt to him.

God, he was such an asshole.

He'd waited outside her work on purpose, knowing it would probably spook her. He'd planned this breakfast for the same reason. She didn't know it yet, but it wasn't going to be what she expected. He'd justified it by telling himself he wanted to see if she had what it took to fit in with the people who mattered to him. He wanted to know if she could roll with the perpetual changes inherent in his life. But the truth was, he was looking for a reason to weed her out. An excuse to push her to the back of his mind and move on.

But that had been before she'd walked out of the building and he'd locked eyes with her. Before those bizarre pangs kicked up. Before she'd smiled and agreed to take another chance on him, even after he'd been a creep and borderline stalked her. And now, he was stuck with his stupid plan already in motion, far too aware of how fully this could backfire on him.

"I didn't know Porsche made SUVs." Her smile felt like sugar and sunshine all wrapped into one beam that pierced his chest. "Sort of an oxymoron, right? When you think Porsche, you think race car. A Porsche SUV is just..." She seemed to take stock of her words and backpedaled. "But...I mean...it's nice."

He stopped at a traffic light and squeezed her hand. "Don't blow smoke. Truth, remember?"

"It is nice. I didn't want you to think I—"

"I'm not that sensitive."

She seemed to like that. Her smile returned and reached her eyes. "Okay."

And they stared at each other for a long, hot second.

"God, you're beautiful." The words were out, floating around the car before Beckett realized he'd said them and not thought them. "Sorry. I've never been really good at keeping inside thoughts inside."

"Thank you," she said softly, then shook her head and looked out the window again. "Where are we going? There aren't any restaurants in this area. Are you lost? I know just about every street in this city."

Of course she did. He'd forgotten all about that.

He released a nervous breath. "Uh..." he hedged. "We're almost there."

"You don't sound as happy about that as you did when you picked me up."

He turned down their final street and slowed. "Yeah, well, that's because I thought there was a damn good chance you were going to turn me down."

She gave him a silly frown. "That doesn't make sense."

Beckett turned into the YMCA parking lot, where balloons and banners for the fundraiser flew. "We're here." He feigned excitement but braced for...hell, he didn't even know what to expect. Anger, disappointment... "Surprise?"

"The Y," she said, part *what the hell*, part humor.

"Let me guess, you've been here a time or two."

"Or ten." She looked over the YMCA, took in the balloons and banners, eyes narrowed. Finally, she shook her head. "Nope, can't figure this one out on my own. You're gonna have to help me."

"We're doing a pancake breakfast this morning. A fundraiser for the Y. We donate things for a silent auction, cook breakfast, then wander around while people are eating and take pictures, sign autographs. The money goes to summer and after-school programs so parents who work don't have to leave their kids home alone. This is our fifth annual."

Her head slowly turned toward him, a furrow dipping her brow. "On a weekday?"

"That's so we can get corporate donors. A lot of Rough Riders fans work in the city and stay late to see games, but they live in the surrounding Metro area. And we discovered that more people showed and we raised more money when we did it on a weekday, because no one wants to commute back into the city on Saturday or Sunday."

She turned her gaze on Beckett. "So, you're telling me that you're going to be cooking and networking at this breakfast? And I'm going to be doing...what, exactly?"

He winced.

She sighed. "Well, this is certainly public. As for the getting-to-know-each-other part..." She shrugged.

He rubbed a hand down his face. "It seemed like a good idea when I first thought of it."

She lifted a brow. "Is that how you got so damned good at hockey? Going with your first idea?"

He grinned, jumping at the chance to change the subject. "You think I'm good?"

"That's what people say."

He deflated. "I'm obviously not as good at other things."

"I don't know about that." She released a breath, leaned against the door, and stared at him. "You are so sweetly flawed."

Donovan, Savage, and Kristoff came out of the building and spotted his car. Beckett's breath leaked out on a groan.

Eden followed his gaze. "This must be the *we*."

"If you want me to take you back, now would be the time to ask."

As the guys approached, Beckett hit the locks, and when Donovan reached Eden's door with a big smile, he found himself locked out.

"Hey, you said to make her feel welcome." His smile fell, and he stabbed a finger at the lock and glared at Beckett. "That's not welcoming."

Eden started laughing. "He's really adorable." She looked at Beckett with a spark in her eye. "Does he have a girlfriend?"

Beckett lifted his hands and waved them in an X. "Wait, wait, wait—"

"For *Tori*."

"Oh. Well then, no. But he's been through a bad divorce recently, so..."

"Oh..." Her expression sobered. "Will you be able to get me home by two? I have class at three, and it takes me an hour to get there."

Beckett had to pick up Lily at school at three. And he'd

already threatened death to anyone who slipped and mentioned her name in the event that Eden showed today. "Absolutely."

She heaved a sigh. "All right, then. Let's get cookin'."

Eden pulled the handle, popping the lock, and Donovan was there to open the door and offer a hand to help her out, as if she were arriving by fucking magic pumpkin coach or something.

Maybe he spent too much time in little-girl land. Puffles, magic pumpkin coaches...

"Dude," Savage called, then gave him double thumbs-up. Eden was already walking toward the Y between Donovan and Kristoff, talking and laughing. "Comin'?"

Beckett stood from the car and rounded the back to pull out the silent-auction donations as Eden disappeared inside. Somehow, that didn't surprise him. What really surprised him was how damn happy he was with her response.

16

E den stood in the industrial kitchen at the Y, wearing a Rough Riders jersey that was three times too big and had Croft emblazoned on the back. While pancakes cooked on the griddle, she tossed blueberries into her mouth and watched Beckett crouch in front of a little boy about seven or eight years old. The child too wore a jersey with Croft across the back. A lot of people who'd come and gone over the last two hours were Beckett's fans.

One of the guys had plugged his phone into a speaker, and an eclectic mix of alternative rock, modern country, hip-hop, and rap played through the space. The Y had opened the huge kitchen they used for cooking classes and events to a series of other rooms where tables and chairs had been set up for diners. Hundreds of patrons had come through the line, been served breakfast by the seven Rough Riders here today, then stayed to snap, chat, sign, and donate.

"This is the last bucket." The female voice drew Eden's gaze. Faith, Grant Saber's girlfriend, plopped a five-gallon bucket half filled with pancake batter on the counter beside Eden.

She sighed. "Oh, yippee."

Faith started laughing, making Eden smile. The woman was beautiful and had an extra sweetness about her. With long blonde hair and blue eyes, she drew a lot of attention, most of which she didn't seem to notice.

"Are you sure these are going to freeze?" Eden asked. "I understand they don't want to waste it, but...frozen pancakes?"

"Sure. You just pop them in the microwave or the toaster."

"If you say so." Eden shrugged. "I don't eat much of anything that isn't prepackaged or premade nowadays."

"You're a trouper. I wouldn't have been so mellow if Grant had introduced the mob to me like this." Faith meant the other Rough Riders, and Eden scanned the crowd between ladling pancake batter on the griddle and tossing on a handful of blueberries. The plastic bracelets created for the event slid along her forearm. She and Faith had donned one of every color, and seeing the rainbow made Eden happy.

Faith sang along with Train's *Marry Me* as she returned to the job she'd been doing before she'd gone to fetch batter and wrapped cooled cakes for freezing. A male voice picked up the lyrics and came up behind them.

Grant pressed a kiss to Faith's neck, and she smiled over her shoulder at the dark-haired Rough Rider. He was a little younger than Beckett, and the love in Faith's and Grant's eyes both softened Eden's heart and terrified her on some level.

Grant set down two stools. "Rest your feet, ladies."

"Oh God, thank you." Eden slid onto the stool and sighed. Tate came toward the grill, still wearing the same grin he'd been sporting since she'd first seen him two hours ago. "Doesn't your face get tired? Smiling like that?"

He reached past her and grabbed some blueberries. "Takes more muscles—"

"To frown," she finished with him, then added, "That doesn't account for gravity," as he tossed the berries into his mouth.

"Smarty-pants." Andre stepped around Tate and grabbed a pen from the counter. His thick Russian accent always made Eden smile, no matter what he was saying. "What the hell you doin' with Beckett?"

"Thank you," Tate said to Andre. "I've been wanting to know but had too many American manners to ask."

"You are welcome," Andre said, serious. "Any time you need my thick Russian skull, you only need to ask."

Laughing, Eden threw a blueberry at Tate. With moves as quick as lightning, he opened his mouth and caught the berry.

"Whoa," Eden said, truly impressed.

He grinned, curled his fingers, and brushed his nails on his jersey.

"Throw me one." Andre told her.

Eden tossed a berry high. Andre bent his knees, opened his mouth, and jockeyed for the perfect spot to catch it. At the last second, Tate slammed the other man with his shoulder, knocking him out of the way to catch the berry himself.

Faith, Grant, Eden, and Tate laughed. Andre was grinning when he shoved Tate. "Cheater. You Americans are a bunch of cheaters." He turned to Eden. "Another. I'm going to show this cheater how to play."

"Game on," Tate said.

Both men crouched in a ready position, just outside the main kitchen area. Before Eden even tossed the first berry, the men were throwing shoulders and grinning like idiots. Eden couldn't help but laugh as she watched the two full grown men turned four-year-olds battling to catch fruit in their mouth. And she got a different view—a positive view—of that competitive spirit all these men embodied. Of course they also kept score and continued upping the ante—three out of five, five out of seven, seven out of nine—until Eden ran out of berries.

When Andre fought off Tate for the last berry, raucous applause surprised Eden, and while Andre and Tate bowed for their audience, Eden took in the spectators with embarrassed heat in her cheeks. But when she found Beckett in the crowd, he was watching with the same joyous smile, as if he'd found her juvenile behavior with Andre and Tate just as entertaining as the others. When he locked eyes with her, she had three startling and profound revelations—one: he wasn't a jealous man; two: he didn't mind sharing the spotlight; and three: it pleased him to see her enjoying herself.

Those had all been problems in her life for as long as she could remember, with either her father, her boyfriend, or both.

"Mmm," Faith hummed at her side. "I know that look."

"What?" Eden said, pulling her gaze from Beckett with butterflies in her gut. "What look?"

Tate and Andre had wandered back into the audience, continuing with photographs and signatures. Eden refocused on the pancakes Faith had saved while she'd been playing blueberry catch.

Faith's blue eyes darted to Beckett and back. "That one. It's the same one I see in Grant's eyes."

Eden almost choked on the berry she'd popped into her mouth. "No. That"—she lifted her gaze toward Beckett—"is not even close to that." She cast her eyes backward to where Grant was washing dishes.

"Maybe not yet. But that," she said with another glance at Beckett, "is how it starts."

"*Pffft*," was Eden's response.

"It's good to see and about damn time," Faith said, then continued before Eden could respond. "Look at him, hauling in the cash. Mr. Smooth."

That made Eden laugh. Beckett was shaking a man's hand while taking a check in the other, his smile on full blast. "At some things, maybe."

"Oh, really?" The interest in Faith's voice drew Eden's gaze back to the griddle. "Tell. I never get enough dirt on that man."

Eden lifted her brows, "That's hard to believe."

"Why?" Faith asked conversationally.

Eden shrugged. "I guess because of the things he does on the ice."

"That's work. They don't take it home."

Her gaze darted to Faith. "No?"

She made a face and shook her head. "Uh-uh. Great, great bunch of men. Definitely a second family." She looked up and smiled as she took in the room. "My dad died several months before I met Grant..."

"Oh, I'm sorry."

She shook her head. "It's okay. He was sick for a long time. He was ready. I wasn't." She finished wrapping a set of six cakes and paused to watch the crowd, a soft smile on her face. "He was my only family. My mom left when I was young, and I didn't have any siblings. Grant has a tense relationship with his parents, so it was just us. Until he brought me into this family. Man, it's really one of a kind. And it only gets better. I think the cohesiveness of the team and their great standings has a lot to do with Beckett's leadership. He's all-inclusive. Ridiculously generous with everything—time, resources, support."

Faith smiled and wrapped more pancakes. "He recruited his sister, who has two young daughters, to be a support contact to Andre's wife, Nika. They're so young and already have one son, another on the way. Nika's told me a number of times that Andre worships Beckett and all the extra time he's taken to mentor him. And I know Nika would be lost without Sarah."

Faith sighed. "This group has completed my life in a way I didn't even know I needed completing."

"Hey."

Beckett's voice startled Eden, and she jumped. Her hand went directly over her heart, and she whispered, "Shit."

"I'm sorry." His voice was soft, his hands sliding down her

arms. "I've got to get better about that. I'll shuffle my feet or something. Are you ready to go?"

"Now? I don't want to leave Faith with—"

"I've got Faith covered." Grant came up to Eden's side and took the spatula from her hand. "Beckett told us you didn't get much sleep on your shift. Thanks for coming out."

"Thanks for having me." Eden hugged Faith and said good-bye to the rest of the Rough Riders, then let Beckett pull her into his side on the walk to the car. She held the wrist he slung over her shoulder and toyed with the red rubber bracelet he'd been wearing since they'd arrived.

"So," he said. "On a scale of one to ten, how bad was it?"

"Depends. Are you asking on a date scale or a getting-to-know-you scale or sheer-enjoyment scale, or...?"

"You ask such difficult questions."

"Well, I really liked your teammates and Faith, so that was a ten. The fun of it would have to be down there somewhere below six, but take that with a grain of salt. Had I gotten more sleep, that score might have been higher. And I think I learned a lot about you, though you learned nothing about me, so I'd have to even that out at a five."

"Not true. I learned a lot about you too."

"Like I can flip pancakes?"

"Like you're easygoing and you have a great sense of humor. You're spontaneous and flexible. You don't hold bad-date judgments against a guy, and you seem to make friends wherever you go."

"That's quite a bit considering we may have spoken a handful of times in the last two hours."

"Observation." They reached the car, and he opened the door for her. "I also noticed you stayed away from the kids. Don't you like kids?"

"A hot grill in a kitchen isn't a safe place for kids." She

steered the conversation in another direction. "Shouldn't they have been in school?"

"The event was considered a community outreach, so the kids who could come with their parents earned school credit."

"Man, you really have this dialed in. Did you bring in some good donations?"

"A lot. We won't have totals until tomorrow, but I feel really good about it." Hanging on to the door with one hand, he asked, "What did you learn about me?"

She breathed deep and looked through the windshield, remembering. And she smiled a little when she said, "I learned your ass looks even better in jeans than dress pants."

He laughed, and she met his eyes again.

"I learned you and your teammates are, indeed, like a motley crew of brothers, and they love you fiercely."

His grin softened, and he nodded.

"I also learned there's a huge heart hidden in here." She patted his chest.

"How's that?"

"You were incredibly patient and attentive to fans. And since you weren't in a kitchen with a hot grill, you got a lot of time with kids, and you're really good with them."

He grinned. "I like kids."

"I also heard how your leadership has pulled the team together into a cohesive unit that's ruling the ratings this season. Overall, I'd have to say I was damn impressed, Mr. Croft."

He stroked her cheek, his gaze lingering on her mouth. "Maybe it wasn't such a bad date idea after all."

"No," she said, "it was still a bad idea."

That made him laugh, and instead of closing the door, he pulled the seat belt over her and leaned in to buckle it. A sweet pang tugged inside her, and she threaded her fingers through his hair. He smelled good, and he was warm.

"There you go," he murmured and pulled back.

Eden reached out and cupped his face with both hands. "You may have questionable taste for date locations, and I did think you showing up at my work was creepy at first, but you managed to pull it out of the fire and make it fun. So thanks for saving me from myself and taking that extra step to corner me."

He grinned. "That has to be the strangest yet sweetest thank-you I've ever received."

"I like to be different."

She pulled him to her for a kiss, and the moment his lips pressed hers, she sighed. And then she needed more. And he kept giving her everything she asked for until their hands were tangled in each other's hair and Eden pulled back, breathless.

He pressed his forehead to hers. "Baby, you are definitely different."

A few hours ago, she'd been ready to write him off. A few hours ago, he'd made her so nervous, she couldn't speak. But now, her craving for him was so strong, it felt like a physical entity inside her body. Now, she wanted to get naked and get him inside her.

"Do you have somewhere to be?" she asked.

"Not until this afternoon."

He kissed her again, forcefully pulled away, and closed her door. Then he paused a moment, hands braced against the car, gaze cast down, as if he were thinking. But he shook his head, met her gaze through the glass, and pressed a flat hand to the window, letting it linger there as he seemed to lose himself in thought another second. Finally, his fingers slipped away, and he rounded the car to the driver's side.

After he'd started the engine, he said, "Okay, where to? Back to your work, or did I quell the creep factor enough to let me drop you at home?"

"Home."

"*Yes*," he said, grinning. "I'm finally doing something right."

She put her address into her phone and turned on navigation so she could relax and soak him in. With Siri guiding Beckett to her house, Eden reached across the console and combed her fingers through his hair at his temple. Suddenly, there was so much she wanted to know about him, she didn't know where to start. She thought about the family he was so close to and the team that considered him their center. She thought about what Faith had said about the group taking her in and becoming her family. And, though Eden had never regretted walking away from her own family in the last two years, her intimate view of Beckett's tight-knit life made her feel lonely.

"You're lucky." The words floated out, melancholy. "You've created a really amazing life for yourself."

"I feel incredibly lucky, but it's not just the life I built. It's more like the life everyone helped me build. Sometimes I think it takes a village to create an NHL player."

"Why's that?"

"It's an *enormous* commitment," he said, his voice heavy with the burden. "In the beginning, it was my parents hauling me to the rink every day, traveling with me on weekends and during the summer. Once I showed promise, there were special coaches and camps and equipment, which cost a hell of a lot of money. There's a sacrifice your siblings make in their lives and your parents make in their marriage and careers because they're pushing you along this path. There are medical bills, long waits in the ER, occasional hospital stays. That's all before I went pro."

He glanced at her, then back at the road. "I only spent a year in the minors before I got picked up by the Rough Riders. Now I have a freaking community of professionals that keeps me moving forward. On the hockey side, I've got coaches and trainers and sports psychologists, always there, always pushing, always honing. I've got the people who hold everything together for me so I can focus on the game—equipment managers, physicians, physical therapists, nutritionists, travel coordinators."

"Jeez." This opened up a whole new window into his life.

"And then there's the personal side," he went on. "To keep me organized and together on that end, I've got an agent, a business manager, a financial planner, an accountant. I've got a housekeeper, who often doubles as a cook and leaves me healthy meals a few times a week so I'm not scrounging and shortchanging my body."

He shook his head. "So, no, I don't do this on my own. This awesome life is in large part due to my amazing family. The other part is due to my professional support. Somewhere in there, yeah, I was born with some talent. And yes, I did spend the majority of my young life on the ice. And I also worked my ass off, and continue to work my ass off. But honestly, none of that would matter without all these other people. They're the ones who created the perfect storm."

"The perfect storm," she repeated, a smile lifting her lips. "I like that."

"That's how it feels. There are a lot of talented hockey players out there, but not all of them have the support network they need to get to this level. When I look back, I swear the stars and planets had to align to get me where I am. I've done my best to try and compensate my family for their sacrifices along the way, try to show my appreciation to my support staff, but it never feels like enough to me, at least not with my family. I can pay my support staff what they deserve, but no matter what I do, I can't give my parents back that time they spent on me. I can't give my sister back my parents' attention."

"So what do you do for them?"

"My first pro paycheck went to buy my parents a house. A nice house, you know? Everything they've always wanted." He huffed a laugh. "And, man, what a fucking struggle to get them to let me do that. You'd think I was asking them to bathe in boiling water. I put college funds together for my nieces. Helped Sarah and her husband buy a house—yet *another* battle. I spend my holidays with all of them, get them to the games as often as they can make it. In the off-season, I try to take my nieces off my sister's hands when I can." He glanced at her. "Her husband is overseas, and it's tough having the girls on her own." He shrugged. "I try to alleviate some of their stresses and concerns where I can. So, yeah, that was the long version of it takes a village to make an NHL player."

She sighed and repeated the words he'd said to her the week before. "Just when I don't think you could impress me any more, you do."

He must have recognized them, because he laughed, and the grin that spread across his face made crazy things happen inside her. Crazy-uncomfortable, thrilling, terrifying things. Then he reached over and closed his hand over her thigh, giving it a little squeeze. The red bracelet still on his wrist seemed to highlight the tan color of his skin and the masculine cording and muscle in his arm. Somehow, that stupid bracelet made him a touch sexier. As if he needed any help.

She was sure he'd meant it to be a sweet gesture, but heat traveled up her thigh and spread between her legs. Eden was damn sure she'd never wanted any man like she wanted Beckett now.

Shifting in her seat, she brought one leg under her and used her knee to lift herself enough to lean over the console and pressed her lips to his jaw. Beckett exhaled, and a little groan floated on the sound. His hand tightened on her thigh.

"Croft," she murmured against his skin. "You kinda make me crazy." And she kissed a path down the side of his neck.

"Halle-fucking-lujah."

His growl vibrated in his throat and made her smile. She

bit the lobe of his ear, then soothed it with her tongue, and Beckett shivered. This big, scary, dangerous hockey player *shivered*.

"I have to ask you a question," she said, pressing kisses to his temple.

He groaned. "Good things rarely start with that statement."

"I want to know if you're claustrophobic."

"Ummmm..." He cast an uncertain smile toward her. "Not that I know of. Why?"

"Because my place is really small. Like shoebox small. And if you're going to hyperventilate, I want it to be over what I'm doing to you, not the small space."

He lifted his hand from her thigh and wrapped it around the back of her head, then stopped at the corner of her street. He turned his head and covered her mouth with his. His tongue dipped inside and stroked hers, followed by a long groan of need that resonated deep inside Eden.

She pulled back. "Drive. Halfway down on the left."

But Eden continued to kiss and lick and bite his neck, and he kept his hand in her hair as he drove.

"Arrived," Siri announced.

He put the car in Park, and Eden was giddy with anticipation. She reached down, unbuckled her seat belt, and found his attention out the window.

Eden followed his gaze. "What?"

"I didn't realize where we were going with all the talk, and then...you, scrambling my brains." He looked at her. "Eden, this is the worst neighborhood in Metro."

She laughed. "You think I don't know that?"

He looked genuinely troubled. "How long have you lived here?"

"About a year." She tried to lighten the mood. "And let me tell you, it's an improvement on my last place."

He reached across the seats to clasp her thigh again. "I

know rents around here are high, but have you thought about looking for another place, in a safer neighborhood?"

A spot inside her warmed. "But if I did that, I wouldn't get to see all those badass dance moves the dealers bust out between sales or have my nightmares cut short by gunfire. This neighborhood has its benefits. Hell, I could stay in my pj's and slippers and hit the 7-Eleven for a six-pack twenty-four seven. And, damn, with my schedule, you can't put a price tag on that kind of entertainment or convenience—"

He kissed her quiet, then met her eyes again. "I'm serious."

She smiled and ran her thumb over his bottom lip. "And I'm serious about getting you out of these clothes." She opened the door, then glanced back at him, gesturing to the car. "Oh, but... this has an alarm, right? And you've got it insured, right? And"—she cocked her head—"does comprehensive cover hubcaps? And wheels?"

"Jesus Christ, Eden—"

She hopped out and shut the door. He gave her the most adorable glare through the windshield—half-frustrated, half-amused. Eden walked backward toward the stairway that led down to her basement apartment, crooking her finger at him. "Out of the car, Croft. We need a little more maneuverability for what I've got planned."

He pushed from the car and locked it as he followed Eden. But he took his damn sweet time, his narrowed eyes scanning every dreary apartment complex, every dilapidated townhome, every barely running vehicle on the street.

She waited at the door. Beckett was on the top step, distracted by a car driving by screaming rap music with a bass that shook the air. Growing impatient, Eden climbed the three steps, fisted the front of his jersey, and pulled him down to the apartment.

"Would it make you feel better to know that the townhome is owned by a little old lady who's eighty-six years old?" she asked. "And that her family rents the basement to me cheaper than dirt so I can be here if Willa needs anything?"

"Not really."

She pressed her body against his, pushed up on her toes, and wrapped her arms around his neck. "She's hard of hearing."

And she kissed him the way she wanted to fuck him—deep, slow, wet, and hot.

He groaned, wrapped his arms around her, and pulled her closer. Finally, his mind was in the right place. She broke the kiss to reach back and grabbed the door handle. His mouth slid to her neck, shooting tingles along her shoulders.

She fumbled to open the door and pulled him into the apartment. It seemed all his worries over the neighborhood had melted in the heat between them. Excitement spiraled inside her. She broke from his mouth to pull his jersey over his head, then kissed a path down his torso while she worked on his belt and jeans.

Beckett swept off the jersey he'd given her, stroked his hands over the tank she'd been wearing under her hoodie, and cupped her naked breasts beneath the cotton. But as soon as she had his jeans open, Eden lowered to her knees, pulling his pants and boxers low enough to free him, and immediately took his hard length into her mouth.

Beckett's whole body jerked, and he swore. And as Eden started moving and exploring, his hands cupped her jaw, stroked over her hair, and drew it off her face. Eden was lost in the salty, insanely male taste of him. Of the silky smooth feel of his cock inside her mouth, on her tongue, sliding along her lips. God, she'd been fantasizing about this all week. Oh, how she loved getting caught up in the passion, in the pleasure, in the escape.

She leaned into him, taking him deep and slow until he filled her throat.

"God, Eden..."

The rough, lust-filled words drew her gaze. Up his gorgeous body, up his ripped abs, up his wide muscled chest, to his eyes, dark and on fire, watching her. She held his gaze as she stroked him and sucked him. Held his gaze as she drove him deep, deep, deep into her mouth again. Held his gaze as fire washed over his features, as his jaw pulsed, as he finally dropped his head back with "God *damn*..."

Then he bent over her, pressed his mouth to her hair, and murmured, "So good, baby. Come here."

He curved his hands around her biceps and gently pulled her to her feet, where he immediately kissed her, stroking her tongue, sucking her lips, and walking her backward to the bed. Then he lifted her off her feet, and she wrapped her legs around his waist.

She combed both hands through his hair and pressed her forehead to his. Sex had never been like this for her. She'd never even imagined sex like this. So fluid. So hot. So all-consuming. So easy. So right. "Want you so bad."

Groaning, he covered her body with his. The feel of him pressing her into the bed made her moan. She lifted her hips, rocking against him. Beckett tugged the edge of her tank down enough to pull her nipple into his mouth while he stroked the other with one heavy, calloused hand. Heat and pleasure shot through her breast, and Eden squirmed beneath him, but he took his sweet time, teasing her with his tongue, dragging his teeth over the hard tip.

"Mmm, Beckett..." she complained.

His hand abandoned her other breast, slid down her abdomen, and pressed between her legs. But it wasn't enough.

"Skin." She pressed her foot to the bed and rolled him to his side, then pushed him to his back. "I need skin. I need you. And I need both *now*."

She pushed off the edge of the bed, found her feet, and

dragged his jeans down his legs. He toed off his shoes, and she ditched his pants. Then she pressed her hands to his legs and purposefully slid them all the way up his amazing body, before lying on top of him. "*Puuuuur-fect.*"

"Not perfect." He flipped her and tugged off her tank. Kissed and nibbled his way down her abdomen while he worked her jeans off, then stood to pull off her shoes, then her pants and panties. "Now. *That's.* Perfect."

He stroked a flat hand over her stomach, between her legs, and slid his fingers inside her.

Eden gasped. Wiggled toward him. "Mmm. Yes."

He wrapped his free hand around the back of her thigh and yanked her to the edge of the bed. Pushed her thighs wide. And dropped to his knees, covering her with his mouth. Heat, pressure, and moisture shocked her with ecstasy. She cried out, arched, and lost her mind until he pulled back. She rolled her head to the side and found him watching her. His tongue slid over her again and again. Eden wanted him inside her, but he wasn't giving her a moment to breathe. With his hot eyes watching her, he flicked her with the tip of his tongue, teasing her higher, higher, higher, and then he kissed her, licked her, kissed her...

"Beck—"

He spread her with his fingers, and her muscles jerked. She drew her arms in, fisted her hands under her chin, and watched him circle the very tip of her clit, slowly, gently, maddeningly, endlessly tantalizing. The sight was sinfully erotic, adding gasoline to her fire.

And when she edged toward climax, he kissed her, licked her, and started the pattern all over again, endlessly patient as he drove her insane. He groaned against her pussy, and the vibrations quivered through her sex.

"Ah God—" Her head rolled side to side; her abdominal muscles flinched and quivered.

Beckett stopped teasing and started eating. Full mouth suction over her, solid pressure on her clit with his tongue. Eden curled toward him in a partial crunch. And Beckett growled, then took her clit between his lips, and—

The climax blasted through her. A hot, wild surge of ecstasy that shot her out of her body. Her muscles contracted, pulling her forward, then throwing her back. She arched, and her thighs came together around Beckett's head. He pushed them wide again and continued to kiss and lick and eat, making her moan and writhe and pant.

Her brain was still floating somewhere amid a white haze when Beckett slid up her body, kissing her everywhere. He framed her face and pulled her in for a hot kiss. He tasted musky and male and thrilling, and Eden needed him inside her, filling her, completing her in the moment. She reached for his jeans on the floor, and Beckett untangled their legs to get out of her way. Twisting to her side, she dragged his wallet from the pocket, then rested on her forearms to search for the condom. She pulled one out as Beckett's body pressed to her back, his lips teasing her neck and shoulders.

When she dropped the wallet, Beckett leaned into her, rolling her toward her stomach. He covered her hand and took the condom, but didn't rush to put it on. Instead, he pushed up on his hands, lifting his weight off her back. Used one knee to spread her thighs, then sank his hips against her ass, rocking into her with a hungry groan. Pulling her hair aside, he pressed his mouth to the back of her neck, turned her head toward her shoulder, and bent over her to take her mouth in a hungry kiss while his hot cock stroked her skin.

She closed her eyes, absorbing the delicious sensations. So many—both physical and emotional—she couldn't understand them all, couldn't categorize them all. She only knew he made her feel intensely sexy, utterly beautiful, and desired to her core. And all that whipped up a wild want inside her.

She broke the kiss to beg, "Please. Inside me."

The sound that rolled in his throat echoed with a primal quality that lit a fire between Eden's legs. He sat back, and the rip-rip of foil made satisfaction settle deep in Eden's body. She pushed up on one elbow and twisted to watch him. The sight of his big, masculine hand stroking the condom on his cock tightened her sex. Then he lifted his gaze to hers and rocked forward again, pressing his body against her.

He kissed her before pulling away and licking his fingers. His hand slipped between her legs and stroked. Eden pulled a sharp breath. Her eyes closed, hands curled into the comforter. Beckett slid the head of his cock over her swollen, slick folds, and a shaky moan passed through her lips.

He pressed into her, and the moan deepened in her throat. She rocked her hips back.

"Want more?" he asked, his voice husky and hungry.

"God, yes."

He gripped her hips and lifted her ass, impaling her slowly. So slowly.

"Man, talk about the best seats in the house. That's so fucking hot." He growled, pulled out slowly, pushed back in just as slowly. "Wish I could watch this show all goddamned night."

Eden whimpered and bit her lip. Beckett moved his hands from her hips to her ass and gripped her cheeks, digging his fingers in until the bite made her moan. Over and over and over, he pushed inside her, then pulled out, stroked her with his fingers, then pushed his cock into her again. Inch by inch by exquisite inch.

"Want more, Eden?"

"Yes," she complained.

Growling, Beckett slid both hands up her back, curved them over her shoulders. Holding her in place, he pushed deep. Pressure spread through her hips. Eden sucked air, and her throat closed. The stretch burned and the utter fullness ached in the most decadent, most thrilling way. Her eyes closed, and she arched. Then let out a moan that came from the pit of her stomach and expressed how utterly mind-bending he felt.

"Is that what you wanted?" he asked, his voice rough, breathless and demanding.

But she couldn't speak.

"Is it deep enough?" A dark sexy edge tinged his voice. "Because I think I can fuck you deeper."

Before Eden could even clear her head, Beckett used his knees to spread her thighs wider. He gripped her waist with both hands and pushed her forward, drawing his length out. The move also arched her back and angled her pelvis higher.

Without warning, he thrust again. His cock burned a path straight through the center of her body and slammed her cervix. Eden cried out in a mixture of pleasure and discomfort. The sensations blended and swamped her. Her head dropped back on a cry. Her hands fisted in the comforter. This was her first glimpse of how addictive sex could be.

The animalistic sound of pleasure in Beckett's throat added heat between her legs. Without releasing her waist, he bent his head to whisper in her ear, "I think I can get deeper. I've still got a good inch until my balls are pressed up against you."

Holy. Fuck. But all she got out was a sound deep in her throat.

"I think that excites you. Your pussy squeezed my cock."

"Yes..."

"What?" He leaned closer, and flexed his hips, pushing him that much deeper and making Eden's eyes roll back. "Yes, what? What do you want, Eden?"

"Every...thing," she forced out. "Give me...all of it."

His growl was hot and pleased and guttural. Holding her hips at that tilted angle, Beckett pulled out slowly, until his tip slipped all the way out of her, leaving her feeling empty. He stroked his slick length across her pussy, dragging himself over her clit and making Eden moan. Pressing back inside her, he drove home in three full, hard pumps.

Thrust.

Thrust.

Thrust.

Eden was shaking and panting, her fingers cramping in the comforter, when Beckett drew out of her and rubbed his wet cock over her pussy again.

"Is that good?" he wanted to know, his voice a hungry growl at her ear.

"So...good."

She rocked her hips to rub her clit against his cock, moaning at the contact.

"Do you want me to keep fucking you?"

"Please, fuck me."

A huff of laughter rolled out. "That is so hot." He bit her shoulder, then licked the burn. "Those words out of your mouth turn me on *so hard*."

She turned her head and met his eyes over her shoulder. "Beckett," she breathed. "Shut up and *fuck me*."

His eyes turned so dark, they looked black. The desire etched in his expression made the need inside Eden boil.

He slid his fingers through her folds, and Eden gasped. Then he stroked her wetness over his cock and eased into her again. Then plunged.

Pain and pleasure spiraled up the center of Eden's body, and she cried out. With both hands at her waist, he held her steady for each hit, ensuring his cock drove deep. His head hammered something inside her that made her want to climb out of her skin to climax. His sac smacked her perineum, titillating her with a little sting on each thrust. Beckett's hands liked to take turns roaming over her ass, his fingers wet from his mouth, stroking her perineum or the rim of her anus in maddening, insanity-inducing, endless circles.

Eden had her comforter twisted into knots in both hands and was using her knees to rock back into his drives before she finally resorted to begging.

"Beckett...God...please..."

He groaned. "But, fuck, it's *so good*."

Eden pressed her face into the comforter and whimpered, absorbing every firework of pleasure. "Can't...wait..."

Beckett drove deep, pressed his chest to her back, and stilled. He slid one hand down her arm, covered her hand, and pried her fingers from the comforter, threading them with his. With her head turned, she found herself staring at their joined hands, their wrists both bound in bracelets from the event. His other arm stretched overhead, his fingers tangling in her hair. His weight sank into her and drove him even deeper, and he settled there a long moment, his heavy breaths in her ear, his quick heartbeat on her back.

Fear burned hot and fast. Eden waited for claustrophobia to close in. But Beckett's fingers flexed around hers, loosening and tightening back up, and affection shoved her fear aside.

She closed her eyes and soaked in the feeling of being so completely...taken. So completely...owned. Something she'd never believed herself capable of allowing again.

"I can't remember...sex being this fucking good..." he panted. "*This* is all I could think about all damn week. Seeing you, talking to you, feeling you. Being inside you. Fuck, this is crazy." Then he turned his head and pressed his mouth to her neck.

Emotions coiled and built and tears burned her eyes. Tears of joy. Tears of appreciation. Tears over the realization that she wasn't as completely broken as she'd believed.

A sudden and fierce affection for Beckett blossomed. Beckett and his confidence, his sweetness, his patience. She'd spent two years hiding from life. A fear only Beckett had been able to break through, allowing her to step back into life. *Really* step back into life.

His groan vibrated over her skin, and he started to move again. But this was different. This was a sensual, deep pull and drive that stole her breath just as intensely as the frenzied grind from before. And, the way it had their first night together, the rhythm seemed to simply glide into place. Eden lifted to meet his thrusts, took his hungry mouth with the same need to consume and be consumed. As their passion deepened, he drove harder and faster, hammering a familiar yet fresh pleasure through her body.

"Eden... Fuck, baby..." His teeth grazed her shoulder. "Wanna feel you come. Wanna feel you get all wet. Wanna feel you squeeze all around me. God, you feel so *fucking* good."

His words kicked the heat up another notch. He seemed to read her every sound, intensifying the strength and speed to drive her directly to the edge.

Her body reached, stretched, tightened. Damn, it was so intense. So all-encompassing. Her free hand clutched at his forearm.

"Oh yeah," he rasped in her ear with a sexy thrill in his tone. "I feel it. Mmm, it's comin'. God, I wish you could feel what you do to me. Open and let go. Let go." He pressed his mouth above her ear. "Let me have you, Eden. All of you."

She relaxed, released her muscles, and his next thrust acted like a bomb. The orgasm exploded deep inside her. She cried out, and her body seized as ecstasy rocketed through her. She choked and moaned. Bucked and writhed. And the pleasure seemed to go on and on and on.

The climax was still twisting and shuddering through Eden when Beckett broke. With his face pressed to her neck, his hips pumped in a fierce succession. His growl vibrated over her skin, and his jaw tightened as he clenched his teeth around curses. His own pleasure ravaged him into tremors.

When he finally collapsed, his full weight on her, Eden sank into the mattress with no complaints. She let her mind slip away, floating on the bliss that always seemed to characterize her time with Beckett.

17

Long, quiet minutes passed while Beckett caught his breath and let his heartbeat come back to normal. But his head was still floating when he eased the weight of his body off Eden, rolled to his side, and pulled her with him. He curled around her, wrapping her in his arms, burying his face in her hair.

"Baby," he whispered, "you fuckin' destroy me."

She hummed, and her hand slid over his forearm, pausing to spin the bracelet still on his wrist a few times. Her own arm was still adorned with half a dozen bracelets in different colors.

God, his heart felt too big for his chest. He ached with the fullness beneath his ribs. Every time he saw her, he learned something new, like peeling back another layer. And his feelings for Eden seemed to be multiplying at a terrifying rate.

He glanced at the clock on her nightstand. They still had time before she had to leave. He kissed her head and whispered, "Want to shower with me?"

When she didn't answer, didn't so much as move, he propped himself up on his elbow and leaned over to look at her. And found her asleep.

His heart squeezed, and a smile lifted his mouth. Beckett pressed his face into her soft, fragrant hair again, trying to make sense of the way this woman made his stomach twist, his heart float, and his body crave.

With a shake of his head, Beckett pushed himself up slowly, trying not to wake her. He looked around the room—really looked—for the first time. And it was even worse than at first, lust-hazed glance.

This wasn't a room; it was a cell.

The basement had cinder-block walls, with two small windows on the back of the town house and two half windows on the front—all of them covered in bars. Exposed plumbing pipes crisscrossed along the ceiling, and utility carpet covered an uneven cement floor. The only furniture was the bed they were on, a wooden nightstand, a metal desk and chair, and one bookcase. And every piece was ancient.

Eden had obviously done what she could to dress it up. Despite the dim, depressing overall feel of the space, it was clean and neat and it smelled nice, filled with a relaxing, breezy floral scent. The walls were painted a pale yellow, adding a little spark. All her books were lined up neatly. Everything on the desk had a place except one textbook, open in the center. There was no kitchen, just a hotplate, a microwave, and a mini fridge.

A strange unease filtered into his post-sex high. He pushed to his feet and turned toward the only other door, which he assumed had to be a bathroom. Pushing the partially open door wide, he clicked on a light. Yep, bathroom. But...man, really nothing more than a toilet, a tiny stand-up shower she could probably barely turn around in, and a single sink basin, its pipes exposed beneath.

A heavy feeling settled in the pit of Beckett's stomach.

He closed the door to try not to wake her and started the cleanup process, hoping to learn more about her from the surroundings. Folded towels sat on the back of the toilet, along with a shower caddy holding her toiletries, because there was obviously no other place to put them.

When he turned on the water, it came out brown, and he let it run until the old pipes cleared. As he cleaned up, he was both confused and...awed. Meeting her, he never would have guessed this was her living situation. She came off as intelligent and well-read and so totally together. He doubted just anyone got into Johns Hopkins' paramedic program. And, frankly, he'd also assumed she'd come from money. Maybe because she hadn't made a big deal out of his apartment or his car. Maybe because she never brought up his contracts or how much he made. Maybe because she'd never asked for or expected anything from him.

He dried his hands and patted his body dry. After only a moment of hesitation, he pulled open her medicine cabinet. Toothpaste, toothbrush, lip balm, Tylenol, Advil, and vitamins. On the bottom shelf there was one tube of mascara, a little bottle of foundation, and a pad of blush.

That was it? Seriously? The women he knew carried more than the entire contents of her bathroom around with them everywhere.

He turned off the light and quietly pulled the door open. Eden hadn't moved. She was still curled on her side, her naked body smooth and sleek and beautiful. Her hair was a tousled mess spilling over the solid yellow comforter that matched the walls.

Beckett glanced at the time, bent over her, and brushed her hair off her forehead. When she didn't stir, he smiled. She could have so easily turned him down outside her work. Or could have told him to take her home when he'd turned into the Y. She could also have interrupted his socializing and asked to leave. But she'd done none of that. And, looking around him, he was beginning to realize that Eden was strug-gling as much as those she'd helped raise funds for today. But she'd stayed on her feet for hours to cook after a long night shift.

And she never asked for anything. Never even hinted that she needed anything. Never got that greedy glint in her eye he'd come to expect in women.

The feeling inside intensified. Man, he admired the hell out of this woman. At least what he knew of her. He couldn't believe how strongly he felt about her after such a short amount of time. But after so many wrong women, it wouldn't take a genius to realize when the right one had wandered into his path, which was good, because a genius he was not.

Beckett pulled on his boxer briefs and wandered to her bookcase to read the titles. Her textbooks lined the top shelf. Topics included anatomy, physiology, advanced first aid, CPR, medical terminology, emergency care in the streets, advanced cardiac support, pediatric advanced life support, pharmacology and drug guides, trauma management, emergency obstetrics, psychiatric emergencies.

"Jesus," he whispered. He got a headache just reading the titles. He'd definitely gotten the intelligent part right.

He crouched and looked at the second shelf. *Brain, Mind, and Body: Healing from Trauma.* The next book in line: *The Power to Break Free.*

He frowned. Those didn't sound like they fit the program. He pulled the book out and looked at the cover, read the subtitle: *For Victims and Survivors of Domestic Violence.*

The way she'd flinched that night in the bar flashed in Beckett's mind, and his stomach went cold. The skin over the back of his neck prickled, and the hair on his arms stood up. A wickedly intense protective streak burned a path through him. He'd known her flinching and startling pointed to something unpleasant in her past, but seeing that vague thought put into the cold, harsh words *domestic violence* made it far more real, far uglier, far more infuriating.

He clenched his teeth and read the other titles in the row. *Domestic Violence Survival Workbook. It's My Life Now, Starting Over After Domestic Violence. Post-Traumatic Stress Syndrome.*

From there, the titles transitioned into a new topic. *Healing After Loss: Daily Meditations. Angel Catcher, a Journal of Loss and Remembrance. Beyond Tears: Finding Light After Loss.*

Beckett's stomach churned, his body flashed hot, then cold, then hot again. His mind tried to make sense of the books. Eden didn't strike him as the kind of woman to regret walking away from an abuser. He couldn't envision Eden mourning the loss of someone who'd hurt her. But maybe the loss of her family when she left California had been harder to overcome than she let on.

He straightened the books and let his fingers float over the bindings, grateful they'd helped her in some way become the strong woman she was today. The woman who now pulled at him in ten different ways.

The covers rustled, then her sluggish voice murmured, "Shit. What time is it?"

Beckett stood. "Only one fifteen. Relax. I won't let you oversleep."

She pulled her hair off her face. "Sorry. I haven't crashed like that in a long time."

The fact that she trusted him enough to relax gave him more of a thrill than it probably should have. "I'm sure you need it."

Sitting next to her, he gathered her into his arms, lay back against a couple of pillows, and pulled her to rest on top of him. She sighed, pressed her face to his neck, and kissed him, then leaned her head on his shoulder.

"Rest until you have to go." He stroked his hands down her back. "Are you cold?"

"Not now." She sounded sleepy and happy. "You're like a furnace."

He chuckled and wrapped her tighter, wishing he could take away all the ugliness in her past. The same way he wished he could wipe away the fears he still saw resurface in Lily's eyes every now and then.

He was thinking about that similarity between Lily and Eden when she said, "Beckett?"

As soon as he refocused on the present, he felt the tension in the air. "Hmm?"

"Is this a...thing?" she said, voice soft and unsure. "Or...not a thing?"

He grinned, but his stomach still flipped and twisted. "Well, this is *definitely* something. So, yeah, I think this is a thing. At least, I'm hoping it's a thing, because I'm already wondering when I can see you again."

She remained quiet for a long stretch, and Beckett let her have the time to sort that out. He had a lot of his own sorting to do. Like when to tell her about Lily. Like how long he wanted to wait before he introduced her to Lily. Like how to figure out how he and Eden could see each other with these insane schedules.

Like why she was living in this hole.

But first things first. "Do you want this to be a thing?"

She smiled, a cute, almost sly smile that made her look so young, but there were still shadows behind her eyes. "Man," she said barely above a whisper. "I..."

When she shook her head, he lifted a hand to her chin, then turned her head until her eyes met his. "Say what you feel, Eden. I'm not going to pounce or argue or try to sway you one way or another. I really want to know what's going on in that pretty little head of yours. I see a whole lot of thought-badminton going on in your eyes."

She inhaled a shaky little breath. "It...scares me."

His heart pulled so hard, he felt the ache all through his body. "I know. I wish I could make it easier."

"It's not your fault."

"I know that too."

Her eyes dropped away, ashamed, and she nodded.

Man, what was it about her injured soul that made him want to hold tighter? Moments like this made him realize how fundamentally Lily had changed him. A year ago, even the hint of drama sent him sprinting the other direction.

Her eyes slid closed in a look of intense longing. "I really, *really* want this to be a thing."

As if a bunch of rubber bands had been holding his heart closed, they all released at the same time, spreading his heart wide open. He grinned and kissed her, and when he pulled back, her eyes were shining instead of dark.

"I hear a 'but' in there," he said, "but I'm going to pretend I don't. That way I can ask if you'd consider coming to see a game? Maybe bring Gabe or another friend who knows hockey? That way they could explain things while they're happening."

Her gaze turned curious and a little guarded. "You really don't mind if I bring a guy?"

Beckett was learning to identify the hot buttons beneath Eden's competent exterior. For a second, he considered cracking the egg and asking Eden directly what happened to her, what she was really afraid of. But he also got the distinct impression that if he pressured her in the wrong way, she'd shut down and they'd lose all the closeness they'd developed.

And he really didn't want to lose this.

"Guys usually know more about hockey than girls. But if it means getting you to a game to actually watch me play, all you have to do is tell me how many tickets you want, and I'll have them waiting for you at the door. You can bring the whole damn ambulance company if you want."

A slow smile softened her eyes. "That would be a little overwhelming. I already lock myself in my bedroom when they throw on ESPN."

"ESPN? Why aren't they watching the NHL network?"

She laughed. "Oh, they do. Gabe's the instigator."

"Knew I liked that guy."

She lifted a hand to his face. "And I know I like this guy." Leaning in, she kissed him again, and the sweetness of it made him ache. But when she pulled back, she said, "Can I think about it?"

Her reaction was as foreign to Beckett as 90 percent of the topics she studied. And a split second of *are we too different to make this work?* passed through his mind before he said, "Absolutely." Then he changed the subject. "Tell me about this place. You've got to admit this is pretty unusual, especially for a woman in this neighborhood. I especially don't like the idea of you walking these streets from Metro."

"It's all I can afford right now." She didn't sound upset or angry about it, just matter-of-fact. "I'm careful. I carry the most powerful stun gun you can buy. And I've got a year of defense and fighting classes behind me. I've also gone out of my way to get to know the people who live between here and the Metro station. We sort of watch out for each other. I have no doubt I'll be getting grilled about the guy with the Porsche before the end of the week."

Somehow that didn't set his mind completely at ease. "You know stun guns are illegal in the District of Columbia?"

She grinned, and a little rebel shone through. "I'd rather pay the fine and stay safe than the alternative."

He sighed. "I suppose me offering a little help to find a safer place for you to live—"

"Would make your family's resistance look like a toddler's tantrum."

He laughed and stroked her face, then pressed a kiss to her

forehead. "I love that tough streak. I just wish it wasn't over a safety issue. Have you always had it?"

"Born that way. Unfortunately, most of the people in my past life didn't even like it, let alone love it."

"Is that why your family's not helping you now? Or can't they afford it?"

She snorted a laugh. "Oh, they could afford it. But what they spent their money on always held an element of self-bene-fit. My father would have paid for a business degree. *Nothing* but a business degree. I got into a handful of top schools out of high school, including his alma mater, Columbia. The funny part is that I wasn't the one who applied. He did. And when I refused to go for business, well..."

She shrugged and sighed. "Doesn't matter now. One of the most important things this job has taught me is how incredibly fragile life is. And how short. How you can be alive one moment and dead the next. Just...gone. No second chances, no coming back. That's it."

Her voice held a deeply emotional note Beckett couldn't quite place. There was a sort of realistic sadness there, but something else too. Something painful.

"So I'm glad I didn't cave," she went on. "But even though I have a tough streak, I have an even wider pleaser streak, and I did spend too many years trying to find ways to make up for that huge failure in my father's eyes. And that turned out way worse."

So he'd been right about her coming from money too. That wasn't making him feel good about the other hunches he'd developed. "Is that why you don't talk to them now?"

"One of many reasons. After two and a half decades of their control, disapproval, and impossible standards, I cut ties. Came here. Started over."

That might be part of the story, but Beckett heard a huge

gap between the impossible standards and cutting ties. He was sure what she was telling him now was the tip of the iceberg.

"And you're doing everything yourself?" he asked. "Paying for school, expenses, on your own? With the money you make at the ambulance company?"

"Mmm-hmm. It's tight, but I manage. I don't need much."

No, she certainly didn't need much. She demanded even less. "Do you miss it? The money, the comfort? I didn't go to college, barely made it out of high school, but this doesn't seem comfortable or safe or conducive to studying. Or even life, for that matter. It's not like you could exactly hang with friends here."

"Depends on the friends." She lifted her face to his again, and a smile curled her lips. "You're here."

He laughed. "Good point."

She stroked her thumb across his jaw. "I prefer this sparse, autonomous life to luxuries that come with a price tag in the form of emotional blackmail. And no, I don't miss material things. Those equate to confinement at best, imprisonment at worst. Material things don't hold any more importance to me than title or fame or money." She shot him a grin. "Sorry, hotshot. I'm pretty crazy about you for you. And, come to think of it, *in spite of* all your trappings."

The thrill that cut through Beckett shocked him. He pulled her closer, lifted her chin, and covered her mouth with his. She opened to him, kissing him with a hunger that mirrored the one stirring in his body again.

Beckett pulled away with a groan. "What I would give for a few uninterrupted days with you."

She thought that was funny. "That's so far out of my realm of reality, I don't even know what that would look like. I like to think I'd be able to take some time off after school, between jobs, but that's probably not realistic."

"You're not staying at Capital Ambulance?"

"They don't offer advanced life support. They're a basic haul-and-drop outfit. As a paramedic, my base rate will double what I make now."

"So, where will you work?"

"I can either work for another ambulance company that employs paramedics or get onto a paramedic rig with a fire department. I'll stay at Capital until I find a paramedic job, but the good ones aren't all that common. I don't want to work for a transporter, where all I do is move people from one place to another. I want a job where I'm working directly with people who need the help."

"The front lines."

"Exactly."

He chuckled. "You've got a little adrenaline junkie in you."

"I guess I never thought about it that way."

"I live it, so I recognize the signs of illness."

She grinned. "I'm nowhere near as sick as you."

That made him laugh. "Truth. I'm terminal."

"No, two years on DC's streets has given me enough of the holy-shit factor. I wouldn't mind a slower pace. Somewhere I actually get a few hours sleep during a shift."

"Metro is so heavily populated. Where are you gonna find that?"

She didn't respond immediately. "Actually, I'm so busy putting one foot in front of the other, I hadn't looked that far ahead."

Her voice was thoughtful, as if she was realizing how her job location could very well interfere with this *thing* they were starting. For Beckett, it was a huge concern. Partially for him, sure. He didn't want to finally find a woman he could fall in love with only to have her move away and make a relationship even more difficult. But more so for Lily. And if Beckett didn't feel comfortable introducing Eden to Lily, how could this thing really be a thing?

"I'm also thinking about continuing on with school," she said, softly, as if these ideas were all gelling now that they'd brought them up.

"For what?" he asked.

She shrugged and looked away, and even before she spoke again, he knew she was going to play this dream down. "I've thought about going further in medicine. Maybe becoming a physician's assistant. My instructors have been trying to sell me on going on to get my bachelor's with the thought of going on to medical school, but that's..." She shook her head. "Unfathomable, honestly." She laughed, brushing the whole topic off with "See why I don't think ahead? It gets messy."

Sure as hell did. Yet after a year of working to instill self-confidence in Lily and encouraging her to dream big, he sure as shit wasn't going to sit here and tell Eden any different.

He tipped her head back, lifting her gaze to his. "Nothing's unfathomable. Especially not for a woman with your intelligence and grit. Go where your heart leads you. We only live once, right?"

The shift in her eyes mirrored the movement in his heart. She had the craziest way of tempting him toward those three words he'd never said to a woman. Often believed he'd never find a woman he wanted to say them to.

Eden pressed a kiss to his lips, then rested her forehead against his. "I better get dressed."

When she pulled away, he added a quick "Can I drop you at school?"

She laughed. "You're adorable. Hopkins is in Baltimore, handsome."

"Oh, right." An hour's drive one way. He'd never make it back to pick up Lily.

"But you can drop me at Union Station. I jump the Acela at two. Gets me to class right on time."

He forced a smile, even though he was pretty sure they were parting again with nothing more concrete between them than when he'd been standing in front of the ambulance company this morning. "Deal."

18

Beckett was weaving his way through downtown DC toward his mother's house when his cell rang through the car's intercom system. Kim's name lit up the dash.

"Shit." He drew out the word with dread, decided he couldn't avoid her any longer, and pressed the button on his steering wheel to answer. "Hey, Kim. What's up?"

"Well, finally," she said, her voice carrying attitude. "I'm in town, and I'd like to meet."

He made one of those I-don't-know-how-I-can-fit-that-in sounds. "This is a crazy week—"

"It's about Lily."

She knew what button to push with him, and it pissed him off.

"She's fine, thanks for asking," he said, still upbeat. "Great, actually. Listen, is this something we can discuss on the phone? Because—"

"It's about the custody hearing. So, no, I think it would be better to do it face-to-face. I'm in the city now." She named a coffee shop. "Or I can grab a taxi and meet you somewhere else."

She was only six blocks away. He might as well get this over with. "No, that's fine. I'll be there in fifteen."

Beckett disconnected and changed directions. On the drive, he considered approaches and tactics to use with Kim. He tried to call Fred, but his attorney was in a meeting. By the time he'd parked, all the happiness and relaxation Eden had created was gone.

He opened the center console and pulled out the school pictures Lily had brought home a few days before. After pulling the order sheet so he could buy more for his family, he headed inside.

Kim sat near the window, legs crossed, foot swinging restlessly. When the door closed behind him, she looked over and smiled. Sitting forward, she clasped her hands gingerly beneath her chin and kept her eyes on him as he approached.

He remembered why he'd found her attractive all those years ago. For starters, she was a beautiful brown-eyed brunette Barbie. She also made a guy feel like he was the only man on the planet, the way she was doing with Beckett now, never letting her gaze waver from him for a millisecond. Back then, she'd had a whimsical country-fresh girl quality with hemp bracelets, holey jeans, and white gauze blouses. Now, she'd graduated to the sophisticated hot-chick zone, decked out in designer jeans painted onto those long legs and a skintight blouse that showed all her cleavage. And she wore more jewelry and makeup than Beckett bet Eden owned.

"Hey," he said, pulling a chair across the table from her. "Long time."

"You look great."

Nope, he wasn't touching that. Instead, he lifted the envelope. "I brought Lily's latest school pictures."

She glanced at the envelope, then laughed. "How...cute. Who would have ever guessed such a badass hockey player would turn so soft over a kid?"

Her insensitivity or attempted jibe or whatever the hell it was didn't bother him in the least. The fact that Kim ignored the photos bothered Beckett far more.

"So, what's up?" he asked, setting the photos aside.

She reached out and put her hand over his. "How are you, Beckett?"

He gently pulled his hand back, but revulsion rolled beneath his skin. "I'm good, but I don't have a lot of time. What did you want to talk about?"

She sighed, and her smile turned petulant. "I know how much Lily means to you."

"Uh-huh."

"And I know this custody issue is important to you."

"It's important because it's the best thing for Lily."

"And I'm inclined to agree to your request if you'd be inclined to agree to mine."

Patience. Patience.

"It's not a request, Kim. We had an understanding when I took over her care last year."

"That was then. This is now. Things have changed."

"You may have a hard time convincing a court of that considering the condition you left her in."

"I really don't want to take this to court, Beckett."

Anger formed a rock in his throat. "What do you want?"

"Five million," she said with a matter-of-fact air. "And I'll sign over custody of Lily. Permanently."

Beckett choked out a laugh at the sheer absurdity of the number. "Five million? Where the hell did you come up with that number?"

"Don't act like that's a lot of money to you." Suddenly, she was disgusted. "I'm not an idiot. The way you're playing, you'll make that in your performance bonus alone this year."

He shook his head. "Even if I did, I wouldn't *buy* Lily from you. Lily isn't property, and this isn't a deal. This is about

Lily's welfare. Lily's best interest. Lily's health and happiness—"

"Don't give me that shit. I know you're not raising Lily. I know you've got a nanny doing all the work. And you're probably also *doing* the nanny on the side. You've probably already got Lily's boarding school all picked out and paid for. You don't want her disturbing your lifestyle any more than I want her disturbing mine."

"About that lifestyle," Beckett said. "What does Henderson think of having to father another man's kid?"

Kim's lips pressed together, and her chin lifted.

"That's what I thought." He picked up his phone and offered her the envelope again. "Would you like any of Lily's pictures?"

"No, I don't want her pictures," Kim spat, furious. "I don't want anything to do with her. But you're going to have to pay to get me to say that on the record."

Beckett exited the café, stalking to his car and wishing he had a game tonight so he could smash some guys against the boards.

Since he didn't and couldn't, he spent the rest of the drive to his mother's talking to Fred, which calmed him down enough to enter the house only a fraction as frustrated as he'd been twenty minutes before.

He heard his sister's voice in the family room and headed that direction. She was on the phone, watching the girls playing in the yard out the window.

Lowering the mouthpiece, she whispered to Beckett, "Griff."

Beckett could tell by her smile alone that Sarah was talking to her husband. "Say hi for me."

He stepped outside, called hello to the girls, and sat on the steps. They yelled back in unison but didn't run to him, and Beckett tried to remember that was a good sign, even if he really did need that hug right now.

The excitement and warmth in Sarah's voice as she talked to Griff made Beckett's mind drift to Eden. And as he watched Lily, Rachel, and Amy play in the leaves his father had raked into piles around the yard, his hopes for the near future plummeted.

Lily's giggle rolled through the air and lightened Beckett's heart a little. She could always make him smile. The screen door closed behind him, and Sarah sat next to him, curling her arms around her knees, her cell phone dangling in her fingers.

"How's Griff?" Beckett asked.

"Good." Her smile looked the way Beckett's had felt a short hour ago with Eden. "Only three more weeks."

Lucky her. "Man, bet it will be nice to have him home awhile."

"More than awhile. He's getting a promotion. He's going to be stationed at the Pentagon."

The Pentagon was a short drive or Metro ride from Arlington, where Griff and Sarah had bought their house. "Hey, that's fantastic." Beckett reached around Sarah's shoulders and hugged her. "Congratulations. Do the girls know?"

Sarah shook her head and focused on the kids. "I'm going to wait until he's home to tell them. Otherwise, they'll ask me a million questions I can't answer."

"And that way, you can say, 'Go ask your dad.'"

"Bingo. Fair warning: he's going to want season tickets."

"I'll wrap them up for him for Christmas." He looked out at the girls again. "Hope I'm on the ice next year, not watching with him from the stands."

"You will be." She knocked her shoulder against his. "You're having an amazing year."

He grinned and nodded, because, yeah, on the ice, he was doing everything he was supposed to do and his game was falling into place. Off the ice... His game had gone askew.

"You're going to have to pull out a rake when they're done,"

Beckett told her. "Or Dad will be all over you. Where'd he and Mom go?"

"I thought I'd leave the leaves for you. And they went out to lunch."

"Good job, sis." It was hell getting their parents out of the house and away from the grandkids, but he and Sarah agreed they needed their own time too.

They sat in a moment of silence while the girls jumped on the swings. But Beckett's mind drifted to Eden and his sensation of being held at arm's length unless she wanted sex. Which was ironic, considering that was really all he'd ever done with women. And that brought his mind back to Kim, and that frustrated the hell out of him.

"Everything okay with the team?" Sarah asked.

"Hmm?" Beckett glanced at her and found that worried crease between her brows. "Oh, yeah. Fine."

"And Kim?"

In an effort to calm Sarah's nerves, he decided to give her the information he'd learned in the car that had calmed his own. "I talked to Fred on my way over. I told him to go all-out, get all the ammunition he could, just in case. He had someone take a statement from the aunt."

"Oh, that's good, right?"

Beckett nodded. "And they're in the process of interviewing people in both her past and current life with as few ripples as possible. He's gathered Lily's medical records and seems confident that if Kim doesn't sign custody over willingly, it will be taken from her."

Sarah exhaled. "That's a relief."

A slight relief, but after two and a half years of dealing with Kim's manipulation, Beckett could feel the other shoe waiting to drop. And his sister didn't need any more worries than she already had, so he hummed an affirmative. "Mmm-hmm."

Another moment of silence lingered before Sarah asked, "Then what's bothering you?"

He shook his head and watched Lily somersault down the far embankment and land in a pile of leaves. "Maybe I should start her in gymnastics."

"She doesn't have time for gymnastics. You've already got her schedule stuffed."

He frowned at her. "Too stuffed? I don't want to stress her out."

Sarah laughed. "Does she look stressed out to you?"

Her cousins had followed Lily down the slight grade, and the three girls were now piled on top of each other, giggling at nothing. A grin broke out over Beckett's face. "No. She looks giddy."

"Then I think you have your answer. But she still doesn't have time for gymnastics. Now what's bothering you?"

Beckett heaved a sigh and leaned back against one of the porch pillars. "It's nothing."

"It's her, isn't it? The EMT."

He smirked. Nodded. Beckett didn't know how to put everything he was thinking and feeling into words. He hadn't even straightened it out in his mind yet.

"You *really* like her." The surprised realization in Sarah's voice drew Beckett's gaze.

"Why do you make that sound as shocking as a fish breathing air?"

"Because this is different. I don't think I've seen you like this since Stacy Dickler bailed on junior prom because of your broken nose. You looked hideous."

He rolled his eyes.

"But you don't look hideous now, and you're making the kind of money women don't chase, they *hunt*. So what's the problem?"

Yeah, that hunting part was a problem. But not with Eden. "She doesn't care about money."

"I like her already," Sarah said. "But that doesn't explain the problem."

He shrugged. "I'm not sure what the problem is. We're good together. Really good. We don't have a lot in common jobwise —she's not a hockey fan—but we have the same values, the same sense of humor. She's smart and sexy, and she doesn't take any shit. Yeah," he said on an exhale, thinking of all the intangible nuances about her that drove his affection deep. "I *really* like her."

"Wait. She doesn't care about money, and she doesn't like hockey? *Why* is she dating you?"

"Ha. Good one." But it got Beckett thinking. Maybe she really *was* only with him for the sex. And didn't that suck donkey balls?

"What's her name?" Sarah asked. "I haven't heard Lily mention anyone."

"Eden. And she hasn't met Lily."

"Why not?"

"Because I don't know if it's going to work out, and I don't want to introduce a woman into Lily's life just to have her disappear, like Kim."

Sarah stared, her brow pulled into the confused how-the-hell-does-your-mind-work look.

"What?" he asked, frustrated.

"The way you're looking at it doesn't make sense. Life, by its very nature, is unstable. Your job, for example, is terribly unstable. You could be traded and moved to the West Coast next week. Our whole family could lose Lily in an instant, which you know would tear us up. But that doesn't keep us from loving her."

She gestured absently. "And then there's Kim. Until you've got her signatures on those custody papers, she could flip on a dime and demand Lily back. And considering it took her over two years to get around to telling you Lily even existed, then forced you to make all the effort in visitation for the next two years, I doubt Kim would be interested in fostering a relationship between Lily and her extended family. But that doesn't keep us from forging a bond with her now."

Beckett rubbed his eyes and nodded, but he was so focused on the potential guilt of hurting his family if he lost the Rough Riders or Kim took custody of Lily that he couldn't figure out what Sarah was trying to tell him.

"And how does that relate to Eden?" he asked, already wincing in anticipation of Sarah's frustration with his denseness.

His sister didn't disappoint. She threw her hands wide. "How in the hell does your brain think so fast on the ice? I don't get it."

"Sarah."

She heaved a sigh. "By not taking the chance, you may not have to deal with the downside of the situation, but you're also missing out on the potential beauty of a relationship. For you *and* Lily. Besides, not having relationships because you're afraid of hurting Lily in itself is hurting Lily. What kind of role model is that? Would you want Lily putting her life on hold the same way?"

He thought about it. "No."

"No. And honestly, as long as you stay in Lily's life, that's all the stability she needs. Look at me and Griff and the girls. Griff goes away for long periods of time. We all live with the fear that one day we'll be told he's never coming home. You come and go from the girls' lives weekly. And they're *fine*. They're happy and well-adjusted and thriving because *I* am their constant."

"You think so?"

She smiled and gestured toward the girls, who were

running to the top of the slope to roll down into the leaves again. "There is your proof."

Beckett imagined introducing Eden and Lily and smiled. Nodded. Excitement sparked at the center of his body.

Lily splashed into the leaves, rolled, and sat up. Grinning ear to ear, autumn leaves stuck in her blonde curls, she looked at him. "Did you see that, Daddy?"

Beckett laughed, then told Sarah, "Maybe you're right."

"Go for it, Beck." She clasped her hands around one knee and leaned back with a sly grin. "If for no other reason than so I can meet the woman who finally got you to walk away from a puck-bunny-threesome offer so you could make out with one anti-hockey chick in the corner. She's got to be something else."

Beckett was going to have to have a talk with the new Russian about keeping what happened with the team in the bars, *with* the team in the bars. "Fucking Andre."

19

Eden walked into the Verizon arena feeling a lot like she had the first time she'd stepped on an ambulance—filled with a mix of anticipation, excitement, and hope, all wrapped up in a straitjacket of fear.

She'd overcome those fears and thrived. Eden hoped she could do the same with Beckett.

"Let's walk around," Gabe said beside her, his excitement palpable. "Pre-skate won't start for another ten minutes."

Whatever pre-skate was. Eden wasn't asking too many questions. She was already overwhelmed. Today, she wanted to get an overall feel for this huge chunk of Beckett's life. Simply making that purposeful decision to take him home, show him who she really was, and love him openly had been a major breakthrough in her life. Now, she was recovering with baby steps.

The halls were filled with a sea of fans in royal-blue Rough Riders jerseys. Excitement crackled in the air. Concession stands lined one side of the row, retail outlets the other side. She followed Gabe into a storefront where he picked up a Rough Riders scarf. While she waited, Eden found jerseys exactly like the one she wore and ran her hand over Beckett's last name emblazoned across the shoulders.

"Aren't you glad I made you wear it now?" Gabe asked, coming up to her.

She grinned. When he'd picked her up, she'd been in a regular sweater. They'd argued for ten minutes over her wearing Beckett's jersey until Gabe had refused to take her to the game in anything else.

"Do you like the guy or not?" Gabe had asked.

"Yes, I like him," she admitted. "But that doesn't mean I want to have his name tagged on my back like property."

"It's not about ownership," Gabe argued, passionate. "It's about support and pride and team spirit. It's about wearing the name of the guy who impresses the hell out of you with his dedication and talent."

That was the argument that made Eden cave. Because when she stripped away her fears, Beckett Croft did impress the hell out of her—in more ways than she could name.

Now, she relented. "Yes, I'm glad you made me wear it."

Gabe grinned and laid his new scarf around his neck. "Let's go find our killer seats." He crossed the aisle and started down the stairs between sections. "Not that you're going to appreciate them," he shot over his shoulder, "since you didn't appreciate standing rinkside."

"Maybe I should have brought one of the other guys," she teased.

"Don't even." He finally stopped and pointed to a row. "Right here." Then he looked at the rink, ten rows and maybe thirty feet away. "Amazing." And cut a serious look at Eden. "I want you to marry this guy. Do you hear me?"

Eden burst out laughing.

"I'm serious," Gabe said.

"I know. That's what's so funny. That and the fact that I'm not marrying anyone."

Their seats were on the end of the row, and as they sat, the lights dimmed. Colored spotlights roamed the ice, and the announcer introduced the Rough Riders. The crowd went wild, buzzers sounded, smoke shot from the ceiling, and the team filed out of a hallway beneath the stands directly across the ice from Eden's and Gabe's seats. The opposing team also came out onto the ice, each warming up at opposite ends of the rink.

The lights came up, the crowd quieted down, and music played over the speakers as the players took shots, passed, and generally loosened up.

Eden searched for Beckett, but the players all looked the same, so she scanned for his number—twenty-two. She found him slapping the puck into the net. He swung behind the goal, then turned and skated backward in a big loop.

His ease and grace and fluidity took Eden's breath. His movements looked effortless and elegant, unlike anything she'd expected. Unlike anything she'd seen in those clips she'd watched. There, his skills had been sharp and choppy and brutal.

Eden felt like they'd only been on the ice moments before they returned to the locker room and the announcer distracted fans with promotional presentations and Rough Riders player statistics on the Jumbotron. Gabe picked up on one of the announcer's threads about the roster and went off on a tangent about players and starters and strings that Eden wasn't interested in following. She was still in awe of how quickly the seats had filled with blue.

So many fans.

Gabe had explained that this stadium was also used by another local NHL team, the Capitals. In the off-season, this was the home court for Washington's local professional basketball team and often hosted major musical headliners.

Gabe said something about Beckett, and Eden cued in to her coworker's dialogue. Turning to him, she said, "What?"

Gabe let out a breath, his lids lowered with a frustrated look. "You said you wanted to learn. If you don't, that's fine. I'll shut up and enjoy the game."

"I do. I'm sorry. This is a little overwhelming."

"I was telling you that this is an important year for Beckett. His contract with the Rough Riders is up at the end of the season. He'll become an unrestricted free agent—"

Eden shook her head and held her hands palms up.

"That means," Gabe went on, "that if he kills it this season, he'll be prime meat, up for grabs come July first. He's getting pretty good money now, but that would set him up for big money. I've seen teams get in bidding wars over defensemen like him. He'll be able to name his terms for the next four to eight years of his life, which is important at his age. And everyone agrees this has been his best season yet. They're talking about him getting chosen for the men's Olympic team."

"Wow." Eden tried to sound adequately impressed, but she'd already reached awestruck saturation. She also didn't want to admit she hadn't even realized there *was* a US Olympic ice hockey team. "What do you mean his age? He's still so young."

"Not for hockey. If these guys haven't been written out of contracts or gone out with an injury by their early thirties, they start retiring. There are very few players in the game in their late thirties. Only a handful in their forties. Beckett's headed into the last phase of his career, and he'll want to go out on top."

She wasn't sure why that made tension pull across her shoulders. Something about the connection between his success and increased violence on the ice wasn't sitting right.

Eden purposely pulled in a breath and cleared her mind of the irrational mental connections. She was really annoyed at how they kept popping up. How deeply they'd been ingrained. How hard it was to reprogram her brain.

Glancing at the clock on the Jumbotron, she was glad there was less than a minute until the first period started.

When her gaze returned to the ice, a group passing her on the steps caught her eye. It was hard not to notice a woman herding three young girls five rows closer to the ice—all four of them with Croft emblazoned from shoulder to shoulder.

A smile automatically tipped her lips up, but a pang stirred in her gut and dragged her happiness away. Eden pressed her hands to the discomfort in her belly and pulled her gaze from the group. She let the therapy and practiced responses take her mind from the painful memories.

The stadium filled with buzzers and sirens and lights. The announcer welcomed the Rough Riders into the rink once again, and Eden sought out Beckett's jersey, then kept her eyes on him as the two teams set up for their face-off.

Even though Eden had played a variety of sports during grade school and high school, she couldn't keep track of anything that was happening—it all happened so damn fast. Half the time, she couldn't even find Beckett.

Gabe's tutoring only confused her more. He spoke a language she didn't know. The referees called penalties she didn't understand. The players had an etiquette she couldn't comprehend. The one that especially puzzled her was the way they all pushed and shoved and elbowed and tripped with what seemed like absolute detachment. The way one would slam the other against the wall, then both men would turn and race after the puck again, emotionless, as if the encounter never happened.

Her mind drifted back to that day at the Y and the way Tate and Andre had jockeyed for berries in a rough but good-natured way. Eden wasn't sure if she should be encouraged or disturbed.

Beside her, Gabe was absorbed, cheering plays, commenting on strategy, and trying to explain it all to Eden.

But the players and the puck all moved so damn fast, Eden found herself constantly lost, wondering what the hell everyone was cheering or booing.

She'd lost track of Beckett again when the stadium exploded in applause and noise and lights. Everyone around her jumped to their feet, and Eden couldn't see anything. She glanced up at Gabe, who was clapping and saying something to her, but the buzzers and sirens were so loud, she couldn't hear him.

He finally sat back down and grabbed her arm, his face bright with excitement. "Beckett scored! Man, what a shot."

People sitting toward the middle of the row came toward the aisle, and she and Gabe stood to allow them to pass. Which made Eden look around. She found everyone squeezing out of the rows and flooding up the stairs. By the time she looked at the ice again, the players were gone. "What's this?"

"Period break." Gabe stood. "I'm going to grab a beer. Want something?"

Eden sighed and sat back. "No, thanks."

She looked around the stadium, feeling frustrated and oddly left out. On the ice, a bunch of kids came out to play hockey. And, Lord, they looked so tiny on the big rink. The thought of Beckett on skates at two years old eased a little irritation.

Then her gaze fell on the girls in the forward rows. Their mom had gotten them cotton candy, and they were pulling off fluffy pieces and stuffing the sugar in their mouths, all while dancing to the music pouring through the stadium speakers.

Eden sighed. They were beautiful. The two older girls had long dark hair. The younger one had a head of sandy blonde curls. And it was the youngest one who tied her heartstrings in knots. Probably because she was so little. Probably because she was blonde. Most of the seats between Eden and the girls had been vacated for the break, and she had nothing to distract her from watching them. Nothing to keep her mind from wondering what her life would be like now if she'd walked out on John one day sooner.

The littlest girl danced a circle while eating pink cotton candy off her tiny fingers. Her gaze caught Eden's and held. A big grin brightened her face. The girl looked like a little cherub and glowed like an angel. Eden felt like a fist reached inside and squeezed in a deeply bittersweet way that spread loss through her.

Then the girl extended her hand toward Eden. "Want some?"

Her voice was as sweet as her face. Despite the hurt, the girl's raw innocence made Eden laugh. "No, but thank you, sweetie."

The woman with the girls glanced over her shoulder and smiled at Eden.

"They're beautiful," she told the other woman.

She beamed. "Thank you." She looked at the girls. "What do you say?"

"Thank you," the older girls said in unison, smiling.

Then the little one followed, with an exaggerated and bubbly "*Thank you.*"

Their mother was pretty, and the two older girls looked just like her. The little one, not so much. The three girls continued to sway and turn circles with their threads of sugar. And Eden continued to watch, trapped in a situation she would never have endured otherwise. When she dealt with children on the job, her mind was already compartmentalized for work, she generally didn't spend much time with them, and she was too busy to let her mind wander. This...this was torture. Maybe if these beauties had been boys, her heart wouldn't be breaking and tears wouldn't be thickening her throat.

Man, Tori was right. Eden needed to get out and live more. School and work weren't giving her the exposure she needed to get over the past. She certainly couldn't hide from relationships and children forever.

Gabe returned, offering her some much needed distraction. Fans refilled the seats between Eden and the little girls. And the game restarted shortly after, restoring Eden with a sense of equilibrium, albeit subdued.

For the remainder of the game, she tried really hard to focus on the plays, on Beckett, and on Gabe's explanations. During the second break, Eden went to the restroom so she didn't have to stare at those little girls again. And by the time the third period ended and the Rough Riders won, Eden thought she might have a better understanding of the game. She definitely had a better feel for the game.

To avoid running into the girls again, Eden quickly slid into the flow of fans making their way up the steps. She stayed close to Gabe as they navigated the mob until he'd used their passes to get them through the restricted access mazes underneath the stadium, where wives and girlfriends—WAGs, Gabe had called them—gathered to meet their men after the game.

Eden didn't love the idea of being lumped in with a group others referred to as WAGs or being seen as someone who waited for "her man." But she'd have to make other arrangements next time, because she was already here.

When they stood at the mouth of the corridor, Gabe asked, "So where are you two going?"

"Out to dinner. I don't know where. Somewhere close, I hope. I'm starving."

"Have fun. Tell Beckett thanks for the tickets and great game."

"Thanks for coming, Gabe."

He laughed and offered an enthusiastic "Anytime."

Stadium staff wandered the halls, and other women and a few children started to gather in the large corridor. Eden wandered toward the end and peered up a staircase that led to a parking lot, which gave her bearings. This hallway wasn't all that far away from the one they'd used to cart Beckett out to the ambulance.

She was remembering that night, smiling to herself, when little voices echoed off the concrete. Eden looked that direction and found the woman who'd been sitting five rows down from her along with the three precious little girls who had nearly brought Eden to tears.

The four females with Croft on their jerseys.

Eden's mind pinged backward, and she realized there hadn't been a man with the group. No husband or father or brother or uncle.

And they were gathered where wives and girlfriends met their men after the game. Wearing Croft jerseys.

Holy shit.

Panic crawled along her shoulders and trickled into the pit of her stomach. The pen and paper in Beckett's apartment flashed in Eden's mind. That night, she'd thought they might have been a gag from his teammates. Then she'd learned of his nieces, and she'd assumed the paper and pen had been left behind when they'd been visiting. But now...

Oh God.

No, no, no.

The girls joined a couple of other boys, and they all ran through the corridor, laughing and chasing each other, their gleeful voices bouncing and ricocheting and echoing. The woman with the trio of girls crossed her arms and watched them play with a serene smile on her pretty face. Another woman came around the corner, and the two fell into an easy conversation.

Eden's brain spiraled for answers. His sister? Could this be his sister and his nieces? But he said he had two nieces, not three. Though the little one could be a friend of the girls. Or the woman could be babysitting.

There were a dozen different explanations to fit this scenario. Logically, Eden knew that. But emotionally, her brain was having a heyday throwing doubt at her, because, honestly, how did Eden know Beckett *wasn't* married?

How good could a quick Internet search be? And how many lovers had John passed off as female colleagues right in front of her face? For that matter, how many financial scams had John covered as legitimate business? How many lies had John twisted as truth?

How many attacks had John sworn never to repeat?

What made Eden think she would be any better at seeing lies now than she'd been able to see then?

The woman followed the girls as they ran down the corridor. Her gaze caught on Eden. And held. After a moment, she lifted her hand to wave. Eden felt as stiff and cold as metal, but she slipped her hand from her crossed arms to wave back.

The metal doors slammed open, and team members dribbled out in small groups. Eden strategically placed herself at the base of the stairs, prepared to bolt. Her mind was now in an intense battle between logic and fear. Surely Faith wouldn't have stayed quiet at the pancake breakfast if Beckett were married. Would she? Then again, Eden knew less about Faith than she knew about Beckett. But Gabe, Gabe would never lead Eden astray. But Gabe was all about the game, not the guys. He probably wouldn't even know if Beckett was married or not.

Still, it didn't make sense for Beckett to have Eden meet him here if he'd known his wife and daughters would be there to greet him. Hell, maybe they were supposed to be out of town and were surprising him. Or maybe he did know they'd be here and this was his ploy to make his wife jealous.

Eden lifted a hand to her temple to stop the spin and whispered, "Or maybe it's just *his sister*."

She didn't know anything anymore. All she could do was

wait. Wait for this sand under her feet to completely shift and knock her on her ass or solidify into concrete.

Eden held her breath as another wave of men passed through the tunnel. And another. People said hello and joked and hugged and talked and made plans. Kids played and laughed. A couple of the guys who'd been at the YMCA said hello to Eden before jogging the steps to the parking lot. No weirdness there. That was a good sign, wasn't it?

She hadn't counted, but she swore most of the players had to be out of there. Where in the hell was Beckett?

"I should leave," she whispered to herself, glancing at the stairs with a fist gripping her gut. "I should go."

The doors opened again, and Eden had convinced herself that if it wasn't Beckett, she was leaving.

When she swung her gaze back, Beckett came through the door with Tate a couple of steps behind him. His gaze immediately homed in on Eden, and a big smile lit his face.

"There you are," the woman said.

Beckett's gaze darted toward her, then the three girls, and his momentum stopped dead. His smile faded into shock.

Eden sipped a breath and held it.

"Man, you're still the last one out of the locker room," the woman said. "Girls, he's finally here."

The three girls turned. The two older ones returned to the woman's side, but the little one, the little one threw her arms in the air, yelled, "Daddy!" and ran full speed at Beckett.

Eden stood frozen as Beckett dropped his bag and caught the little girl with a grunt and "Jesus, Lily..."

Daddy?

Daddy.

Eden turned and hurried up the stairs. She wasn't thinking, just moving. *Away, away, away. No, no, no. How did this happen? How did this happen?*

"*Eden!*"

Beckett's bellow hammered her heart into overdrive, and she flinched, pulling her shoulders up and fisting her hands. She had to force herself not to run, but rushed along the fence line of the parking lot. With no idea where the hell she was going, she kept her focus on putting distance between her and Beckett and his family before her mind started working.

"Eden." A woman's voice startled her, but Eden didn't stop moving. She was behind Eden, her footsteps quick. "Eden, wait."

A hand touched her arm. Eden spun and backed away. "I'm sorry." The words came out breathless. "I didn't know. I swear I didn't—"

"I'm not his wife," she said, her expression as compassionate as her soft voice. "I'm his sister. Sarah."

Relief swept through Eden. Her knees buckled, and she grabbed the chain-link fence to keep from falling and focused on the black pavement. "Oh, *thank God*."

"And two of those girls are mine," she said. "My daughters Rachel and Amy."

Which meant...

In her mind, she saw that sweet little angel running to Beckett. Saw Beckett, in his slacks, dress shirt, and tie, hair still damp from the shower, drop his bag and catch the girl like he'd done it a million times.

A hard knot balled beneath her ribs. Eden lifted her head and looked at Sarah. "He has...a daughter."

Sarah nodded. "Lily. She's *amazing*. I'm so sorry we blindsided you like this. I didn't know you were coming tonight, and I didn't tell Beckett we were going to be here either. It was one of those last-minute things... God, I feel so bad..."

Lily.

Even her name broke Eden's heart.

"It's not your fault." Eden released the fence. "I have to go."

She turned.

"Eden, wait." Sarah came around and stepped in front of her. "Don't go. I'll take the girls home. I promised them ice cream after anyway. You and Beckett can still—"

"No." The word came out as a pained whisper. "No, we can't."

20

Beckett crossed his arms on his knees and rested his forehead there. Cold from the concrete steps in front of Eden's door had seeped through his pants and frozen his ass half an hour ago. But he was going to fucking sleep here if that was the only way to get her to open the door.

After forty-five minutes of trying to talk to her, he was now reminding her he was still there every five. If he'd known this was how he was going to spend his night, he would have stopped to pick up a blanket and some water.

He lifted his head. "I'm still here."

Beckett didn't even wait for a response, just put his head back down.

Footsteps shuffled on the sidewalk behind him. The hair on his neck prickled. *Ah, fuck.* Beckett lifted his head and glanced over his shoulder. Two men stood three feet away. It was almost eight p.m. now and the streetlight shone at their backs, so Beckett couldn't see much of them.

"What's up?" he asked congenially, as if he sat on stoops in the hood in his suit all the time.

"Who are you, man? And why you been sitting here?"

"Friend of Eden's." He sighed and shifted to put his back against the iron railing. "And I've been asking myself that for a while."

"Friends let you in. We don't like you hanging here. This is our territory. Take your fancy ride and get."

"Sorry, I'm not going anywhere." To ease the sting of confrontation, he said, "Don't worry, I'll keep it down. Don't want the cops coming to bust up my party."

"You're stalking," the shorter guy said. "You can go to jail for that."

"I'm waiting," Beckett told him. "Big difference."

"Fuck this, man." The taller guy stepped over Beckett's legs, jogged down the stairs, and pounded on the door. "Yo, Eden. You want me and Arturo to get rid of this guy for you?"

"Yes," came from behind the door. The first word he'd heard in over an hour.

Tall guy stopped at the bottom of the stairs, hands on hips. "You heard her."

"Tell me something," Beckett said. "When you and your girl are having a fight, do you listen to everything she says?"

"Nah."

"And don't you both say things you don't mean?"

"Sho."

Beckett lifted his hands with a shrug.

The tall guy turned back to the door. "Eden, are you sure you don't want to come out and talk to this dude? He's been out here a long time, and it's like twenty-nine degrees."

"Yes," she said. "I'm sure."

"Twenty-five, feels like nine," Beckett corrected, "and I didn't bring my snow-camping gear."

"Would you all leave me the h-hell alone," she yelled. "Some of us h-have to work tomorrow."

The catch in her voice told Beckett she'd been crying, and that cut at his heart.

"Ouch," tall guy said.

"Whoo-wee," short guy added. "What did you do to piss her off? She's always in a good mood."

"I'm special like that." Beckett pulled at his hair, which was sticking up in all directions. Then called to the door, "And it's only eight o'clock."

They all stared at her door for an extended moment, and when it didn't open, tall guy crossed his arms and asked Beckett, "What you do for a livin' to buy that fancy Porsche?"

"I play hockey."

"Hockey?" He shifted and angled his head to get a better look. "How come I don't recognize you?"

"Probably because we wear helmets, move real fast, and are usually covered in cuts and bruises." He held out his hand. "Beckett Croft."

The expression on tall guy's face went from skeptical to no shit in a split second. He laughed and took Beckett's hand. He did some kind of secret hood handshake and slapped Beckett on the shoulder, laughing. "Look at this, Arturo. Beckett Croft is in our hood. You had a great game tonight, bro."

And the conversation progressed from there. But only for about two minutes.

Eden's door flew open. "*Stop.* Just fucking stop already."

Her hair was up in a ponytail, and she was in sweatpants and a sweatshirt. And she'd definitely been crying. Her face was red, her eyes puffy.

Beckett's heart plummeted to his stomach. He should let her go. She didn't have room for this kind of turmoil in her life. Neither of them did.

"Robby and Arturo, thank you for checking on me, but get the hell out of here." And she turned back inside, leaving the door open.

Robby sucked air through his teeth. "Good luck with that, bro."

Beckett sighed and stared at the door while the other guys retreated.

"Twenty-five, feels like nine," she called from inside. "Come in or stay out, but close the damn door."

Kennedy was back. The tough chick who'd put him in his place that first night. Beckett sighed, stepped into the basement, and closed the door behind him.

She was sitting at her desk with her back to him, elbows planted on the desktop, hands clasped near her mouth. "You lied." She shook her head. "I can't do lies."

Now she only sounded half-tough. And half-shaky. "Baby, I didn't lie."

She cut a look over her shoulder.

"I swear I was going to tell you about her tonight at dinner." He slid off his blazer and laid it on the bed, then moved to the corner and sat. With his forearms braced on his knees, he clasped his hands. "What's really going on, Eden? This reaction is pretty extreme. I understand the initial fear that I might have been married, but once that was cleared up..."

"You first. Why wasn't she the first thing you told me about? Why wasn't she the only thing you talked about?"

The way she said it conveyed the message that Eden believed Lily should be the center of his world. He was glad to know they shared that value, but there was a big puzzle piece missing in the picture that made up Eden Kennedy.

"I've filed for full custody of Lily, and the hearing is coming up soon. Her mother hasn't contested it so far, and I don't want anything to change that, so I'm keeping Lily very under the radar until the hearing is over and custody is finalized."

"Were you married?"

"No. Her mother was a woman I had a casual night with on the road when I was nobody, still making next to nothing. I was a stepping-stone on her way up the professional athlete chain to bigger, flashier stars. And I was fine with that."

"Why isn't she fighting you for custody?"

Beckett shook his head and looked at his hands. "Kim wants what a lot of women who chase after professional athletes want—money, fame, a lifestyle. Lily wasn't planned, and a kid gets in the way of a lot of things. For Kim, Lily got in the way of finding a sugar daddy. She's got herself a very rich football player right now. Taking Lily back would jeopardize all that."

Eden's expression compressed into agony, and she rubbed her eyes. "God, I *hate* people sometimes."

Beckett got that. In her job, he could only imagine what she saw on a daily basis. "That's not even the worst of it."

"What does that mean?"

"I didn't know Lily existed until she was almost two and a half, and Kim showed up on my doorstep looking for child support. When she thought I was nobody, there was no point in tracking me down. But after news got out that I'd signed a nice contract, she was all over me. I told her I wanted a paternity test, but one look at Lily, and I knew. She looked a lot like my nieces as babies. I told Kim I'd give her child support without lawyers if she gave me visitation. She was all too happy to hand Lily over to someone else. I learned later she did that a lot. For extended periods of time.

"By the time the paternity test came back, confirming Lily was my daughter, I was already head over heels in love with her. I filed for joint custody but had to fight Kim for it—not because she wanted Lily, but because she wanted my money. When Lily was almost four, Kim and I hit a rough patch with visitation. She kept making excuses why Lily couldn't see me—playdates, birthday parties, vacation. I hadn't seen her in a month when a stranger showed up at my door with Lily."

Beckett would never forget that day. Never forget the sight of his daughter. Just the memory enraged him. "She was wearing torn, filthy clothes, had scrapes on her knees, hands, and face, knots all through her curls, a green runny nose and was coughing like a seal."

"Shit," Eden whispered and pressed her forehead to her hand.

"The woman who brought her turned out to be Kim's aunt and told me Kim had dropped Lily off with her over three weeks before and vanished without a word since. When I took Lily to the doctor, she had bronchitis, pneumonia, double ear infections, pink eye, and was so dehydrated, she had to be hospitalized for two days. Once again, after the fact, I later found out Kim had gone on a Vegas bender with an Argentinian soccer player, which was why she kept telling me I couldn't see Lily."

He paused and studied his hands. "I told Kim that if she tried to take Lily back, I'd have her arrested for child endangerment and neglect." His stomach knotted. "The thought of doing that to Lily's mother still makes me sick, but I would have done anything to keep Lily away from her."

A moment of silence passed. The room felt heavy with sadness and turmoil. "It's ugly, heavy stuff, and we already have a fistful of challenges facing us. I don't want to give up and let go. I'm crazy about you. But I don't want to hurt you either."

She took a deep breath, and air hiccupped into her lungs, the way Lily's did when she cried hard. Thankfully, that hadn't happened in a long time.

"This"—she gestured toward herself—"isn't all your fault." Her voice was soft but flat, like she'd gone numb. "I mean, *most* of this isn't your fault." She didn't look at him. Her gaze lowered to her desktop and the textbook there, her fingers toying with a corner of the page. "My last boyfriend...was abusive." She lifted a shoulder as if to discount the horrendous statement. "But that isn't what's held me back most. If it had just been the abuse, I'd have moved on by now."

Her breathing grew shallow, and a tear leaked from the

corner of her eye. Beckett was at a total loss, with no idea how to manage his own sudden rage while being considerate of Eden's distress. He felt as inept as he had the first time he'd taken Lily in his arms.

Beckett leaned forward and reached for her, but Eden lifted her hand in a stop gesture. "I need to get this out."

"Okay." He clasped his hands between his knees.

"I was..."—she cleared her throat—"pre—" Her voice cut out. She closed her eyes and tried again. "Pregnant. I was...pregnant."

She paused to take a breath as if the words had been monumental to get out. They sent a cold trickle of dread down Beckett's spine.

"We weren't married, but he was a family friend, my dad's work colleague. My parents liked him; we'd been dating over a year. I thought— Doesn't matter. I was wrong. He wanted me to have an abortion. I refused. That was the first time he hit me." She licked her lips. Took a breath. "I wrote it off to the stress, the shock. I thought him wanting the abortion was a phase and that he'd come around. But while I was waiting, he was drinking. When he drank, we argued. And when we argued—"

"He hit you," Beckett finished, barely able to keep his fury in check.

Eden nodded and took a deep, shaky breath, then blew it out the way a sprinter would after a hard run. As if it had taken all her energy to get that much out. Her hand was shaking. And Beckett ached to take her in his arms, but his own hands were clenched so tight, his fingers had gone numb.

"I should have left him sooner." Her eyes closed on a look so agony stricken, Beckett saw the next blow coming, and he couldn't do anything about it. "But my parents adored him. And I'd finally found a window of approval in their eyes." She shook her head. "I waited too long. I was packing my things when he came home early from a business trip. We got in the same old fight over the abortion. To get him off my back, I told him it was too late to have one. He was livid. I've never seen anyone so angry. He...backhanded me across the face, and I fell down a flight of stairs..."

Her voice faded into anguish, and Beckett couldn't take it. He dropped to his knees, covered her thigh with his hand, and squeezed gently. Then waited while she pulled herself together enough to go on.

"The placenta was damaged," she said softly, "and the baby died."

"Eden..." He had no words and ended up pressing his face to her arm.

"I was over five months along, so even though she'd passed, I had to give birth to her. And they let me hold her after. She was a little bigger than my hand." Eden opened her hand, palm up. "Her feet reached my wrist. And, God..." She closed her eyes. "She was perfect. So utterly perfect." She opened her eyes and the slightest smile played on her lips. She even had hair, this wispy little crown of blonde..." She covered Beckett's hand with hers and curled her fingers around it, her gaze distant. "I named her Summer, because she was due in July."

After a moment, when she didn't go on, Beckett lifted his hand to her head and pulled her into him. He kissed her hair. "Baby, I'm so sorry."

She nodded. Another quiet stretch passed before she said, "Lily was sitting five rows down from me and Gabe at the game. I kept trying to ignore her, but I couldn't. She's so small and blonde, and God, she's radiant... I kept thinking how Summer would be two years old now..."

He pulled back. "God, I wish I'd known my sister planned to bring the girls tonight. The team saves a certain section for family tickets."

Eden didn't meet his eyes. "I'm sorry. I thought I'd found a way to deal with it and move on. But I obviously haven't. And Lily...she's too..." Pain etched her brow. "I'm not ready..."

"Hold on." He took her chin between his fingers and lifted her head until her gaze met his. "You don't have to make that decision right now. And you didn't really get to know her. I have yet to meet someone she doesn't instantly wrap around her little finger, including every damn member of my team."

A smile quivered on Eden's lips but disappeared within a second. "You've worked hard to get her to a good place, Beckett. I don't want to do anything to mess that up."

He threaded one hand into her hair. "You won't. You can't. My family and I have created the strongest base she could ever need. She's solid and secure and happy, even with all the turmoil in her background. Even with my crazy schedule. She's not that fragile. And neither are you." When Eden's gaze lifted to his, he said, "You are one of the strongest women I know. And you don't have to move forward alone."

She sighed but didn't resist, giving Beckett hope.

He glanced at his watch. "Why don't you come pick her up with me?"

She gave him an intensely skeptical look.

"It would really help me out with my sister," Beckett said, begging a little. "She was so pissed when I met up with her after she'd gone after you." He winced, remembering. "If the girls weren't with us, I'm pretty sure she would have decked me."

Eden huffed a surprised, amused "What?"

"She said I should have told you about Lily. Told me I screwed up something that could have been special. She really liked you."

"She couldn't. We talked for two minutes."

"You make big impressions in a short amount of time. Think about our first two minutes together."

That got the stress in her expression to soften, and the first real smile he'd seen all night lightened her face. "There's my girl. I knew she was in there." He kissed her forehead. "What do you say? Come meet my family?"

"I don't think—"

"By now, Sarah's probably got my parents all pissed off at me too." He lifted his brows and gave her his best hopeful plea. "Come on, be a lifesaver, baby."

"I can't. That's too—"

"Hey, we agreed we've got a thing here."

"I think we agreed we both *wanted* this to be a thing, not that it actually *is* a thing."

"This *is definitely* a thing. And when people have a thing, they meet family and friends. So meet them. If it doesn't turn out well or you feel weird or Lily still causes you more pain than pleasure after you've spent some time with her, then we'll, you know, call off our thing. And you can say you tried. *Really* tried."

She got a pained look on her face. "Your family's going to think I'm—"

"Beautiful, sweet, smart—"

"A nut case," she countered, making him laugh.

"Believe me, I know my family. And they're going to love you."

21

Eden stared out the window at the moonlight on the Potomac as they crossed the Fourteenth Street Bridge. She didn't know what the hell she'd been thinking when she'd agreed to this.

"Don't even think about it," Beckett said, drawing her gaze. "Do you have any idea how cold that water is right now?"

His allusion to thoughts of bailing into the Potomac made her smile. "You have to admit, it's not a bad idea."

"You're right. It's a *terrible* idea." He reached over and took her hand, then brought it to his mouth for a kiss. Curling his fingers around hers, he rested them on the center console. "Relax, baby. We are a super-casual family."

She shook her head. "I'm not at my best."

"Yeah, you are," he said seriously. "You just can't see it."

Eden looked out the passenger's window again, overwhelmed by Beckett's acceptance of her history. Of the way she shied away from the most important person in his life. This visit to his family was as risky to their current relationship as an avalanche to a skier.

And Beckett was the crazy-ass daredevil looking over his shoulder and laughing as the mountain tumbled after him.

"Where is your ex now?" he asked, jerking Eden in a completely different direction. "Did anything happen to him? I mean legally?"

"Yeah." This she could answer with an element of satisfaction and pride. Nothing would bring Summer back, but at least Eden had reaped justice for her. "He's in prison serving fourteen years for second-degree murder."

Beckett's head swiveled toward her, his mouth open. "Seriously? That's...I don't want to say awesome, because nothing about this is awesome, but it so refreshing to hear the system actually worked."

"When you force it."

"Meaning?"

"My father had considerable influence with the district attorney, and both my parents sided with my ex."

"*What?*"

"They said I shouldn't have gotten pregnant. Then they said I should have had the abortion. Then they said, well, what did I expect putting him under all that pressure?"

"Jesus Christ," Beckett bit out. He rested his elbow on the window ledge and rubbed his forehead.

Eden appreciated Beckett's anger on her behalf, but she couldn't let herself get caught up in it or she'd sink like a stone. "So I cracked open my trust fund to hire an attorney powerful enough to get past my father's pull, and he convinced the DA to file charges. And when I found out how hard John was going to fight it, and how limited the DA's resources were, I drained my trust fund to keep my attorney on the case. He did the research and put together the supporting documentation necessary to make sure John got the maximum sentence. My lawyer did everything but actually try the case."

"It really sucks that you had to use money that could be

helping you now to put that bastard where he belongs. But on the other hand—"

"It was gratifying to use my parents' money to do it," she finished.

"Exactly."

And, dammit, this was why she was in the car, driving to meet his family. He got her. He wanted her. He accepted her, flaws and all.

She laid her head against the seat and soaked in the sight of his handsome profile as they made their way through Arlington toward the suburbs. "Do you like being a dad?"

"Oh, man." He shook his head. "I *love* being *Lily's* dad. That kid is the absolute light of my life. She turned my world upside down, and I can't get enough of her. Everything I do or don't do revolves around what she needs, what's best for her."

The overwhelming joy in his voice filled a dark space in Eden's heart and made her smile.

"I couldn't manage like I do without my family, though. They watch her when I'm on the road. They help me get her to special classes while I'm at practice. They come to my place and tuck her into bed for my home games. I cover the mornings and get her to school, and we spend most weekends together, depending on my schedule."

"Gabe said something about your contract coming to an end? What's going to happen then?"

"Yeah." He sighed the word, heavy with stress. "This is the last year in my contract with the Rough Riders. I'm at a mid-level age and have a lot of good years left. But the better I play this year, the better my options for the coming years will be. And what I really want is an eight-year contract with the Rough Riders. If I can't get that, I'd take one with the Capitals, because my priority is to stay here so Lily can stay close to our family."

"What if you don't get that?"

He sucked air between his teeth and shook his head. "I can't think like that right now. I'm livin' like I'm going to keep doin' what I'm doin' until I'm not doin' it anymore."

He took a few turns on streets in an upscale neighborhood with large houses on spacious, thickly treed lots, then finally started up a long driveway. "Here we are."

The house at the end of the drive, nestled into a gentle hill, was the stuff *Architectural Digest* covers were made of. Multiple levels, lots of glass, a curved main stairway, and double, heavily carved, wooden entry doors reminded Eden of the homes she used to breeze in and out of without noticing all the gorgeous details. Exterior lights, landscaping, and stone pavers created an elegant yet calming welcome.

Eden must have missed something somewhere. A house like this here cost at least a million if not more. "This is the house you bought for them?"

"Mmm-hmm. Wait till you see the back porch. Amazing view of the Potomac. I could sit out there all day."

He came to a stop in front of the triple garage.

"Didn't you say you used your first professional paycheck for this?"

"Yeah. I wasn't making as much then, but the signing bonus helped."

She pried her gaze off the house and looked at Beckett with her mouth open but thoughts jumbling. "Hockey players must make a hell of a lot more than I realized."

He met her gaze with a look she couldn't read. A little amused. A little questioning. Maybe a little sarcastic? "You don't know how much I make?"

She frowned. "How would I know that?"

"It's public. All you have to do is google my name and NHL contract and you'll have as many details about my hockey contract as I do."

"That's stupid. Why is it public? It's no one else's business."

His mouth kicked up in the cutest lopsided smile she'd ever

seen. He laughed and leaned over the console, pressing a soft kiss to her lips. His were warm and gentle and felt so good on hers. She wanted to sink in and stay there. When he pulled back, he met her eyes and murmured, "Have I mentioned how crazy I am about you?"

Eden's heart twisted. Emotions and logic tangled. And she groaned.

Beckett's grin sparkled in the darkness. "You're crazy about me too." He kissed her again. "Come on," he cajoled in that low sexy voice that made heat burn between her legs. "Admit it."

"*Pffft.*"

He kissed her again, cupping her head in that way that made her feel precious. Opening his mouth over hers and pressing hers open. Sliding his tongue inside and stroking hers until she sighed out a moan and leaned into him.

"Mmm." He pulled out of the kiss slowly, leaving Eden a little dizzy and a lot hungry. "Let's get inside before I change my mind about this visit and take you back home."

He turned and got out of the car, leaving Eden with a fresh batch of what-the-hell-am-I-doing nerves bubbling to the surface. This was a futile effort. She didn't want serious. She didn't want attachments or commitments. She certainly didn't want a freaking family.

A flutter of panic attacked her stomach as he opened her door.

When she turned toward him, he stroked a hand down her arm. "Hey, relax. Really, this doesn't have to be a big deal. How many places have you walked into, interacted with people, and walked out? Hundreds? Thousands?"

"Not thousands." She breathed deep and forced a smile. "But you're right. I'm fine."

On the walk to the door, he curled his arm around her shoulder and pulled her close. "Be forewarned, it will be noisy and chaotic. My mother will try to feed you, and my father will try to ply you with alcohol."

She was smiling when she walked up the elegant curved front steps. Before they reached the front door, a squeal eked out from somewhere inside, followed by a chorus of giggles.

Beckett grinned at her. "Told ya."

She laughed, but a knot had already formed in her gut and her hands curled into fists.

He leaned forward to open the door, and his smile turned smirkish. "I'm also going to get the 'Beckett Thomas' as soon as I walk in."

The door opened, and a soft ping sounded somewhere close, signaling their entrance. He pressed a hand low on her back and led her into the foyer.

He'd barely closed the door when a woman yelled, "Beckett Thomas..."

She sounded older than Sarah, and her tone clearly indicated he was in trouble.

Beckett sighed, then yelled, "Sarah, you're such a tattle—"

"Daddy!" The excited voice came along with Lily sprinting along the marble tile, full speed.

Beckett crouched and caught his daughter the same way he had inside the tunnel earlier, smoothly, easily. He tossed her in the air, drawing a round of giggles, then settled her in his arms.

Lily pushed her hair from her eyes and looked at Eden with a smile like pure sunshine. "Hi," she said. "I saw you at Daddy's game."

"Lily, this is my friend, Eden."

"Hi, Lily." Eden smiled, and now that Beckett was holding her, Eden could see some of him in her pretty face. She had his dark eyes, her face the same soft triangular shape. And good Lord, but she was beautiful. Her dusty blonde curls were a wild halo around her head, and her little teeth gleamed when she grinned.

The pain Eden expected to stab her heart didn't come. The knot in her gut was still there, but her attention was diverted from the discomfort by a woman's voice moving through an adjacent room Eden couldn't see.

"Don't even think about grabbing her and jumping in the car, Beckett." Her voice was stern but not mean. "We need to have a—" She came around the corner and into a wide arched opening. Her gaze settled on Beckett, then jumped to Eden. "Oh." She stopped, planted her hands on her hips, and tilted her head. "Hello."

Eden smiled at the woman. She was pretty, like her daughter, with a short, layered head of silvered gold hair and light eyes. Which might explain Lily's blonde hair. "Hi."

Sarah appeared behind her mother, darted a look at Eden, then grinned at Beckett, shaking her head. "Oh, man. You slithered out of that one." She looked at Eden. "He owes you."

"He certainly does," his mother agreed with a less than pleased look at Beckett before offering her hand to Eden. "I'm Tina."

"Eden. Nice to meet you."

The two other girls who'd been with Sarah earlier in the evening drifted in, and she introduced her daughters as Rachel and Amy.

"Sarah tells me you're an EMT," Tina said.

"What's an EMT?" Lily wanted to know.

"Eden works on an ambulance," Beckett told her. "She helps sick and hurt people and takes them to the hospital."

His mother was still holding Eden's hand when she darted a look at Beckett, then told Eden, "I'll bet he didn't tell you I was a nurse for twenty years."

"Oh...no, he..." Eden glanced at Beckett and found him grinning. Grinning ear to ear with a glint of I told you so.

His mother drew Eden's hand through the bend of her elbow and walked her through the foyer into a short hallway.

"Spent a few years in the ER too. We haven't put dinner away yet. Have you eaten?"

"Actually, no, but I'm okay. I'm not really—"

"Nonsense. We have plenty. Do you like pie? I made an apple cranberry." She grinned, and Eden instantly knew where Beckett's smile had come from. "I'm taking cooking classes at Sur la Table, so I'm always using the family as guinea pigs."

"Don't let her fool you." A man's deep voice drew Eden's attention to the kitchen, and her assessment of the home's value rose from a million dollars to two million. It was huge and stunning. Sparkling quartz countertops, top-of-the-line stainless appliances, hardwood floors, rich cabinetry, and high ceilings. "She's an amazing cook." Beckett's father was a few inches shorter than his son and roughly the same age as his wife. And Beckett had gotten his dark eyes. "And you'll need wine to go with the pie. Do you prefer a dessert wine or something different? We've got a nice Bordeaux and an unoaked chardonnay I just opened."

Before Eden could answer or introduce herself, Lily said, "Grandma, I want pie."

She sounded so different from when they'd walked in, Eden turned to look at the little girl. She had her head tucked under Beckett's chin, and she yawned. He swayed gently the way so many parents did unconsciously. The image was worthy of a *Sports Illustrated* cover highlighting an article on the human side of NHL's most brutal players.

Every soft emotion inside Eden surged to the surface. Her heart tugged and twisted.

"Sounds like someone didn't eat any dinner," Beckett said.

"I did too." Her pathetic attempt at arguing drew smiles all around the kitchen.

"Barely," Tina said, with an overwhelming amount of love in her eyes. "Want to try to get a few more bites of turkey in? I'll put whipped cream on your pie."

Lily groaned.

Beckett chuckled. "I think she'd fall asleep face-first in that whipped cream before she got any into her mouth."

"Crash and burn," Sarah said, pulling out a chair at the kitchen table and taking one of her daughters into her lap. "Dad, I could use a hot chocolate and Baileys." She lifted her brows at Eden. "Does that sound good? I bet you could use a drink. Beckett has that effect on people."

Eden and Tina laughed. Beckett rolled his eyes. His father grinned.

"That sounds amazing." Eden glanced at Beckett's father. "If you're making them. Otherwise, any wine is perfectly fine."

"Irish hot chocolate for the ladies," he said, and extended his hand across the sparkling black quartz countertop. "Jake."

She took his hand in a firm shake. "Eden."

"Welcome, Eden."

She'd barely released Jake's hand before Tina pulled out a chair for her. "Come sit. I'd love to hear about your job. Which ambulance company do you work for?"

All eyes were focused on Eden, and she couldn't remember the last time she'd felt so self-conscious. She'd changed into jeans and a sweater and pulled her hair up into a bun before getting in Beckett's car. She'd even spritzed on some five-year-old perfume. But no matter how she packaged herself, she knew inside, she was subpar tonight.

Sarah's daughters returned to the living room, where a movie played. And Eden managed the casual chat about her work and Tina's nursing. Then Beckett opened the door to a path leading down the rabbit hole.

"Eden's in paramedic school," he said, easing into a seat with Lily on his lap.

His mother gasped with pleasure, and her bright eyes sparkled with approval. "Really. How exciting. What made you want to go into the field?"

The question hit her sideways. It wasn't one she'd ever been asked and one she hadn't anticipated. "Um, a while back, I was in an accident, and the paramedic who was there really made the situation a life-changing experience. It made me want to be there for other people."

She glanced at Beckett, hoping he'd pick up the conversation and steer it somewhere else so she didn't have to answer any more detailed questions about the accident. Otherwise, she'd have to start lying, and she sucked at lying.

He met her eyes and added, "And the program is through Johns Hopkins."

She offered a grateful smile, which he returned.

"Oh my," Tina said, taken aback. "That program only takes the best. Your parents must be so proud. Where are you from, Eden?"

Criminy. This was why she stuck with school and work. Because conversations with new acquaintances led to a past she wanted to forget.

"California." She smiled for Beckett's mother. "Unfortunately, my parents and I aren't close like you and your children."

Her brow fell. "Oh, what a shame." She shook her head and patted Eden's arm. "Their loss, sweetheart. You're delightful."

Heaviness weighted her stomach, and darkness crept into her heart. She'd been trained and groomed to be delightful. And, yes, she could pull out those traits and manners at will. Yet it had never been enough for her own parents. And her continued attempts to please them had ended up costing her own daughter's life. So she didn't feel the least bit delightful. She felt like a complete fraud in the face of authentically wonderful people.

But she offered a humble "Thank you."

"Son," Jake called from the kitchen. "What can I get you?"

"A brush." The tinge of frustration in his voice drew Eden's gaze. "And some scissors. What the heck did you women do to her hair this time?"

"No, Daddy." Lily slapped both her hands on top of her head, blocking his fingers before he could take out the first brightly colored elastic. "I like them."

"Okay, okay. I won't steal them, baby. Just fix them before you fall asleep. Otherwise, you're going to wake up with your hair in knots around the rubber bands. Remember the last time that happened?"

Lily whimpered, and her hands slid from her head and dropped to her lap in an exhausted gesture.

Beckett grinned at Eden, and the pure, raw joy shining through hit hard enough to topple her. "Sixty to zero in three-point-two seconds."

Despite the dual fists gripping Eden's gut and heart, she laughed.

"Grandma, can I have pie? Please?" Lily asked, half plea, half whine, making everyone in the room smile.

"One piece of turkey?" Tina asked sweetly.

Lily huffed, and her face fell into a pout. "Fine."

Laughter Eden didn't know was coming rolled out of her, drawing everyone's gaze. She covered her mouth. "Sorry. That was *all* Beckett right there."

Which made the rest of his family laugh. And when she glanced at Beckett, the look on his face, one of raw affection and open joy, flipped Eden's stomach inside out.

They stayed there in the kitchen, chatting about Eden's future plans, Sarah's teaching, Jake's coaching, and all the kids until the glasses were empty, the pie was long gone, and Lily was asleep in Beckett's arms.

Eden had fallen far too comfortably into a little fantasy of what it would be like to belong to a family like this when Beckett said, "It's getting late. I'd better get Eden home and this little one into bed."

Hello, reality. Hello, dingy basement, gunfire alarm at two a.m., invisible personal walls at school and work, and long hours alone, cramming information into her brain.

This wasn't her family. She didn't belong. The clock was about to strike midnight, and Eden's Porsche was about to turn back into the subway.

At the front door, his family surprised Eden yet again by not just saying good-bye but hugging her. Even Beckett's father tossed an arm around her shoulders and pulled her in for a quick squeeze and a quiet "Keep him in line, now."

They bundled up, and Eden followed Beckett to his car. He opened the back hatch and dragged out a booster seat with one hand, Lily securely tucked close to his body with the other. While he positioned the chair in the backseat on the passenger's side. Beckett belted Lily in, tucking her blanket beside her. Eden crossed her arms against the cold and watched him, admiring how careful and gentle and sweet he was with her.

When he closed the door and turned to Eden, she said, "Can you drop me off at the Foggy Bottom Metro? I can't stand the idea of you having Lily in the car when you're driving through my neighborhood. I know I joke about how bad it is, but I'm very aware of the crime, and you are a prime carjacking target. Even the thought of—"

He cupped her face in both hands and kissed her. Eden suddenly couldn't focus on anything but the warmth of his lips. The feel of his fingers stroking her cheeks.

"Mmm." She curled her fingers in the front of his jacket and leaned into him. God, this was so dangerous. *He* was so dangerous.

He pulled out of the kiss slowly and just enough to whisper, "I want you so bad, I haven't been able to think about anything else for the last half hour."

Then he kissed her again, hungrily, stroking his tongue into her mouth. She opened to take him, to give back, instantly flooded with need. He tilted his head and took the kiss deeper while covering one of her hands with his and guiding it to his erection. The feel of him, hot and hard beneath his slacks, made Eden ache to feel him filling her, and she automatically tightened her fingers around him. Beckett moaned into her mouth.

Fuck, this man was such a rush.

He pulled out of the kiss and looked down at her with that lusty sparkle in his eyes. "I don't plan on driving through your neighborhood. The talk about taking you home was for my parents. I plan on taking you straight to my bed after Lily's all tucked into hers."

After the painful, tumultuous day, Eden melted at the thought of being wrapped in Beckett's arms, warmed by his body, and driven to levels of pleasure that made her mind stop —stop thinking, stop worrying, stop second-guessing.

But by the time he'd helped her into the passenger's seat, her brain had cleared, and before she could say anything, he closed her door and walked around to the driver's side. She waited until he'd started the car before she said, "Honestly, there is nowhere I'd rather spend the night than in your bed, but I'm not sleeping with you while Lily's home."

He glanced over his shoulder to back from the drive and lifted one brow at her. "And why not?"

"What do you mean why not? Do you always have sex in your house when your daughter's in the next room?"

"She's not in the next room, she's all the way across the apartment in her own suite. And you're the first woman I've brought home since I took full custody of Lily. Besides, couples have sex with children in the house all the time. How do you think siblings are made?"

She opened her mouth but came up short on an argument. He had a point.

"You haven't had much kid experience," he said, his tone

both sweet and amused. He reached across the console and squeezed her thigh. "She's been playing with her cousins all day. She's not going to wake again until I prod her for school in the morning. Not when I carry her from the car. Not when I change her into pajamas. Not when I tuck her in. She's out for the night. When she stays with my sister or my mom, she's sometimes restless, but when she's home with me, she never wakes at night. Believe me, I've done this a hundred times over the last year. I know."

Eden turned and glanced back at Lily. The occasional streetlight illuminated her sweet face through the window. "She's amazing, Beckett."

"Thanks, I agree. She means everything to me."

"And your family..." She pulled her gaze off Lily and looked at Beckett's profile as he drove. "I can see why you turned out so great."

"I wasn't always great. In fact, I was an egotistical ass my first few years on the Rough Riders. Immature with lots of money and everyone telling me what hot shit I was. I was a little prick, and too busy to see my family much, which made it even worse because they're the ones who keep me grounded." He shot a grin her way. "And speaking of my family, they loved you, just like I said they would."

"They're so sweet." She reached out and stroked his cheek with the backs of her fingers. "I'm sure they love all the girls you bring to meet them."

He covered her hand with his and brought her fingers to his lips for a kiss. "Baby, you're the first woman I've brought home since I learned to drive in high school."

"What?" Her heart made a funny skip. "Why?"

They started over the bridge, and the moonlight on the Potomac reflected into the car, illuminating Beckett's handsome face.

He shrugged. "I was too busy with hockey in high school to

have a girlfriend. Was drafted into the NHL before my twentieth birthday. Was wild for years. And this job, it makes relationships hard. Hard to find and hard to keep. I never wanted to go through the headaches I'd seen other guys go through."

"Like what?"

"Fighting, affairs, separations, divorces, child custody battles, though I got sucked into that last one anyway. The stress of the job, the ups and downs of the season, the job insecurity, the constant travel and the moods that come with it all, they're rough on everyone. Don't get me wrong, there's no better job in the world for me, and it has its perks—the money, the fame, the sheer fun of playing hockey. But honestly, the rest of it sucks. And it especially sucks for the families of the players."

Eden was thinking about all that when Beckett passed the Metro station. "Beckett—"

"I'm telling you, she's not going to wake up."

"If she does, I'm leaving."

He shot a fiery grin at her and lowered his voice. "Can't wait to get you naked."

22

Beckett carried Lily into her room and laid her on her pink satin bedspread under her pink tulle swag canopy.

"Oh my God." Eden's whisper came from the doorway, where she stood looking around the room.

Beckett had to admit, it was even a little much for him some days, and he'd had lots of time to get used to it.

"Yeah." He turned toward a dresser and pulled a nightgown —Lily's favorite pink one with sparkles all down the front— from the bottom drawer. "I let Sarah and my mom decorate. That's the last time I give them free rein with my credit card when they're buying for Lily."

At the bed, he knelt on the floor and pulled Lily's shoes off, then dragged her pants down and eased her arms from her jacket and T-shirt. Once her nightgown was on, he pulled down the covers, then picked her up and gently laid her head on her pillow, then tucked her soft blanket next to her and pulled the covers over her.

He straightened and stared down at her. Lily filled his heart in so many ways. He couldn't imagine living without her. If Kim pushed, he was going to unleash the wrath of his wealth on her.

Eden moved to the foot of her bed. "I can't believe how hard she sleeps. Won't she have to go to the bathroom?"

He shook his head. "All the girls stop getting drinks at eight p.m. She was wetting the bed almost every night when I got her. Stopped right about the same time she stopped crying every night."

Eden stroked a hand up his back and leaned into him. She pressed her head to his biceps. "You're such a great dad. She's so lucky to have you."

Warmth gathered in his heart. He turned and slipped his arms around her. "You couldn't give me any bigger compliment. Not even if it was about hockey." He walked her backward toward the door, whispering, "Unless it's how well I make love to you."

He used one hand to close Lily's door at his back. Then he leaned down, tightened his arms, and lifted Eden off her feet. She wrapped her legs around his hips and her arms around his neck.

"Are you sure?" she asked, still whispering. "I really don't mind going home. We can find another time—"

He kissed her again, showing her exactly how sure he was. And Eden opened to him, sank into the kiss, and moaned. Beckett lit up like a struck match. She was so raw. So vulnerable, yet so strong. A complex contradiction in so many ways. And right now, she wanted him. Knowing that want had grown so intense he'd become a need shot a hot thrill through his veins.

She slipped her hands down his shirt and worked on the buttons. He closed his bedroom door, and instead of laying her on the bed right there, he walked her to the side where the windows cast quiet lights of the night across the room. He released her enough to let her slide down his body until her feet touched the floor, then pulled her sweater over her head, followed by the camisole underneath. Kissing a path from her ear to her shoulder, he unclasped her bra and let it fall off her arms. Moonlight spilled over her beautiful face, her full breasts, her flat belly.

"God, you are gorgeous." He let his mouth move over the soft mounds of her breasts, and closed his teeth over one nipple until she gasped. Then he released her and spiraled his tongue around the tight bud until she moaned. And started all over again on the other side.

He loved the way she shivered, the way she clenched her hands in his hair, the hungry kitten sounds she made. Loved her smell, her feel, her taste. And as she worked his clothes open, pushed her hand into his pants, and closed her fingers around his cock, he definitely loved the way she handled him.

Fire burst through his groin and spread. Pressure built across his hips and collected at the base of his spine. Beckett worked her jeans and panties down her legs, which dislodged her hand and gave him a moment of relief. She'd taken off her boots at the door and now stepped out of her jeans.

Crouched there, he looked up at her. "You look amazing in the moonlight."

She smiled and combed both hands through his hair.

Beckett kissed his way up her body, and when she took his mouth with enough passion for Beckett to drown in, the urgency kicked up a notch. He pulled his wallet from his back pocket and broke the kiss to pull a condom from the folds.

"Let me this time," Eden said before taking it from him and ripping the package open. Her hands were steady and sure, exactly what he'd expect of a competent EMT. But she wasn't the least bit medical when she slowly stroked his cock as she rolled the condom over his length, making him see stars.

When her fingers hit the base of his cock, he gripped her waist and dragged her up against him. Her lower belly cradled his erection, creating a delicious gentle pressure. With one arm holding her close, he slipped the other into her hair. "You fuckin' make me crazy, Eden. I just want more and more and more."

"Take all you want," she said, her eyes reflecting the same desire, heating Beckett to the core. "I'm yours."

His heart skipped a beat.

A little voice whispered in his ear, *Yes.*

Before he could even think about getting out of his clothes, Eden walked him to the edge of the bed. She pressed both hands to his abdomen and eased him down. "Lie back." The words were more of a sultry suggestion than an order, and the look in her eyes matched the tone, spurting gasoline on his fire. "You played hard today."

She leaned into him until Beckett's back was against the mattress and she hovered over him, propped on elbows and knees. He reached into her hair and gently pulled at the elastic band holding it in a bun. The thick mass fell all around her face, making her laugh, and Beckett pushed it back with both hands. Then he drew her to him and kissed her, her lips still curved under his.

His life was perfect. Right this minute, playing for the Rough Riders, living close to his family, Lily happy and safe in her bedroom across the apartment, Eden loving him in his bed —his life was fucking perfect.

Too bad every single one of those elements was on the verge of change.

Beckett tilted his head and opened to Eden with an urgency to hold on to this. Hold on to her. She read his need, and her humor melted as she put equal passion into their kiss. He loved the way she seemed to know what he wanted or needed without having to ask. The way she fulfilled his wishes so completely. The way she was now, stroking her tongue against his while she slipped one hand between their bodies and rubbed his erection.

She positioned her body over him and eased back, pushing

the head of his cock into her heat. Beckett opened his eyes and found her gaze on him as she took him deeper. He clenched his teeth around a groan. His hands slid down her body, and he gripped her hips, pushing her slowly, steadily onto his cock.

Eden's eyes rolled back before they closed on "*God.*"

A little negotiation with their bodies, and he was imbedded deep inside her, surrounded by tight, wet heat that made his breath come fast and his heart hammer. And tonight, something that had been growing between them spilled over for Beckett.

All his life, sex had been sex. Sex had been inserting tab A into slot B, repeatedly. Sure, some women turned him on more than others. Some women were more playful or more creative or nastier than others. But in the end, sex was still sex.

Until now. Because as Eden straightened over him, with her hair falling around her face and the moonlight and city glow cast across her beautiful body, Beckett knew this was different. Eden was different. And something Grant said when he'd returned from the Christmas break last year with Faith beside him returned to Beckett now.

"*Sex is just sex until you have sex with someone you love. Then you're talking a whole different hockey game. Then you're talking the Stanley Cup of sex.*"

And as Eden rocked her beautiful body to pump him in and out of her succulent heat, the emotions swirling inside him jacked his physical excitement, pushing him toward orgasm at an exponential rate.

He pulled himself into a sit-up, wrapped one arm around her, cupped her neck with the other hand, and kissed her. Deeply. Tenderly.

"God, Eden..."

"Mmm." Her hips quickened. She pressed her face against his neck. "Beckett," she whispered. "So good."

This was crazy. Nothing pushed him over the edge this fast.

Nothing but the feel of Eden's pussy clenching around his cock. The bite of her nails at his shoulders. The vibrations of her pleasure against the skin of his neck.

She must have felt it too, because she rose fast. Her hips quickened, her moans deepened. And within minutes, she squeezed his cock.

Beckett's climax slammed through him like a bomb in his pelvis. It exploded deep in his body, streaked up his spine, through his cock, down his legs. The pleasure shattered his brain into tiny pieces that glowed bright white and drenched his body in carbonation until every inch of his skin tingled.

Eden kept one arm clasped around his neck, her breath hot and quick against his skin. She was quiet, and Beckett felt something shift between them. A seriousness that seemed to weight the air.

He'd never been in love before, but somehow he knew this was that feeling that made the guys around him do stupid, crazy things. 'Cause, yeah, he could envision himself doing stupid, crazy things for Eden to hold on to this. To hold on to her.

Only his life wasn't his own to wield anymore. He had Lily to think about.

So instead of letting the words roll out like he wanted, Beckett eased back, cupped her face in his hands, and kissed her, then whispered, "You are so amazing, you humble me."

And she smiled. The simple sight swamped him with emotion.

Oh, hell yes. He was most definitely in love.

23

E den and Tori were pulling out of the hospital parking lot when their pagers sounded again.

Eden, filling out reports in the passenger's seat, closed her eyes on a groan. Tori swore.

"You've become a total jinx," Tori said. "We all agree. Every shift from hell has one common denominator: you."

"Wow, you're giving me a lot of credit." Eden covered the iPad and pulled out her phone for directions to the call. "And while I deeply appreciate the confidence, if I had that kind of power, I'd use it to have the universe orchestrate my life in a whole different way."

She picked up the radio to tell the dispatcher they were en route to the call of yet another *woman down*. Then told Tori, "Nothing like going straight from the hood to the Ritz." With a few quick clicks on her phone, Eden pulled up photos of the house. And in between Siri's directions, Eden said, "It's a huge brick colonial surrounded by a white picket fence. Middle of the block on the right."

Tori wove through the streets of downtown DC, picking up

their earlier topic of discussion: Beckett. "So when are you two going out again?"

"Tomorrow night," she said, smiling at the thought. She'd woken and showered with Beckett early that morning, leaving for work before Lily had stirred. "He's got a game tonight, then home to Lily. He's off tomorrow. We're meeting a few other guys on the team and their girlfriends and wives for dinner."

"I'm so happy for you," Tori said, entering the affluent Spring Valley neighborhood of Washington, DC.

"I'm...cautiously optimistic. I'm having to force myself not to jump in with both feet. It's hard. He's tempting in so many different ways. But this whole thing still scares me."

"I think that's normal. And smart too."

Eden gave her a smile before they pulled into the home's driveway and bailed from the rig to grab equipment from the back. But she knew she was all talk. She was already head over heels for Beckett, which scared the living shit out of her. Yet holding her feelings back was like trying to get an IV in a guy on PCP.

They loaded equipment on a gurney and approached the sidewalk. The house's interior lights glowed golden in the night, and the lights from the ambulance shot strobes of red and blue across the brick. Eden slowed as they reached the gate. "Hold on."

After a quick glance around the neighborhood, she scanned the home's lush front yard encompassed by the fence again. Huge rhododendrons and hydrangea plants were scattered among various trees and shrubs. In the dark, she couldn't tell if the backyard was also open to the front, but she didn't see a fence separating the two.

Shifting the oxygen tank into one hand, she used the other to shake the fence gate, rattling the hardware as she watched the shadows for movement.

"What are you doing?" Tori asked.

"Checking the dog's friendly meter."

"What dog?"

"Look at the other houses. Only one other fence I can see. If there's a fence, there's usually a reason." Eden did it again, adding a whistle. No dog appeared. But no one stepped out of the house either. And Eden's trouble meter flared orange.

She unlatched the gate and pushed it open. "Stay here a minute," she told Tori. "And keep this exit clear."

Eden was at the stairs, about to take the first step toward the front door, when she heard a low growl from her right. Her trouble meter jumped to full-blown red. Fear skittered down her neck and flooded her chest. She turned toward the sound and caught sight of the dog jumping from around the corner of the house.

Eden stumbled back a step, holding the oxygen tank out in front of her. The dog was big and dark. But it was his ferocious bark that pounded down her spine and lifted the hair on her arms.

He lunged, teeth bared in a snarl. Eden shoved the tank at him, hitting the dog and knocking him back. But he was on his feet in seconds, meaner than ever.

"*Shit.*" She sidestepped back toward Tori with the metal tank keeping the dog at bay until she'd slipped through the gate again. Tori slammed it behind her, and Eden stumbled into the street, panting, shaking, her heart pounding in her ears.

The dog jumped at the fence, barking and snarling. It was a Rottweiler, and his teeth glowed white in the night. Eden's adrenaline felt like octane in her bloodstream when a man stepped out of the house and yelled, "What are you doing out here? My wife needs medical attention."

He was middle-aged and arrogant. Eden could hear the you-work-for-me attitude in his voice. And after almost getting mauled by his dog, yeah, that irritated her.

"Get your dog out of the front yard so we can pass, sir."

"Don't be stupid. There isn't anything wrong with the dog. Just come in."

Stupid? Eden's ire mounted. "Secure your dog. We're not entering the property while he's loose."

Before she could instruct Tori, her partner got on the radio to dispatch and requested law enforcement backup.

"What's your name, sir?" Eden asked.

"What difference does that make?"

Great, a rich arrogant prick. More concerned with being in control than the state of his wife. All too familiar to Eden.

"Sir," Eden said, searching for patience, "please come get your dog and put him in the backyard so we can take care of your wife."

"Excuse me." Another man's voice at Eden's right drew her attention from the house. He was in his early fifties with graying hair and a friendly face. "Hi. I live right next door. Butcher knows me. I feed him when they're on vacation. I can put him in the backyard."

"That would be great," Eden said.

"Darrel's a real asshole," the man said, voice lowered, "but his wife is a really good person and a dear friend of my wife's. Please take care of her."

And with that, he turned to the fence, talked to the dog, and managed to grab his collar before opening the gate, then led the dog toward the side yard.

Eden glanced at Tori. "Let's go."

"Do you want me to cancel backup?"

"No." Eden had a bad feeling about this.

As they approached the stairs again, the man reentered the house with a muttered "About fucking time."

Eden stepped through the front door, and the opulence of the home's interior registered instantly. Dark hardwood, light furniture, everything in its place. A showroom. Her tension mounted.

"Where's your wife, sir?"

"Kitchen." He jerked a hand somewhere toward the back of the house, then pulled out his phone and dialed. Then paced the living room instead of leading them to his wife.

Eden darted a look at Tori, and they shared thoughts without words.

They found his wife easily enough, laid out on the kitchen floor, twisted to lie half on her side, half on her back.

"Ma'am?" Eden dropped to a crouch and pressed her fingers to the woman's neck, relieved to find a pulse. "Can you hear me?" She glanced at Tori. "Pulse is weak."

Tori crouched at the woman's head and turned her ear to the woman's mouth. "Breathing." She grabbed the C-collar and glanced at Eden. "Did you see his hand?"

Eden nodded, flashing back to Darrel's raw knuckles and the blood spatter on the sleeve of his dress shirt. She pulled the penlight from her pocket as Tori lowered the backboard to the floor.

"Ma'am, can you hear me?" Leaning over the woman, Eden scanned her face where a cut bled over her left cheek, one from the corner of her mouth. Injuries Eden knew too well. She snapped on her penlight, lifted the patient's eyelids to check her pupils, and found them unequal and nonreactive. Bad, bad news. "Head injury. Let's move."

Tori clicked the C-collar into place, and together, they carefully rolled the woman onto the backboard.

Eden collected their jump bag as Tori secured the woman to the board.

"What was law enforcement's ETA?" Eden asked.

Tori's head came up, her gaze swinging toward the front door. "I think they're here."

"Thank God." She grabbed one end of the board, Tori took the other, and they lifted the woman to the gurney. "Let's go."

On the way out, they found one police officer talking to the husband, who barely glanced at his wife on the stretcher. At the ambulance, another cop approached as they loaded her inside and handed Eden a piece of paper with notes on it.

"What's this?"

"Her info. Name's Margaret Baxter. Thirty-two." His face was grim. "We've been here a number of times. Her husband won't give you any information, and he makes sure she won't wake up for a while. By the time this hits the DA's desk, Baxter'll have it all smoothed over with a handshake and a smile."

Eden's stomach plummeted, and her head filled with flashbacks of John and her father.

The cop shook his head. "I'm just waiting for the day I find the medical examiner's rig in the drive instead of an ambulance."

"We're doing our part to make sure that's not today." Tori slammed one of the back doors. "You do yours to make sure that's not tomorrow." Then she cut off the view of the cop by slamming the other.

Eden's mind fragmented a little. Tori hopped into the driver's seat, turned over the engine, and flipped on the sirens.

That cleared Eden's head. She picked up her radio mic with one hand and kept her fingers on the pulse at Margaret's neck with the other. Monitoring Margaret's breaths, Eden contacted the local hospital's emergency room. "Capital to base."

"Base. Go ahead, Capital."

"We've got a thirty-two-year-old Caucasian female found unconscious at the scene." She repositioned her fingers on Margaret's neck to get a better heartbeat with dread sinking in her gut. "Initial exam showed lacerations and bruising to the face. Pupils uneven and nonreactive. Heart rate fifty-two and weak. Respirations ten and—"

Margaret's chest stopped moving, and Eden broke off, waiting. After a second that felt like a minute, Eden grasped her arm hard and gave her a shake. "*Margaret.*"

No breathing. And the heartbeat beneath her fingers faded to nothing.

Eden dropped her radio and told Tori, "She's coding."

She pulled her shears from the holster on her waist and cut Margaret's blouse up the middle, catching her bra on the way. She spread the fabric wide and found a series of bruises marring Margaret's skin, some old, some new.

Tori picked up the radio from the driver's seat and continued communications as she drove. "Capital to base, patient is coding. Administering AED."

Muscle memory had Eden reaching for equipment without thought. She threw open the defibrillator's case, hit the power button, and slapped leads on Margaret. Placing the paddles diagonally across the heart, Eden hammered the pulse button.

Zzzzap.

Margaret's chest rose a fraction of an inch. Eden moved one hand to the woman's carotid. "Come on, Margaret."

The slightest thump tapped her fingers, and relief sagged Eden's shoulders. "I've got a pulse. Still no respiration. Starting rescue breathing."

Tori relayed the information while Eden covered Margaret's mouth and nose with a mask and breathed for the woman. She checked for a pulse in between breaths.

"Almost there." Tori's words still hung in the air when too many milliseconds passed between beats in Margaret's neck.

Frustration sang through Eden's body. "She fucking coded again."

"I'm pulling into the parking lot."

"You're going to have to take me with her." No time for the

defibrillator. Eden pushed to her feet, bent over Margaret, piled her hands on top of each other, and leaned her weight into the pump.

One, two, three... She counted silently to herself, more to keep focused, to keep her mind compartmentalized so she could function, than to keep track. Now, it was about keeping the blood flowing through Margaret's heart, body, and brain until the docs could pull out the big guns.

"Come on, Margaret..." she told the woman as Tori came to a stop. Eden climbed onto the gurney, straddling Margaret with her knees while continuing compressions. "Don't let him win."

Eighteen, nineteen, twenty.

By the time Tori opened the back doors, Eden's arms burned, her shoulders ached, and sweat collected on her back.

"Comin' out," Tori warned.

Thirty-one, thirty-two, thirty-three.

Eden used her tired thigh muscles to balance as Tori pulled the stretcher from the rig, then jogged toward the ER.

Four nurses and two doctors met them at the doors and swept them into the nearest trauma bay. A nurse lowered one arm of the gurney. Another slapped more leads on Margaret's chest. One of the doctors prepared the defibrillator paddles.

Sixty-five, sixty-six, sixty-seven.

"Tell me when," Eden said.

The doctor nodded. "Go."

She sat back and rolled off the gurney. Tori was there to stop her momentum.

"Clear," the doctor called before placing the paddles the same way Eden had.

Pu-chunk.

Then silence as everyone watched the monitor.

Nothing.

Eden's hands fisted. Every muscle in her body was strung wire tight.

Fight, Margaret.

"Again," the doctor said. "Clear."

Pu-chunk.

Silence as everyone watched the monitor.

Beep.

Beep...beep...beep.

Eden's muscles went weak. She bent at the waist and pressed her palms to her knees. Which was when she realized she was shaking from fatigue. Panting from exertion. Nauseous with relief.

"Good job, ladies," one of the doctors told Eden and Tori.

They nodded and exited the trauma bay, sharing a subdued high five.

"Take a breather, grab some water," Tori said. "I'll get things put back together."

"Thanks."

In the restroom, Eden splashed water on her face. She pulled out her bun and collected the hair that had fallen out, winding it into a knot on the back of her head again.

When she looked in the mirror, Eden found her own familiar face staring back, cheeks flushed, skin glowing from the workout. Yet she didn't quite recognize herself. She felt like she was looking at a stranger. Yet not. More like a familiar stranger.

What the hell was a familiar stranger?

She shook her head and let her gaze roam to her uniform while her mind drifted over the last twenty minutes, and emotions bubbled to the surface. Emotions she couldn't identify. This tangled mess and out-of-body sensation came sometimes after intense situations like the one she'd just experienced. They came when she faced dangerous people or when she'd narrowly escaped a dangerous situation or when someone died and she brought them back. Or when they just died.

Feeling the way she was feeling while dressed the way she was dressed, entrusted with the responsibility she was entrusted with, made her feel like a fraud. Like a sheep in a superwoman's clothing.

Eden pressed her eyes closed, breathed deep, and forced the insecurities from her mind. She exited the bathroom, and checked on Margaret. When she found that the doctors had her stabilized, Eden wandered toward the exit. But Tori had stopped at one of the last empty ER exam rooms and stood at the open door, staring up at the television in the corner.

"I'm ready," she said behind Tori. When her partner glanced over her shoulder, the look on Tori's face tightened Eden's stomach. "What?"

Tori stepped farther into the room and gestured to the television. "Beckett."

Eden's first emotion was fear. Fear he'd been hurt in his game. The channel was tuned to NHL, and Beckett's team headshot was on the screen. Another photo had been posted opposite Beckett's, one of a gorgeous brunette. The headline underneath read: Croft's Former Girlfriend Alleges Abuse.

Eden's stomach chilled. She crossed her arms. "Can you turn it up?"

Tori picked up the remote off the empty bed and raised the volume.

"...they evidently have a child together," one newscaster was telling another, "a daughter Croft has had custody of for nearly a year now. Croft has kept that very quiet, and you've got to wonder why."

Eden's stomach coiled with tension.

"We've discovered a custody case filed with the courts," the other newscaster went on, "that shows Croft is going for full custody of the child. The woman in this case, Kim Dixon, is currently living with Raider running back Henderson Mitchell. She alleges that while seeing Croft six years ago, he was abusive. When she found out she was pregnant, she broke off the relationship because she feared for the child's safety."

"No." Eden shook her head.

"Of course," the sportscaster continued, "this story just broke, and comment from Beckett Croft will have to wait as he is currently battling the Boston Bruins, and arguably playing one of the best games of his season. This wouldn't be the first time a sports figure became violent off the field or, in this case, off the ice. That said, Croft has no history of violence, and Dixon herself admits she never reported the abuse, though she does have this photo from a trip to the emergency room after an alleged fight with Croft while they were dating."

The brunette's beautiful face was replaced with one taken in a hospital gown. The sight of her injuries made Eden pull in a sharp breath. She had a cut and swollen lip, a bruised and swollen eye, cuts on her cheekbone and her brow. And what looked like fingerprints ringing her neck.

"Shit," Tori whispered, her hand lifting to her own throat.

"More recently," the first newscaster said, "Dixon reports that after allowing Croft the chance to get to know his daughter, he is now trying to take her from Dixon by claiming she is an unfit mother. Dixon met with Croft the other day at a café in DC to discuss their custody arrangement. Dixon claims Croft tried to buy her off, offering her five million dollars to sign over full custody of their daughter. She provided this photo as proof of that meeting."

The headshots vanished, and an image of Beckett sitting across the table from Kim appeared. By the cut, style, and length of Beckett's hair, Eden thought it looked like a recent photo. He was wearing his jersey, something he did only for events...

Her mind darted backward to the YMCA charity drive. To him wearing his jersey that day. And Eden scanned the photo again. Her gaze slid down his outstretched arm and his hand holding the file folder, and held on the red bracelet around his wrist.

This photo had been taken after he'd left her bed. After he'd dropped her off at Union Station. A stab of betrayal pinched her gut before she could institute rationale to stop it. He'd told her he had something he had to do that afternoon. What he had to do hadn't been any of her business.

Unless he'd been lying to her this whole time. Unless he was capable of abusing a woman. Neither of which she'd believed possible. But Eden saw things in the street every day she'd never believed possible. She'd never believed John capable of hatred and abuse and ultimately murder. She'd never believed her parents capable of betrayal and abandonment. She'd never believed herself capable of standing strong against the most important people in her life, walking away from it all, and starting over with nothing.

She might not want to believe Beckett was capable of abusing a woman, but he'd said himself that he'd been a very different man when he'd been dating Kim, and that finding out about Lily had changed him. In fact, Eden was pretty sure he'd called himself a selfish prick.

Eden crossed her arms tighter, confusing the hell out of herself.

"Eden?"

Tori's voice dragged her back. "What?"

"Are you okay?"

She shook her head. "I...don't know."

"Did you know about her?"

"Yes." Eden looked at the screen again, where the image of Beckett and Kim at the café stole her attention. He had an envelope in his hand, and he was offering it to Kim, whose expression and mannerisms clearly demonstrated she didn't want whatever was in it. "But his version of events is very different from these. He said Kim told him about Lily to get child support. He said he had to fight her for partial custody, and that she abandoned Lily on Beckett's doorstep a year ago. I didn't know about this meeting. I don't know anything about a deal. And he certainly didn't say anything about her abuse allegation. He said they had a one-night stand, and that was it."

"What do you believe?"

Him. She believed him. Everything in her gut told Eden that Beckett was the real deal, from the way he cared for his daughter to the way he loved his teammates.

But her gut had been wrong before. She was, admittedly, terrible at seeing through lies and facades, especially when they involved a man she cared about.

"I..." The pain in her chest made her grimace. "I don't—"

Their pagers went off.

Tori ripped hers off her belt. "You have got to be fucking kidding me."

Eden released a breath and turned from the room. "Let's go." She pushed the gurney toward the exit. "I'm going to have to stay busy tonight."

24

B eckett had this. He *had* it. If he could get this fucking
Bruin's right wing off his back.

With two minutes remaining in the tied game, Beckett
swung behind the Bruins' net. Leaning toward the pipe, he cut
off the wing. The other man slid behind Beckett and came up
on his right. Another Bruin came up on Beckett's left.

He'd been slamming his heart out all goddamned game. He
didn't want to go into fucking overtime.

He passed to Kristoff, who did what the kid always did, the
freaking magician, and faked two other Bruins, enabling him to
pass to Hendrix. Who slapped the puck back to Beckett as he
swung behind the net in the opposite direction.

Beckett saw a hole. Took a sharp turn. Flipped the puck
over the goalie's shoulder.

And scored.

Triumph surged through Beckett. The stadium roared to
life. And he pumped his fist before his other four teammates
closed around him for a group hug. They patted his helmet and
congratulated each other on great work.

But when he returned to the bench, Tremblay didn't look

happy, and he didn't offer his typical praise for a win either. And when the guys fell into line on their way to the locker room, Tremblay barked, "Beckett. My office. Now."

Savage and Donovan frowned at Beckett. "What the fuck did you do?"

Beckett had no idea. He lifted his arms out to the side. "Nothin'."

"Something happened off-ice during the second period," Hendrix said. "Paul relayed a message, and Tremblay hasn't been happy since."

Fuck. Beckett handed off his stick, helmet, and gloves to Savage and made his way to Tremblay's office, scouring his brain for something he could have done over the last twenty-four hours that would piss off his coach to this degree. But there had been nothing. Not even in the last week. Hell, not in the last month. He'd been a model hockey player, and this had been the best goddamned season of his career.

So when he stepped into Tremblay's office where his coach paced and ordered Beckett to close the door, then into a seat, a sick knot formed in Beckett's gut. He did as told, but his mind jumped to Lily. To his family. To Eden. To how his awesome life would fall apart if his coach had pulled him in to tell him he'd been traded...

Tremblay faced Beckett. "Tell me about Kim Dixon."

Beckett's mind skidded to a stop. Scrambled to make sense—

No fucking way.

"She's a one-nighter from years ago," Beckett said. "What about her?"

"She's making much stronger accusations than being a one-night stand."

Dread swamped Beckett like a flood. "Holy fuck." He ran his hand over his mouth. "What is she saying?"

"That she is Lily's mother. That she left the relationship

because you were abusive. That you recently tried to pay her five million for full custody of Lily."

"*Whoa.* Nothing after her being Lily's mother is true. I never touched her after that night, I sure as shit never hurt her, and she met me at a café last week to tell me that she'd sign over custody of Lily if I paid her five million, not the other way around."

"What about the abuse allegation? Ted's going to go ballistic when he hears about this."

The team's owner was an extremely conservative man who monitored all the players' behavior on and off the ice. One who wouldn't put up with anyone tarnishing the team or the club's name.

"It's bullshit," Beckett said, growing angry. "I've never hit or hurt a woman. I've got a mother, a sister, two nieces, and a daughter. You know me. You know I would never—"

"You were pretty wild in your younger days, Beck. And men do stupid things when they've had too much to drink and are overstimulated by a good or bad game."

The statement hit Beckett in the gut. "I may have been a little wild, but I've never caused any trouble. Are you saying you believe that shit? After seven years with me? You believe I'm capable of that?"

Tremblay sighed. "No. I don't. But I also don't know how I'm going to convince Ted of that. So you'd better get this shit straightened out, because I can only do so much on your behalf. If this accusation doesn't get cleared up, we both know you won't be seeing an offer come July."

"This is fucking bullshit." Hurt blended with rage. Beckett stood, shoving the chair back so hard, it toppled. "I've played for you and Ted for seven fucking years. I've given you my all and more. Then *one* woman comes out with *one* lie, and I have to be the one to restore my credibility?" He stabbed a finger at the air. "*That* is *bullshit.*"

He walked out, letting the door swing wide and slam against the office wall. Livid. He was *livid*. Out of his mind *furious*. He'd spent a lifetime maintaining his integrity. He might have been wild for a few years, but no wilder than any college kid. And far less wild than most other athletes. How *dare* they question his credibility. And Kim. That bitch wanted to try to bully him into *paying* for their daughter? Fuck that. *Fuck her*.

He strode into the locker room with red hazing his vision. His heart beat in his ears. Sweat rolled down his face, his back, his arms. He opened his bag and pulled out his phone. Before he could dial Fred, a dozen messages popped up— texts and voice mails from his parents and Sarah as well as Fred.

Kim had purposely leaked this story while he'd been on the ice. That goddamned wicked—

"Henderson kicked her out."

Donovan's voice jerked Beckett from his misery. He turned his head and found his friend's serious gaze on him. "What?"

"That's why she pulled this stunt," Donovan said, voice low, gaze cutting around the locker room before coming back to Beckett. "I called around. Henderson broke it off with her and tossed her ass out of his house. She's living in a hotel. She must think this is her ticket to some fast cash."

Beckett squeezed his eyes shut and gritted his teeth to keep his voice down. "That narcissistic *bitch*."

Hendrix came out of the shower and dried his hair with a towel, then dropped it around his neck. "We all pay to play, Beck. It's your turn."

Beckett faced Hendrix, a guy he'd played with for four years. A guy whose family knew Beckett's family. A guy he'd treated like a brother. "What the fuck does that mean?"

Hendrix shrugged. "Hey, relax. I'm just sayin'—"

"You're sayin' you think it's true. You're sayin' that just

because a woman goes on air and spews up bullshit that makes it truth."

His teammate got a stupid look on his face and shrugged. "Well, they don't go through all that for fun."

"No, you idiot, they go through it for the money. And the manipulation. Jesus Christ, you've got your head up your ass." Growing angrier by the second, he turned and found everyone in the locker room looking at him. He threw his arms wide. "Anyone else want to throw away all they know of me from working side by side for years over a single allegation from a gold digger?"

"Jesus, Beck," Hendrix said, "relax—"

"Easy for you to say, isn't it?" He swung back to face Hendrix. "You don't have any kids at risk here, do you?"

That shut Hendrix up. In fact, it shut the whole locker room up.

In the silence, Beckett told everyone in the room at large, "In the future, if anyone here doubts my character, I'd appreciate it if you'd be man enough to bring up any issues you have to my face and not talk about me behind my back. That's called respect, for those of you who like to gossip like little girls. I treat you with respect, and I expect you to treat me the same. If I find out you're acting differently, we'll take it outside, after hours. Am I clear?"

A combination of subdued "Yes, Cap," "Affirmative, Cap," "Clear, Cap," rippled through the room, and the guys went about their business.

Beckett took his phone down the hall, where the team often extended their workouts and stored equipment. He dialed Sarah and paced.

"Hi," she answered, her voice tense with fear.

"Has she contacted anyone in the family?" Beckett asked.

"No, but the media have tried, and they're already outside, lining the streets in the neighborhood. But worse, Lily was coloring in the family room while we were watching the game, and when it came on, we were all so shocked, we didn't turn it off before she heard too much."

"*Fuck.*" His stomach rolled. He closed his eyes and braced himself. "I haven't seen the news. How did she take it?"

"Um...not well. She translated what she heard into the fear that Kim was coming to take her back and seriously freaked out. Like, full-on panic-attack freaked out. I've never seen her like that."

Beckett's heart broke for his daughter. "Does she need to go to the ER?"

"There were moments when we considered taking her, but we talked her down to a lower ledge, and the girls distracted her with games. But I do think you're going to have to take her to the doctor tomorrow. She's living in this jumpy state of terror, clinging to everyone. It's even worse than after Kim abandoned her last year."

A sound choked out of Beckett's throat, and tears stung his eyes. "God*dammit.*" He took a breath. "I'll be there as soon as I can."

He hung up, rattled by his fury. An entire year of consistency and finesse and patience and therapy ground to dust in minutes simply because Kim wasn't getting her way.

Beckett really had to work to collect all his rage before he dialed Eden. She didn't answer, which didn't surprise him. He knew she was working tonight. When her voice mail picked up, he soaked in the sound of her voice. He hadn't realized how badly he needed her support until right now. How badly he wanted to hear her tell him it would all work out, that he wouldn't lose Lily or his contract or the respect of his team over this out-of-the-blue, unsubstantiated lie until he'd heard her voice.

"Hey, it's me," he told the recorder. "I know you're probably busy as hell, but if you get a few minutes free, could you call me? I could really use to hear your voice tonight, and I need to talk something over with you. It doesn't matter how late. Thanks. Bye."

Then he lowered his phone, took a breath, and dialed Fred with a murmured, "Time to let the dogs out."

25

E den sat on the corner of her bed with her phone in her hands. She was still in her uniform and really wanted to drop back and fall asleep. Work had given her two hours of rest, and she hadn't been able to stop thinking about Beckett and this damn scandal since she'd heard of it in the ER. She'd heard his message around eleven p.m. the night before but hadn't felt ready to return the call without more information, which, of course, she hadn't had time to dig up. Until this morning.

And she still found herself caught in limbo. Because from what she'd been able to find out about the situation, both Kim's version of the story and Beckett's version of the story were credible. As a woman who'd been abused and been made to feel like it had been her fault, Eden felt a certain obligation to take every woman's abuse allegation at face value.

Only, in this case, that meant doubting a man she'd fallen in love with at some point over the last few weeks. A man who'd given her the safety and belief she'd needed to take another chance at life.

She pressed one palm to her forehead and closed her eyes. God, she was so confused.

A knock on her door brought her head up. "Eden?"

Beckett's voice shot a jolt of fear through her. Then she immediately felt guilty over the knee-jerk response. Still, her belly tightened as she stood and moved to the door—and not in the excited way it usually did in anticipation of seeing Beckett.

She opened the door, and he turned from staring at the street. The look on his face broke her heart. His eyes were dull and pained. His handsome features etched with fatigue and misery. He was wearing jeans and a T-shirt under a hooded sweat jacket, and his shoulders were hunched against the cold.

"Oh, Beckett..." She stepped out and gripped handfuls of his jacket. "Are you okay?"

He wrapped her in his arms and pressed his face to her hair. "What a fucking mess."

His voice was heavy and rough and turned Eden inside out. He smelled clean and male and familiar, and the thought of losing him tore her apart.

"Where's Lily?" Eden asked.

"My parents'." He loosened his arms and looked down at her. "The media is everywhere, even at her school. I couldn't send her even if she wanted to go, which she doesn't because she's scared Kim's going to take her away."

Eden's gut twisted, and she pressed a hand to the pain. "Do you want to come in?"

He shook his head. "I need to get back to Lily. I just wanted to see you. You didn't call me back. You must have had a busy night."

Eden nodded, and Beckett pulled her close again, holding her as if drawing energy from her. God, her heart ached. And her mind warred, one side trying to convince her she could love him even if Kim's story was true, because he really was a different man now. But another side told her she was being stupid and weak and opening herself up to being a victim again.

"Is it true?" The forces battling inside her pushed the words from her mouth.

He pulled back, his eyes clouded with confusion. "What?"

"Any of what Kim is saying?"

A flash of disbelief traveled through his eyes a split second before an indefinable sharpness hardened his expression. His hands tightened on her arms. "Are you asking me if I tried to *buy* Lily from her? Or are you asking me if I *hit* her?" He paused only a second. "Or are you asking *both*?"

The anger in his eyes unnerved her. "It was a long time ago. You were a different man, you said so yourself. People have different ways of seeing things. Maybe you don't even remember it happening that way—"

He dropped his hands from her arms. "Because it *didn't* happen that way."

His bark made her flinch, and he took one big, deliberate step away.

Panic flared in Eden's gut. "Beckett—"

"You know me," he said, pained, serious, and angry. "You know who I am, Eden. I opened my entire life up to you. You met my family. You've seen me with my daughter."

Shame leaked into the mess of emotions eddying inside her. "I can't just ignore—" She let the rest of her words evaporate on her exhale, knowing he'd take them wrong while he was so upset. "Can you come in just for a few minutes? Can we talk about this? I really want to talk about this."

"What's the point? There's nothing I could show you that you haven't already seen. Nothing I could say to you that you haven't already heard. You already know me. *You* of all people — How could you *possibly* think—" He shook his head and lifted a hand toward her. "Never mind. I don't even want to know."

So much hurt and disappointment filled his voice, his expression, it tore at Eden's gut. "Beckett, please—"

He turned toward the street. "Good-bye, Eden."

He took the stairs to the sidewalk in two big steps. Before Eden had recovered from the blow of good-bye, Beckett was in his car, pulling away from the curb.

And gone from her life as quickly as he'd entered.

26

Beckett stared at his fingers tapping on the arm of the chair. He wondered if Eden was working tonight. Wondered how she'd done on that big physiology test she'd had yesterday. Wondered if she missed him, or if she still believed the worst of him and thanked her lucky stars he'd bailed.

"Beck."

Thoughts of Eden snapped off, and Beckett refocused on Fred across his wide desk. "Yeah."

"Did you hear anything I just said?"

Beckett rubbed his face with both hands and sighed. "Sorry. Haven't gotten much sleep."

Between Lily's restless nights and Beckett's regrets over Eden, he was seriously sleep-deprived.

"Well, it's not hurting your game any."

No, his games were his opportunity to take out his frustrations. His opportunity to push all his troubles aside and focus on something he could control. And he played harder than ever. But the last week without Eden in his life was long enough for him to realize he'd fucked up big-time. That expecting her to rally behind him the day after Kim's news had broken was unreasonable and insensitive.

"I heard you through the part about Kim's press conference."

"Then you missed my comment about your brilliant move to call Henderson. His corroboration of the information we had from others put the last nail in Kim's coffin."

Beckett shook his head. "I'm so glad this didn't go to court."

"Agreed," Fred said. "I'll have all the legal documents finished up by the end of the week. Once Kim's press conference airs, this mess will be behind you. You and Lily can move forward without worrying about Kim popping up in the future. The Rough Riders can sign you again without worrying about your image."

Beckett sighed and pushed to his feet. "I can't thank you enough, Fred." He reached across the desk and shook his attorney's hand. "I don't know what I would have done without Lily."

Fred grinned. "I'm glad you'll never have to find out."

Beckett walked out of Fred's office wishing he'd never have to find out what he was going to do without Eden too.

27

E den paced the concrete path beyond the mouth of the tunnel the players used to exit the Verizon arena, waiting for Beckett. Twenty-three players had already passed her, half of whom she knew now and said hello to. But with every passing moment, her nerves coiled a little tighter. Not only was she starting to think coming here was a really stupid idea, but coming on one of the coldest freaking nights this winter had been *beyond* stupid.

She repositioned her scarf to cover more of her face and continued pacing. Five more minutes. She'd give him five more—

The doors scraped open again and Eden's stomach flipped. This was it. And after the initial burst of nerves died, she relaxed into the anticipation of getting rid of this horrible guilt. Two sets of footsteps echoed through the tunnel along with the low hum of male voices.

Eden wandered toward the tunnel as they grew closer and met Beckett and Tate at the entrance. Both men stopped. She couldn't read Beckett's expression.

"Hey," she said.

"Hey, Eden." Tate stepped up to her and gave her a hug. "Good to see you."

Gratitude warmed her chest. "You too."

"Later," Tate told Beckett, who lifted his chin in answer.

Tate wandered toward the parking lot, and Eden and Beckett were left alone, staring at each other.

Finally, a soft smile lifted his lips. "Hi."

Nervous laughter escaped on a whispery huff of air. "Hi." Another moment of silence while they held each other's gaze. "You don't look surprised to see me."

"The guys texted me that you were here."

"Ah." She laughed. "Right."

"Eden—"

"I just—"

They spoke at the same time. But Eden pushed on. "I know you probably don't want to hear what I have to say, and I realize it may not matter to you now, but I think it's important for you to know because it might be something you can find value in when you look back." She stopped only long enough to draw breath. "I'm here to apologize for doubting you."

He stepped forward and opened his mouth to speak.

Eden held up a hand. "I don't expect you to forgive me. It was wrong and so hurtful. It wasn't meant that way, but that doesn't matter either, because I know that's how it felt. And you were right, I do know you. My heart knows you. But I was letting my head lead because I was afraid to trust my gut. But I know my gut was right. And I'm so very sorry for judging you and judging you wrongly. So, yeah, I wanted you to know that I don't doubt you, no matter what Kim says."

She needed to turn. Needed to walk away. Needed to let him move on.

Turn. Walk away. Move on.

Biting the inside of her lip, Eden dropped her gaze to the concrete and the exterior light pooling on the ground blurred in the tears gathering in her eyes.

She started to turn, but Beckett's hand closed on her arm.

"My turn," he said.

He dropped his duffel and wrapped her in his arms so tight, he pulled her off her feet. A half laugh ebbed from her throat, and she wrapped her arms around his neck.

He pressed his face to her hair and murmured an emotional "I've missed you so fucking bad."

That did it. Her tears spilled over her lashes, and the sobs she'd been holding back all week rolled out. And nothing in the world felt better than having Beckett's arms around her when she needed him.

He set her on her feet but continued to hold her tight and stroke her hair as her emotions quieted.

"I was coming to see you after the game, because I was wrong too." He eased back and cupped her cheek, wiping at her tears with his thumb. "Given who you are, what you've been through, you weren't wrong to wonder. And I want you to know that however long it takes for you to feel comfortable, for you to believe in me, I'll wait. I don't care if it takes a week or a month or a year, I'll give you the time you need to find the truth, because I love you, Eden. I love you, and I don't want to live without you any more than I want to live without Lily."

Another sob bubbled from her throat, this one from an abundance of love. She slid her arms around his waist and held him tight, unable to get words out of her thickened throat.

"I have the entire legal file in the car," Beckett continued. "Kim's holding a press conference Monday, recanting her allegations. She's signing custody of Lily over to me permanently in lieu of criminal charges. And she's not getting a dime. You can read her statement—"

"I don't need to read it. I have no doubt." She lifted her gaze to his and framed his face with her hands. "My heart knows." She pulled his lips to hers for a kiss and murmured, "And my heart knows I love you. So very much."

EPILOGUE

Three months later.

If Eden slid forward another inch, her butt would fall off the seat. She had one hand curled into a fist, the other arm curved around Lily's waist where the girl sat on her lap.

"Come on, come on, come on..." she murmured, watching Beckett toggle the puck between the front and back side of his stick blade as he sped down the ice.

He hit some resistance in the form of the Indians center and passed to Rafe. A left wing stole the puck from Rafe, but Beckett was already swinging behind the net and slammed him into the glass, freeing up the puck for Rafe again.

All the players closed in, the tension ratcheted up, and people in the forward rows stood.

"Eden," Lily whined, leaning right and left. "I can't see."

Eden stood, lifted Lily into her arms, then hoisted her onto her shoulders. No doubt she wouldn't be a favorite of the people behind them, but with everyone standing, a girl had to do what a girl had to do to see her man. And let his daughter see her dad in action.

"Eden," Tina said beside her. "You're going to hurt yourself."

"I'm okay," she told Tina without taking her eyes off the action. "She's nothing compared to the patients I lift at work. Can you see your daddy now, Lily?"

"Yeah, I see him. I see him," she cried with excitement. "He's got the puck."

"Two minutes," Sarah said on Eden's other side, voice tight.

"He's got this," Jake said from the other side of Tina.

With thirty seconds left, an Indians defenseman took Beckett down hard. Eden sucked a breath and grimaced. But as he went down, Beckett reached with his stick, shoving the puck toward Tate, who scooped it up, skipped it toward the net. And scored.

The whole stadium surged to their feet. Bells and sirens and lights and smoke filled the space. On the ice, the guys skated into a circle. Around Eden, Lily, Rachel, and Amy covered their ears.

With the second period over, fans started toward the stairs and refreshments and restrooms. The teams skated off the ice. And Eden sat back down, surrounded by Beckett's family with his daughter still on her lap.

Eden wrapped Lily in a bear hug and rocked her side to side. "Your daddy's killin' it on the ice tonight, baby."

She giggled and looked over her shoulder. "You know what that means."

Eden leaned back and grinned, and she and Lily responded together. "Ice cream."

Then high-fived each other.

But Eden also knew that meant something extra special for her tonight too. After games—win or lose—Beckett always brought more energy to the bedroom. And Eden's whole body tingled in anticipation.

"If you're headed out to the refreshment stands," the announcer's voice came over the stadium speakers, "you may want to wait, because we have something *very* special planned for tonight's second-period break."

"Oooh," Eden said, pulling Lily close. "What do you think it is?"

"Excuse me, Ms. Kennedy?" Eden turned toward the aisle where one of the Rough Rider cheerleaders stood, a big smile on her perfect young face. "Can you and Lily come with me?"

"Um..." She looked at Sarah, then at Tina and Jake, searching for guidance. When she got none, she turned back to the girl. "No, I don't think so. Thanks."

"Eden." Sarah laughed, surprised by her refusal. "Go."

"Mmm, nope." She shook her head. "I didn't even want to go out on the ice to throw your brother's injured butt on a gurney. I sure don't want to go now."

The cheerleader continued to cajole Eden.

The announcer's voice boomed over the sound system. "It looks like our participant needs a little encouragement, folks."

On the Jumbotron, Eden's name flashed in sparkling lights, and the crowd chanted along with the appearance of her name.

"E-den. E-den. E-den..."

Eden's mouth dropped open, and she looked at Beckett's parents again.

Tina's eyes sparkled with her grin. "Go, Eden. Don't keep the fans waiting."

"Oh, jeez." She covered her eyes. "I'm going to kill Beckett."

"Come on, Eden." Lily slipped off her lap and pulled on Eden's other hand.

With a groan, she relented, passing Sarah with "Your brother is so dead."

As soon as Eden appeared rinkside, the fans applauded, and she wondered if they knew what was going to happen even when Eden didn't. Though she couldn't imagine how.

She and Lily stood at a door leading into the rink from the

center of the longest side while more cheerleaders rolled out a thin red carpet, ending at center ice.

"Just walk to the end of the carpet, Ms. Kennedy," one of the cheerleaders said, all bounce and smiles.

Eden set her eyes on that spot in the carpet, told herself Beckett was going to become her sexual slave for a month to pay her back for this stunt, and took a deep breath. Lily's hand tightened in Eden's and her other arm circled Eden's thigh. "Eden?"

When she looked down, Eden saw Lily's nerves had risen too. "Come here, baby."

Eden picked her up and carefully remained on the red carpet as she walked out onto the ice.

When she reached the end, Lily said, "I can get down now."

Eden set Lily on her feet but held tight to her hand as the announcer welcomed Eden and Lily as Beckett's girlfriend and daughter. The fans cheered—for what, Eden had no idea.

"Now, please welcome back to the ice," the announcer said with drama and flair, "our own Beckett Croft."

Beckett skated onto the ice from the opposite side of the rink—sans gloves, stick, and helmet—and the crowd went wild. He made a graceful loop around the arena, waving to fans, his grin wide and carefree. He easily jumped the carpet and completed the loop as the announcer quoted Beckett's stats and claimed this as the best year of Beckett's career with league record-breaking possibilities well within reach.

"This is Croft's seventh year with the Rough Riders," the announcer said, "and seven is definitely his lucky number. Just days ago, he received news he was chosen for the men's US Olympic team."

The audience cheered, and this time, Eden released Lily's hand to applaud as well. She still felt so blessed to have been with him the day he'd gotten that thrilling news.

"And tonight," the announcer continued, "Croft has chosen

to complete his trifecta of awesomeness with those he loves most, Eden and Lily."

The lights dimmed, and spotlights focused on Eden, Lily, and Beckett.

Eden's nerves rose to the surface of her skin and jittered. Her stomach knotted. From twenty feet away, Beckett took another smooth curve and headed back toward them. At ten feet away, he dropped to one knee and slid the remaining distance, coming to a stop at their feet.

Lily covered her mouth, giggling. "Hi, Daddy."

Her voice came over the speakers, and light laughter rippled through the audience.

"Hi, princess. Ready to do this?"

She nodded.

He opened his arms, and she climbed into his lap.

Now Eden had nothing to do with her hands. She was burning up, which had to be impossible when she was standing on a huge slab of ice. And her stomach was jumping like she'd swallowed a gaggle of frogs. But knowing anything she said would be heard over the speakers, she didn't utter a word.

Beckett reached out and took her hands in his, then Lily added hers on top, and the sight of her small hands with theirs pulled hard at Eden's heart. She'd come to love Lily madly within weeks of committing to Beckett.

He smiled up at her, his eyes soft and brimming with emotion. The quiet spreading through the stadium felt deafening.

"Eden," Beckett finally said, "you make me happier than I've ever been."

Lily nodded. "Me too."

Another ring of laughter came from the seats, and tears swelled in Eden's eyes. She bit her lower lip to hold herself together.

"I love you with all my heart," Beckett said.

"Me too," Lily added.

Eden couldn't hold back a laugh, which pushed the tears over her lashes.

"Oh no, Daddy," Lily whispered, her eyes round and worried. "She's crying."

More laughter from around the stadium.

Beckett chuckled and pulled a small box from somewhere beneath his uniform. "I think those are happy tears, baby."

Eden's gaze held on the tiny square black box, and her stomach triple-flipped like a damned gymnast. Then she looked at Beckett. And he was grinning. Grinning in that affectionate way that told Eden he did indeed love her with everything he had. Everything he was.

Holy shit.

Holy. Shit.

Lily took hold of the box, and Beckett helped her open it. The gorgeous diamond band sparkled up from a bed of black velvet, taking Eden's breath. She lifted her hands and tented them over her mouth, shaking with emotion. "Oh my God."

Her whisper shivered through the stadium.

Beckett held Eden's eyes when he asked, "Will you stay with us forever, Eden? Will you marry us?"

Lily looked up at her with the same loving, longing expression as her father and said, "Will you marry us?"

Emotion overwhelmed her, and when she tried to answer, she got caught in a mini hyperventilation episode. It took her several excruciating seconds filled with fluttering hands and tearing eyes before Eden could control her voice well enough to rasp out, "Yes." She took another breath and repeated, "Yes, *yes.*"

She crouched and wrapped her arms around them. "I love you both, so much."

But her words were drowned in the crazy applause raising the roof, so Eden turned her head and kissed Beckett. As much as she wanted to devour him in front of everyone, she was well aware of the families in the audience, not to mention his own daughter right there.

Their daughter now.

When she pulled back, Beckett took the box from her hand, pulled out the ring, and slipped it on her finger, then kissed her again. "I love you, Eden."

The three of them pushed to their feet together. Beckett held Lily in one arm and used the other to lift Eden's arm overhead to a raging crowd. She grinned at Lily, whose smile was so bright and so pure, it swelled Eden's heart.

"These women," he yelled to the fans, "make me better in every way. They make me stronger, tougher, and faster. Who's ready for round three, Rough Riders fans?"

The rumble that erupted through the building shook the floor like an earthquake and made Lily cover her ears.

With a grin and a kiss, Beckett handed Lily over to Eden and skated backward toward the tunnel leading to the locker room. Eden stepped back behind the wall with Lily in her arms and was greeted by Beckett's parents, sister, and nieces with more hugs and more love.

Across the ice, Beckett punched a fist in the air, yelling, "*Unleash—*"

And the entire stadium joined him with "*The fury!*"

ABOUT THE AUTHOR

Skye Jordan is the *New York Times* and *USA Today* bestselling author of more than thirty novels.

When she's not writing, Skye loves to learn new things and enjoys staying active, so you're just as likely to find her in the ceramics studio as out rowing on the nearest lake or river.

She and her husband have two beautiful daughters and live in Oregon.

Connect with Skye online

Amazon | **Instagram** | **Facebook** | **Website** | **Newsletter** | **Reader Group** | Tiktok

ALSO BY SKYE JORDAN

ROUGH RIDERS HOCKEY SERIES

Quick Trick

Hot Puck

Dirty Score

Wild Zone

PHOENIX RISING

Hot Blooded

Shadow Warrior

Hell Hath no Fury

Wicked Wrath

FORGED IN FIRE

Flashpoint

Smoke and Mirrors

Playing with Fire

WILDFIRE LAKE SERIES

In Too Deep

Going Under

Swept Away

NASHVILLE HEAT

So Wright

Damn Wright

Must be Wright

MANHUNTERS SERIES

Grave Secrets

No Remorse

Deadly Truths (Coming Soon)

RENEGADES SERIES

Reckless

Rebel

Ricochet

Rumor

Relentless

Rendezvous

Riptide

Rapture

Risk

Ruin

Rescue (Coming Soon)

Roulette (Coming Soon)

QUICK & DIRTY COLLECTION:

Dirtiest Little Secret

WILDWOOD SERIES:

Forbidden Fling

Wild Kisses

COVERT AFFAIRS SERIES

Intimate Enemies

First Temptation

Sinful Deception

Made in the USA
Las Vegas, NV
05 May 2024

89563850R00166